HOLIDAY COUNTRY

HOLIDAY COUNTRY

İNCİ ATREK

FLATIRON
BOOKS
NEW YORK

HOLIDAY COUNTRY. Copyright © 2023 by İnci Atrek. All rights reserved. Printed in the United States of America. For information, address Flatiron Books, 120 Broadway, New York, NY 10271.

www.flatironbooks.com

Designed by Jen Edwards

Library of Congress Cataloging-in-Publication Data

Names: Atrek, İnci, author.
Title: Holiday country / İnci Atrek.
Description: First edition. | New York : Flatiron Books, 2024.
Identifiers: LCCN 2023016828 | ISBN 9781250889461
    (hardcover) | ISBN 9781250889478 (ebook)
Subjects: LCGFT: Bildungsromans. | Domestic fiction. | Novels.
Classification: LCC PS3601.T73 H65 2024 | DDC 813/.6—
    dc23/eng/20230613
LC record available at https://lccn.loc.gov/2023016828

Our books may be purchased in bulk for promotional, educational, or business use. Please contact your local bookseller or the Macmillan Corporate and Premium Sales Department at 1-800-221-7945, extension 5442, or by email at MacmillanSpecialMarkets@macmillan.com.

First Edition: 2024

10 9 8 7 6 5 4 3 2 1

For Müjgan

HOLIDAY COUNTRY

1

THE SMALL CLUB

A man stands at the top of the ladder, blocking my way out from the sea.

"You must be Meltem's daughter," he says. He places a hand on each side rail and leans in toward me. "In fact, I'm sure of it. I can tell by the way you swim."

It's mid-July, and even though I have never seen this man before, I can tell that he's spent long days in places of summer. His irises are too bright for such naturally dark features. His beard is coarse with salt, and his unkempt hair curls under his ears and traces, just for a moment, his jawline. Around his neck is a shark tooth on a leather string, an interesting choice of accessory—a child's accessory—for someone my father's age.

It's one of the many things I still haven't gotten used to around here. In this country, especially in this small town, all collisions are considered an invitation to conversation. Instead of getting easier over the years, like I thought it might, masking my irritation has only gotten harder. I climb out and motion for him to step aside, joining him on the dock. Then I gather up the two triangles of my bikini, give them a tug, and squeeze. A small rain empties out onto the wooden planks.

"Yes," I confirm, feeling his gaze on me. "Meltem's my mother."

His eyes widen. Though a moment ago the relation was assumed, it's now dawning on him that he really is of the age to know a woman with a nineteen-year-old daughter. *Time passes, buddy. Get used to it.* I nod to indicate that the ladder's all his, then make a left on the T-shaped dock, walking down its length toward the Small Club. His footsteps trail my lead. Their hurried thuds are almost indistinguishable from those of the boys who dive off the dock in exaggerated acrobatics—though of course his are heavier, and pound over and over on the land, far from any silencing edge. Perhaps he's heading back for his towel, as there should be no rush to catch me; we still have seven weeks before I disappear. All of us in the neighborhood run into each other continually, moving in circles from the water to the café to the market to the park and around again. I pass the showers, the changing rooms, the lawn speckled with striped sun beds. When I start up the steps to the Small Club's beach café, the man grabs ahold of my arm, and I turn sharply. Large strokes of sunlight have already erased my footsteps. His eyes peer into mine, and he blinks once, twice. I hold my gaze steady, then jerk my arm out of his grasp. He lets his hand fall to his side.

"What's fascinating," he says, sounding lost in a memory, "is that you don't look like her at all. Not like she used to. It's all in the way you move." The heat from the sun-boiled steps is too much, and I hop from side to side. "Yes," he murmurs, continuing his inspection. "Yes, yes. That's it. There's something in the movement."

I stop moving. The way his voice dipped into the past and his eyes fix onto my body almost makes me believe that he does indeed have some claim over me. An arrangement we'd made long ago that I'd since forgotten. I start to feel uneasy, but shut off the sensation by focusing on the hot pain at my feet.

"I'm an old friend of Meltem's," he says, as if this means something. All of my mother's friends are old friends. She has yet to make a new friend in her American life. This is despite having moved continents over two decades ago, despite having raised me all those years in California. "I had heard that she had a daughter, but I wasn't expecting to meet you on my first day in Ayvalık."

I wonder who's watching, and glance over at the Small Club's café. In the far corner, Aslı sits alone in her tiger-stripe bandana, camouflaged in the chaos of nylon beach bags and magazines spread across our table, the towels draped over the plastic chairs. Steadily, she taps an index finger on a can of Nestea Peach as she surveys the scene, her face half hidden behind a newspaper. Her expression is a clear signal that she is available for rescue, should the situation warrant one.

Does the situation warrant a rescue?

No. I am not afraid of anything during the summers, surrounded by the sand and the sea. By the neighbors who watch everything unfold from their sun beds and terraces, timing their blinks so that the gossip is comprehensive. But as the man continues to search my face with his bright eyes, something in me leaps at the suggestion that I was being sought, and have now been found.

I think through my next sentence carefully before I speak, keeping my voice level. "You should not grab girls you do not know." I choose a formal pronoun, pointedly addressing the man as a stranger, a respected elder. This is one of the things I admire about my mother's native language: the dichotomy between what is said and what is meant. I smile, pleased at having regained control of the situation—it's not something that happens often, here.

Whoever this man is, he's definitely a newcomer to our little neighborhood, our *site*. Had I seen him during my previous summers here, I would have remembered. An old friend of the family from İstanbul, vacationing in our seasonal town. I mentally flip through my mother's photo albums stored in our California home—I'd pored over them enough growing up that I'd all but committed them to memory—but can't find a sepia match for his face. No likeness in any of the photos taken at her alma mater by the Bosphorus, by the gilded gates of her high school in Beyoğlu, or from the beach scenes of her childhood vacation home on the outskirts of the city. His presence was not among the memories she chose to keep.

"What's your name?" I ask. Out of the corner of my eye, I see Aslı move to get up, but I shake my head to let her know that I'm fine. "I'll tell my mother that you're here."

"There's no need," he says, and heads back to the dock for his swim while I remain where I am, my feet on fire. "I'll stop by sometime. I know where the house is."

"Everyone knows where our house is," I call out after him. The sentence comes hurling out of me differently than I mean for it to, childish and petulant instead of powerful and indifferent. He turns to me, then shakes his head and chuckles. I shut my eyes and hate myself for how I always use the simple words. My American tongue cracks and guesses where it should flow and pop, and because I cannot properly place my inflections, I often leave conversations with the same questions I had upon arrival. We are at week five of my summer now, so I have managed to slip my accent out of the basic phrases, perfected the cadence of the hellos and the good-evenings and the orders of tea, *tost*, and coffee. When I keep things simple, no one can tell that I don't belong here. In the longer conversations, sounds mix and mangle in my throat on the way up, and my personality gets lost in the shuffle. I am not myself when I speak Turkish, though every summer, I get just a little bit closer.

In the summer, when the days are sticky and cannot separate from themselves, my linguistic progress becomes its own calendar. Aside from that, the only other way to tell time in this town is through the sun's demarcations on the skin.

I am now a toasted golden brown, my body glowing like a candied chestnut and my hair lightened from the sun and the bowls of water inside which I boil daisies, then rest my head. I learned the daisy trick from my mother, though she also taught me that the sun not only beautifies; it destructs as well. Flakes of burnt skin have already peeled off my shoulders, and the remaining topographies are encrusted with salt water. I don't mind the peeling, though. It's a small price to pay for these long days of summer bliss.

My mother's skin, sadly, is charred. The summers of her past caught up with her in her middle age. She used to rub Coca-Cola all over her body, she told me, then bake until she swore she could hear a sizzle. These days, the color she used to crave manifests as deep lines in a leathered face. Now, on our annual summer trips to Turkey, she stays inside my grandmother's seaside villa until late afternoon, and only then travels to a secluded section of the beach, several meters north of the main dock. She then pitches a tent of pink and green, colors that do not even attempt to blend into the seascape. There she is in the water now, underneath her large sun hat, rising and falling with the waves. All this protection, too late in the game. My mother always forgets that she cannot turn back time.

I walk back to our table, Aslı's eyes following me each step of the way. "Who was that?" she asks as soon as I'm within earshot, slapping her palm against the table in a series of staccatos. "Who was *that?*" She stands to get a closer look. The man who says he once knew my mother walks down the dock, his back to us and his eyes on the horizon, toward the far-flung islands. Despite his age, his body is lean, his saunter nowhere near the hesitant waddle of first-timers shyly approaching their first swim of the season. It's clear that he's no stranger to the water. His back, its muscles carved into shape-shifting geometric figures, glistens in the sun.

About a quarter of the way down the dock, he slows down, then takes a giant leap forward. Then another. And another, shortening the time between each, the sound of his footsteps chopping the heaviness of chords into the elegance of a trill. Once on the edge, he springs into the air with full confidence. For the briefest moment, he floats above the Aegean, then bends his body into a flawless dive.

"Who cares?" I say. I pull out a chair for myself and sit down, leaning my neck all the way back. Upside down in this way, I catch the eye of a waiter and signal for a deck of cards.

"Right away, Miss Ada," he says, and scurries off.

I stroke my arm where the man had latched onto me, where salt now dries into thin vapor trails. In my mind, I replay his perfect dive. Showing off like a teenager. There's no urgent need to tell my mother about our encounter; she'll find out soon enough.

After all, in this small town, nothing stays a secret for long.

⚓

Everyone knows where our house is because it's the best-situated villa in the whole *site*, this development of two hundred or so similarly styled summer residences. It's directly—and I do mean *directly*—across from the Small Club, whose oleander-lined entrance marks the beginning of the day. To start your day, you must walk past our front terrace, where one, two, or all three generations of us will be watching you. The *site* itself is a twenty-minute minibus ride north of the Ayvalık town center. It spills downward from a hilltop, collecting in pools where the land levels off—most centrally, at the market, which is semicircled by a crescent moor of dilapidated athletic courts.

In our neighborhood, the basketball hoops have no nets, and spectators sit upon layers of sunflower seed shells, cracked, then spat out the night before by teenagers perched on its concrete bleachers (my friends and I are responsible for many a shell). The volleyball court next door does have a net some summers, though instead of fine-grained sand, it stretches over a field of dead grass, similar to the surface of the soccer field across the street that's always sprawling with kids in mismatched jerseys. The tennis courts, farther eastward on the slope, sparkle in comparison.

Between the soccer field and the sea is the children's park, where the most important moment of my summers took place. When I was eight years old, my grandmother sold her property in Datça, in a fairly new *site* where I had no one to play with but the street cats, and bought the Ayvalık villa. I was thrilled to be surrounded with kids my age, and though I clung to my mother the first day at the beach, I gathered my courage and marched, head held high, to the park in the evening. A girl on the monkey bars immediately caught my attention. She had bruises along her arms—from falls and fights, maybe—and her lips were pursed in concentration as her body swung from one metal rod to the next. I stood underneath her and introduced myself. "I'm Ada from California," I said. "We just moved here."

The girl dropped down. "You're not from California," she said, looking me in the eye. Her face was wild and angular, lit aflame by the slowly setting sun. Suddenly I no longer felt safe. "You're a liar. I can tell you're a liar. I bet that's not even yours, it's too beautiful for you." She pointed to the end of my braid, at the rhinestoned emerald green hair tie I had borrowed from my mother.

"No, I'm not a liar," I said, unsure where the conversation was going.

She laughed at the way I couldn't roll my r's. Then we faced each other and I sensed a terrible heat radiating from her. "Give me that," she said, and yanked the tie from my hair. She laughed as my braid started to unravel. It was a loud, ugly laugh, more of a bray than anything human. What would I tell my mother? I ran away to the swing set, but she followed me, insistent on total destruction. "If you love God," she said, "you'll get off that swing and let me have it." My green stones shone in her hair. I didn't know how to argue with her logic. I left the park and walked home with my head down.

I returned to the park the following evenings because I didn't want to tell my mother that they hated me here. I would sit and cry by the slide, where the mean girl would approach me with her friends and demand that I recite "askerler dörder dörder yürüyorlar" (the soldiers are marching by fours) and other tongue-twisting phrases so they could laugh at my r's again. On the fourth night, I watched her hang upside down on the monkey bars, that glint of green in her ponytail, while her friends cheered. Behind them, from the shadows by the fountain at the edge of the park, a girl stepped forward. She wore a terrycloth headband pulled down to her forehead. She carefully tracked the sway of long hair that hung like a pendulum from the monkey bars, her eyes narrowed like a hunter's. Then, in one quick movement, she reached up and pulled down my beautiful green hair tie. The mean girl screeched a long, deafening screech, but she couldn't drop down in time, and knew the battle was over.

"I'm Aslı," the girl with the terrycloth band said, crouching down next to me by the slide. She opened her hand to reveal the glittering stones with a conspiratorial smile, then introduced me to her twin brother, Bulut, and their cousin Ozan, who had been sitting with her by the fountain. Ozan told me that the girl and her family would soon move away to a different *site*, that there was nothing to worry about. They all said they liked my large eyeballs, long lashes, and pointy chin. "You look like a beautiful fish," said Aslı. "Fish are very important in Ayvalık, in the Aegean. That witch can go, but you will have to stay." I got up from the grass and hugged them all. They walked me to the market and asked what my favorite ice cream was, then pooled their pocket money to afford the strawberry Cornetto. Never once did they laugh at my mispronunciations, my dumbfounded look in response to words I'd never heard before, having only the vocabulary of the summers and my mother to build upon.

That winter, all winter, I practiced rolling my r's until they were perfect.

Beyond the children's park spreads the sea, and along the seaside promenade the last and most important points of interest reveal themselves. On the north end of our *site* is the Big Club, where grandmothers and grandfathers dine to live music and play hands of cooncan. Behind the Big Club stretches Sıfır, the abandoned beach. As it lies at the edge of our neighborhood and the beginning of the next, nobody has reason to swim there, and its dock remains broken and unmaintained. Then, back to the southern end, us, and the Small Club. These "ends" I speak of are relative; it is a five-minute walk between the two. But, of course, everything moves slower in the heat.

I lean over our table and consider my fortune. My deck of cards has been arranged clocklike with a thirteenth pile in the middle, and droplets of salt water fall from my hair, mottling the faces of numbers and royalty. The top card in the middle pile is the first to be overturned and placed on its hour—say, a three of diamonds to be placed at three o'clock—then a card from that hour's pile is overturned and moved accordingly. I made my wish when I cut the deck, whispered the fortune that I wanted to be mine. For my wish to come true, the last card to be revealed must be a king. I take a sip of iced tea and press the cool can to my forehead, considering the probabilities.

Aslı asks me what I wished for. She is very interested in my recurring wish, asking me about it every time I lay out the cards, though I have yet to give her a straight answer. I smile and wait for the usual round of guesses, during which she watches my face closely. Besides my boyfriend,

Ian, who's back in California, Aslı is the most perceptive person I have ever met. She's aware that a question strategically phrased will always reveal its answer. A stark refusal to confirm or deny, an involuntary twitch at the mention of a sensitive topic—every response is a tell, if one can read it right. I keep my face tilted toward the cards just in case one of her guesses lands close to the truth, but so far, I've been pretty lucky.

"You wished for . . ." She stares into the middle distance and sucks in her cheeks. I am flipping, placing, hoping. The Small Club pulses around us, at its peak in the late afternoon. A pigtailed toddler with a floatie on each arm belts out a made-up song as she waddles among the tables; a woman in a baseball cap and aviators barks orders at a pimpled waiter; a group of younger girls run through a dance routine farther down on the lawn. Near the kitchen, Bulut and Ozan twist and jam foosball handles with such force that the table rattles and the woman in the baseball cap turns her attention from the hassled waiter to them and holds up a hand, yelling, "Enough now!" Just then, Bulut scores, ending the game. He howls and bangs his fists on his bony chest to celebrate his unlikely win. Ozan sneers and begrudgingly pulls a beer out of the café's fridge. He shoves the bottle of his lost bet into Bulut's chest, nearly knocking him over, then kicks the leg of the foosball table on his way back to us. The two resemble an unlikely duo from a children's book: Bulut scrawny and hairless with a protruding Adam's apple, his body all angles, while Ozan rarely shaves off his black beard, and is muscular and stout from years of disciplined chest presses. Ozan even has a tattoo, a line from a poem on his left shoulder: *Above all, the seagulls.*

Aslı watches the whole scene with a disgusted look. "Oh!" she says, her face brighter now. "Your wish is for Ian to come visit."

I laugh, flipping over a queen. I hadn't even considered Ian. "Talk about the twilight zone. I already have enough trouble adjusting. Him here, too? Just imagine. He's interning in San Francisco this summer anyway. Busy."

"He didn't even ask to come along on this trip?"

"It didn't come up. I mean, I didn't offer. We've only been together a year, not even. Since . . . October, yeah." One of hearts, two of hearts, three of spades. If Ian came here, he would expect me to show him this country, and I have nothing to show. I am far from conquering life here, not yet at the point where I can invite someone else in. It would be the ultimate embarrassment if my boyfriend, who knows my confidence in California, the strong praises I sing of my mother's homeland, caught a glimpse of all the things I do not yet know.

"Still, that's long. He didn't think it was weird, being separated for three months?"

"Not at all," I say, though I'm not so sure my nonchalance alleviates her concern. "This is here and that is there, and he is there." It comes out sounding pathetic in Turkish instead of cryptic like I wanted it to, but Aslı is good at understanding what I mean. She smiles somewhat pityingly and doesn't prod, and I return to another attempt at rewriting my future.

A month before we left for Turkey, my father expressed concern that my mother took omens too seriously. That was the same week he admitted his affair. The infidelity was news to both of us, though looking back on it, I realized it would have been impossible for my mother's long sojourns in Turkey and her depressive episodes to have slipped by without consequence.

The day the omen arrived, all three of us were in the kitchen. My mother was inspecting the dregs in her coffee cup, searching for shapes. "But when it comes down to it, you *do* agree that it's all a bunch of horseshit, right?" my father pressed. He came up behind her and cautiously rested his hands on her shoulders. She immediately shook them off, and they fluttered in the sky like frightened birds before he shoved his hands in the pockets of his jeans. His eyes dimmed, trying to interpret the interaction. He could never understand the pull of defeat my mother felt as the years went on, her confusion over how her body could still possibly be desirable to touch. I had grown up witnessing this push and pull for years, and only after I met Ian did I realize that theirs was not an ideal partnership. I began observing them more closely, trying to identify the problems.

One problem was that my father and his family are from Michigan, where people do not tell their fortunes.

"Some things *are* written," said my mother, turning the demitasse over in her hands. "And you can't change them, no matter how hard you fight against it." She set her cup back onto its saucer and twisted around to look my father in the eye. "Once you learn to accept your fate, you'll find that you see signs for it everywhere. Instead of being frightened that most things are already laid out for you in your life path, you'll feel a sense of relief and oneness with the universe. The universe speaks in the most unexpected of ways. You'll learn to take things a bit more as they come, to accept them instead of getting frustrated. Like you usually do." Then she gave us both a good-natured smile, a shade friendlier when she turned to me, because I was already one of the converted.

"Fine, sweetheart," my father said, sounding weary. "Tell us then, what's it say?"

My mother tilted her demitasse toward him. "Notice here?" she asked, gesturing with her pinky to a mound of dregs inside her cup. "It's dark, three-dimensional practically. That means that there is something brewing inside me. A worry, an anxiety that I've been suppressing. And here, we see two shapes. One small, one big. The small one is doing something to the big one, it has something in its hands. First a knife, then a . . . heart?" She peered in for a closer look.

Certain shapes in coffee fortunes have specific meanings, my mother explained. Like birds and good news, or a clean white space signifying a pure heart. All the rest is based on the fortune-teller's instinct as her eyes sweep the insides of the cup, taking in the images streaked by the grounds while it's set upside down to cool. In that sense, the fortune cannot actually exist without its fortune-teller.

"No, I understand now," my mother said, nodding. "I was right. Initially there's a stabbing from behind; then, behold, a heart appears."

"Machiavellian?" I ventured.

"Quite possibly," my mother said.

"Very imaginative, all this drama. If I had known such mumbo jumbo was permitted, I would have set up a business in clairvoyance instead of microchips," my father joked. He adjusted his glasses to fill up the space where nobody laughed.

My mother was quiet for a while, rotating the cup. "Yes, I see. It's a declaration of love disguised as a betrayal."

"What's this about love and betrayal?" My father's voice peaked, and I giggled at the unexpected pitch.

"Did I stutter?" my mother asked. It was one of the phrases she had picked up from me during my preteen years. In alternating languages, my mother and I are the limitations of each other's thoughts. My father stared at her, her jarring shift in tone having stunned him into silence. "A declaration of love. Disguised. As a betrayal," my mother repeated. Then she picked up the cup and saucer, ran the water in the sink, and carefully rinsed out her future.

A few days later, when my father buckled under the pressure of the fortune and confessed his infidelity, I was surprised at the shock on my mother's face. Hadn't she seen it coming, just the other day? I started to wonder whether, as she stared into the demitasse, her intuition had revealed a distinctly separate meaning for that smudge of a scene. A very different type of love, perhaps; a very unexpected act of betrayal.

She did not care so much who the woman was, my mother said, because it didn't matter. The action had been a cry for help, not a change of heart. She needed time to determine whether the marriage was worth saving. On my end, I refused to visit home for the rest of the school year. From time to time, I would drive by my father's office in Cupertino out of a morbid curiosity. I didn't know what I expected to see, but I never saw it. I caught a glimpse of him once, heading out to lunch with his cofounder, but never her. Gazing at that sleek, imposing building, I let myself imagine what a different sort of life would be like: if my mother had integrated, invested in a career; if she and my father had started off on more common ground.

My third king arrives. I place it in the middle of the pile and pull an unturned card out from underneath. Four of hearts. The current moment, the transition of the day. When the siesta in the air-conditioned bedrooms comes to an end, when the pastries for teatime are starting to be considered. I place it on its hour and move swiftly through the remaining cards.

"You wished for your parents to get back together?" Aslı asks, watching me carefully.

"They are together," I snap, and Aslı perks up, though this is not my secret. I take a deep breath, slowing down. "Though I'm not so sure they should be. They're just on a break as she thinks through things this summer. I keep telling her that what he did was unforgivable, but she's crafty and keeps making excuses for him." He had flown her overseas mere months after they had met, dropped her off at the edge of a new continent, where they tied the knot within the year. You could see the distance between them in the wedding photos: him, the wild red hair of a studious engineer, face and freckles bright and dumbfounded with luck, and her, a darkened olive, hair melting into skin, the only brightness a shining sword of hope in her eyes. At the altar, he promised a devotion whose difficulty he could not have fathomed.

In the hours he spends with us outside the office, my father is kind and generous. However, financing three months of separation from your wife and daughter takes a toll regardless of your intentions. It took me many years to understand how hurtful these summers away were for him, but by then, nothing could stop us from getting on that flight every June. The call of the Aegean, of my grandmother, was loud and clear. Why did they lean so heavily into a marriage that would destroy them both? Equally guilty, at first glance. But my father's power, his money, the fact that everything took place in his homeland and not hers, placed all culpability firmly in his court.

My mother's adjustment to America was a sacrifice that deserved more than what he had given her. I will not forgive him for it.

Bulut and Ozan come back to the table and pull out their chairs, Bulut still looking smug from the win. "We have an idea we want to talk to you about," he says.

"*You* have an idea *you* want to talk to them about," corrects Ozan. "And besides, there's no way they'll agree." He reaches across the table for a book he'd been reading, but his eyes are on Bulut's beer. In a second, he's snatched the bottle, chugged it down, and slammed it on the table. Bulut cries out, and Ozan's voice returns to its usual, playful lilt. "Actually," he says, "you never know with Ada, do you?"

The final king arrives too early. Aslı notices this and frowns, but I shrug it off. It doesn't matter. I've been wishing for the same thing all summer, and I have yet to end on a king. I gather up the deck and turn my attention to my friends.

"That's right, you never know," I say. "I'm a wild card."

2

THE ISLAND

A sea-cold hand on my shoulder, and the conversation stops before it can begin.

"Look at you all, fresh-faced as flowers." My mother's voice slips into the cadence of mine and my friends', but the authority of her tone lifts it above ours. With her other hand, she reaches across the table and turns over the newspapers, books, and magazines sprawled across its surface, reviewing what we've chosen as our summer reading. She nods, a silent comment on the selection, then taps a fingernail on the lone hardcover. A hefty book with a tangerine dust jacket. "Who's reading this?"

Ozan reluctantly raises a hand, as though in class. A tome in the months meant for play—Ozan's well aware that my mother does not approve. My mother is a woman who spends her California afternoons on the wicker love seat of our sunroom, working through a dog-eared collection of Mallarmé. She had attended one of the French lycées of İstanbul, and her taste in literature remains heavily foreign. But she never reads during the summer.

"I always have to soak up every minute of these Ayvalık months," says my mother. "I could never pass time alone in the dreamscape of a book. When you retreat into yourself in that way, allow another time and place to take you, aren't you refusing what the current moment has to offer? The days here pass too quickly for me to ignore them." She gives a disappointed half smile, and I understand what she means. We both feel a responsibility to make up for lost time. She for an entire lost life. "The original"—she taps again on Ozan's book—"is in French, were you aware?"

Ozan nods, visibly relieved to be spared further lecture.

"Ada's first crush in middle school was French. Remember him, Ada? My husband and I also met in Paris, two travelers on a rooftop bar. Though I have to say, he was far from being my first crush." She forces out a laugh to draw attention away from the flippant tone she used for the word "husband." Her alternating attempts to unveil and mask her looming decision make me cringe. I do so blatantly. The woman he had been sleeping with was American. A client, it turned out, of the company. They'd met at a business dinner at Evvia, the Greek restaurant on University Avenue where a date had taken me before prom and the waiter had sketched an archipelago of islands on the paper tablecloth to show me where his family was from. I'd yelped when my pita bread leaked a trail of tzatziki from Antiparos to Naxos, and he'd come over and drawn it all again on the other side. My father couldn't respect any delineation, rumbling over the borders without much thought as to why they were there, perhaps assured that he could rearrange them later. He overlaid the personal with the professional. He displaced my mother, but allowed her three months of the year in her home country, adding to her confusion. Nothing was sacred.

The affair was short-lived, but an indiscretion nonetheless. I never met the woman, though I am certain that she was everything my mother wasn't. Happy, most likely. The type who allowed men to caress her naked neck, nape to collarbone. Lived driving distance from her mother, supported with the familiarity of the life she had been born into.

Leave him and move on, I want to tell my mother. But I can't. Not in those words. It's difficult, as a daughter, to nudge parents toward the break. It is devastating to witness her sadness.

As for my first middle school crush, I remember him well, though I no longer remember his name. Whoever he was, I had asked my mother to teach me French words so that I could seduce him. She had offered up only pleasantries, and I had scowled at how she hoarded her knowledge, scattered only what was trivial and useless. *Bonjour, ça va?* How far could anyone get with that? But I managed. We made out for a full semester, until the international exchange period was over and he returned home. I remember how I had skipped swim practice to let him touch me in the music room after school, his hands up my crushed velvet shirt and my back pressed up against someone's bassoon case. How he had gotten so caught up in the moment that he mumbled something to me in French, forgetting who I was and what I could understand. That night I had gone home and knelt beside my bed and, opening up my hands like a book, whispered, "Please oh please oh please continue mistaking me for someone else forever."

I sigh and reach my arms out over my mother's shoulders, cradling her neck in my hands. My mother's face has always intrigued me; its weathered look, her loose curls framing it like a storm at sea. She's wearing a swimsuit I hate, this gray-and-navy tankini that ages her. I was told by the women in our Turkish-Californian community that before I was born, during the first five years she was with my father, my mother had been gradually declining into a different person. They insinuated that my conception was the fault line, that it was my birth that ultimately shattered her.

They told me my mother used to be someone who looked after herself. Cold creams with flakes of gold, an array of pots and potions lining the double vanity of the bathroom. My arrival, unfortunately, aligned with the more prominent manifestations of the sun's handiwork. I was born at the same time the years began to carve themselves outside of her eyes, down and around her lips. That's when her skin began to slacken, the women told me, and she started to shop for turtlenecks, collect silk scarves. When she could no longer comprehend her new relationship with the sun or with her body, she forced a punishment upon herself for the decay. My mother got rid of everything that had once made her feel beautiful, of any worth. She stopped exercising, rubbing away at her tightly drawn outline. One of my earliest memories is my mother slumped over the bathroom counter as I peered at her from the edge of the doorway. "What's the use," she had cried, holding tubs of her golden creams under a running faucet. "What's the use anymore?"

My mother turns back to Ozan. "Anyway," she continues, "there's no need to read when you're already in paradise. Books are for when you don't like where you are. Look, look at where you are!" She throws her arms open to express the expanse of the beauty we should all behold. The sea glitters in response, then is immediately ruptured by the cannonball jumps of teenage boys.

"I suppose we can get rid of these distractions," Aslı says, and sweeps her hand to knock the collection of literature to the ground. "Long live summer!" she yells. We all cheer, and my mother beams. Then she reminds me that the Small Club is serving *çipura* today, and that she's ordered three whole fish to be delivered to our house for dinner.

Oh, shoot, I tell her. I completely forgot. Noticing that she's unconvinced, I smack myself on the forehead for emphasis.

Just then, a waiter comes by and sets the meal I had ordered earlier in front of me: one mint lemonade and two Ayvalık *tosts*—large, panini-like sandwiches with sausage, ketchup, pickles, tomato, and extra mayonnaise—wrapped in recycled paper. My mother is incredulous.

"Ada, sea bream is the jewel of the Aegean," she says. "If this coast is known for anything, it's known for its sea bream. You're not honestly telling me that you'd rather fill up on *tost*?"

"To be fair, Meltem *teyze*, Ayvalık itself is specifically more famous for its *tost*," says Bulut. My mother arches an eyebrow at him, acknowledging the fact without conceding the win.

I forgot, I repeat, because really, I had. You can't expect me to—ow! My mother's fingernails dig into my shoulder. I flinch myself out of her grasp and gaze up at her. She's muttering something unintelligible, and her eyes are fixated on the other side of the café, beyond which groves of olive trees stretch southward, lining the coast. Between the groves and my mother is the man with the shark-tooth necklace. Even though he is far away, even though he is doing nothing but staring out to the sea, the effect of him there, inside her summer, seems to destabilize my mother. As the others continue talking, I gently take her unsteady hand in mine. No one else seems to notice the pallor of my mother's face, the tremor of a smile that is too frightened to take shape. I silently, and immediately, forgive her for her condescension regarding the sea bream. Is this my fault? Should I have prepared her for the eventual encounter? But there's no way I could have anticipated this reaction. I could not have realized that though this man might want to see my mother, she might not want to see him. I feel guilty for the secret, as though, by keeping this from her, I'd created a rift between us.

"*Allah belanı versin*," my mother curses, and her expression settles decisively into anger. Her words are so fragile that they are little more than an exhale. They fall to the ground like snowflakes. "You've got to be kidding me."

She tries to step forward, but because I am in her way, she walks straight into my chair. Then she blinks, noting the barriers, and works her way around the table. She nearly loses her balance again as her sandals catch onto one of the magazines on the floor. "What in the world," she says under her breath, kicking away the humor weekly she'd tripped over. "What in the world are you *doing* here?"

The man sits alone, his bare feet propped up on the empty chair across from him. My mother comes up from behind, blocking a segment of light from his peripheral vision, though it should barely be noticeable. There is too much movement in the café for her presence to have much significance. She waits until he finally senses that he's not alone and turns around. For a moment, they stare at each other. But it is not the type of stare that locks out everything else in the world, the type that causes sounds to collapse into themselves and the background to lose focus. Each can surely still smell the salt of the sea; they both still have one foot in the real world. In their gazes, my mother asks a question, and the man stalls. She smiles expectantly, tenderly, but there is no sign of recognition on his face. I nearly turn away, uncomfortable witnessing the unrequited emotions. Never have I seen her look at anyone like that before.

Something significant must have happened between them, once. I shudder, adjusting to my own suggestion. My mother's past has always held for me a vague and perfect history, those now inaccessible years where she had blossomed.

I think of how the man had noticed me in an instant from afar, from the movement of my head emerging from the water. I want to apologize to my mother for the fact that he had recognized me, but not her. But the searchlight of my mother's smile does not falter. Then something catches.

"Oh, but it's you—Meltem!"

The man lifts his feet from the chair and stands to embrace my mother. They kiss on the cheek, his hand hovering slightly over her arm as he leans in. There is a sort of pride in his smile, a sense of self-congratulation, perhaps, that an old friend can still note the resemblance from his youth. He motions to the chair, but my mother politely shakes her head. She gestures behind her toward our villa, then off into the distance where you can see the colors of her tent, establishing her life here in its spatial elements. Not once does she point toward me. I am used to these moments when my mother forgets she has a daughter, but they are not supposed to happen now. This man has milked it back out of her, thick in the stretch of summer when my mother is supposed to be mine again. The bad moments are only supposed to happen at the very beginning of our trip.

Our annual flight path: San Francisco International to Flughafen Frankfurt Main to İstanbul Atatürk, via Lufthansa. This is how I learned the German words for safety, emergencies, and the forbidden. Gifts in particular were unacceptable—"Gift" was German for "poison." No *gifts*! I'd screech, bouncing near a signpost of prohibited items. But we have *gifts*! We are carrying *gifts*! Other parents might have celebrated this wordplay, marveled at my precocity. But during those moments in my younger years, in the space between departures and arrivals, my mother remained indifferent. I'd wait for the gentle press of her palm upon my face, for its eventual tensing and small squeeze, her usual way to request that I stifle my silliness, but it never came. Not at the airport. Never, not once, at the airport.

For the first four years of my life, my mother did not take me to Turkey or speak to me in Turkish because my father believed that children raised in multilingual homes become slow learners. Later, when my mother noticed the mental acuity and linguistic skill of another Turkish-American child, she packed our bags and took me on my first flight. "I spoke to you throughout the entire journey," she told me. "Both legs." She recounted every Nasreddin Hoca fable that she knew and sang national songs in a quiet, beautiful voice as we unwrapped the foil from our chicken schnitzels. When she was at a loss for words, she read out loud from the in-flight magazine, translating every article, cover to cover.

But my mother's concern with the oversight began and ended with our first trip. After that, the winds shifted. Once we were there, she immediately lapsed back into her old life. The life where her mother had controlled her, where she was very clearly a daughter and nothing more. My grandmother laid on the guilt for the lost years, I fell in love with the sea, and it quickly became evident that we would return. Each time we left, my father stayed home to keep his business running. He was never interested in coming with us or meeting my grandmother, who had made it abundantly clear that she blamed him for her longing and loneliness.

For all of our following travels to Turkey, my mother showed no trace of her initial enthusiasm for my cultural education. She had been reminded what it was like to be home and treated the journey with a gravitas that was extreme, even considering her usual stoicism. At the waiting area by the gate, the seat next to hers was the last to be filled, if it was filled at all. The chill her body emitted saw to it. In the boarding queue, passengers understood the expected radius of proximity and adjusted themselves accordingly. And though I always stood next to her, of course, the distance between us while in transit was more prominent than any physical space. It was a vast field of disinterest. Almost as if I were someone else's child. An airline representative once kneeled down beside me and asked if I was traveling alone. I pointed up to my mother, who didn't turn around, because she wasn't my mother, I realized. My mother had already boarded the plane, had somehow navigated the labyrinth of fatigued and impatient passengers to make her way down the jetway. It was only when she had buckled her seat belt that she remembered she had a daughter and realized her daughter was not behind her. In Arrivals, as we waited for our suitcases to cycle through, I would gaze at the rows of unclaimed luggage. Desired, for some reason or another, at the start of the journey; unwanted or forgotten at the destination.

Each trip brought with it the painful reminder that I was not a natural extension of my mother's life; I appeared only after she took the fork in the road to become somebody else. When she traveled back into her past, there seemed to be no place for me. I, with my right-handed fork-wielding and loud indoor voice, my space-filler "ummms" and construction paper cutouts of Pilgrims, was clearly part of her new world. The pain of the dichotomy was in its temporary abandonment, but its heartbreak lay in the fact that the rupture occurred where it did—in a country that mocks, in tiny, piercing ways, every attempt at my integration.

Upon landing in İstanbul, my mother's discomfort peaks, then fades once a night and a morning has passed in my grandmother's winter condo. It finally crumbles when we leave on our eight-hour bus ride, always in the same blue-and-white branded vehicle, down the western coast of the country, off to the summer villa. My mother always reserves spots on the right-hand side of the bus and claims the window seat for an uninter-rupted view of the sea. My own view is mostly of the back of her head, and I put together the seascape from around her outline. When we breach the limits of the metropolis, she will unclasp her purse and take out a package of cream-filled cookies, unlatch my tray table, and place it silently on top. It is, I have learned, her way of apologizing.

I watch now as my mother points again to the villa, taps at her left wrist with an index finger, and says goodbye to the man she once knew. I observe his face carefully as she leaves, trying to figure out what has passed between them. He seems content, almost complacent.

"Ada?" Bulut's voice hooks and drags me back to our table, where Aslı has now neatly stacked the books and magazines. "You want to hear about this idea, or no?"

As she passes us, my mother raps on the table without breaking her stride. "Save some space for your sea bream," she calls out over her shoul-der. I try to sense whether there's a shake in her voice, but her volume overpowers any discernible emotion. What did the man say to her? "Grandma's not going to be too happy about a full stomach."

Grandma's never happy about anything, I yell back. My mother disappears down the oleander path. Then I turn to Bulut. "Okay, tell me."

Bulut leans into his chair to balance on its back legs, and Aslı instinctively shoves him forward. "You know the islands?" he asks.

There are three of them that are ours. Or at least that we call ours, the islands that we know for sure aren't Greek. The closest one is out from the left of the dock, and slopes into twin barren mounds, resembling a rocky moon landing. Nobody knows the actual names of any of the islands, but around our *site*, that one's known as Barren Island. The second and third islands are multiple times farther than the first, and much larger. If you stand at the edge of the dock, you will be directly across from the second farthest, which is round and smooth, plopped in the water like a scoop of ice cream. That's Ice Cream Island. The third, much farther out toward the direction of the Big Club, is lush and green, allegedly home to a small tribe of turtles. Turtles are generally spotted closer to the Mediterranean, so one can never be too sure of the facts. All we have to go off of are the reports from occasional explorers on Zodiacs. Turtle Island, we call it.

Of course I know the islands.

"Oh, you moron, is that what this is?" Aslı drops her head into her folded arms, and a mass of unruly black hair spills out on the table. "Bulut still wants to do the swim to Barren Island," she explains, her voice muffled. "Yesterday, when we were getting *lahmacun* from the market for dinner, the *lahmacun* maker's kid was bragging about how he had swum there once. You know Bulut, he believes whatever he wants to believe, but ask anyone in the whole *site* and they'll tell you that that kid's a world-class liar. He's ten years old, how can a kid manage that distance? Bulut, why can't you just be happy swimming to the raft like a normal person?"

The wooden raft is a twenty-second swim from the dock, and that's if you're slow.

"Learn to keep your mouth shut for a minute," says Bulut, and I silently agree, eager for him to continue. "Whether or not he actually— whatever. That's not the point. The point is that he gave me the idea. It's doable, you can see it, it's honestly right there. Right. There. How long can it take to swim, two hours? Three, at most?"

"Three hours is too long for the water to stay calm," says Aslı. She places her palms flat on the table and slowly raises her body, her stomach grazing the edge as she looms over us. "You've been coming here for years. I get it. You feel comfortable. Why wouldn't you? But notice the perimeter of what you're used to." She gestures to the Small Club, its lawn out front. The shark-tooth man, now ordering coffee with the air of a local. The changing rooms, the showers, the beach beyond, the dock, the raft where someone's grandfather is tanning on his back. "*Those* waters," she adds, stretching out her arm, indicating the faint shadows across the gulf, "are not a part of what you know. Don't fool yourself."

Bulut makes a face and peels away a strand of hair that has slicked itself onto his beer bottle. "One day you're going to be bone-bald and we're all going to be relieved," he says. "Don't maintain eye contact with my sister, Ada. You'll turn to stone."

As Aslı and Bulut argue, I continue to feign indifference. I rest my chin on Ozan's shoulder as he reads his book next to me. From what I can tell it's the fictionalized story of a famous astronomer. My lips move silently to shape out the long, agglutinative words. Here is a new suite of vocabulary, a different continent of lexicon from the lands I'd navigated. The Turks of California never speak in scientific jargon. In fact, their diction rarely strays from the boundaries of family life, of cultural events, of questions and concerns regarding their children. *Which one's the garlic yogurt?* Or *Lale's son forgot to wish us happy* bayram, *he pocketed the holiday money without once kissing our hands.* The older generations who left their country are stunted by the departure; they undergo a clean break from the flux of the rhythms and vocabulary of their homeland. They can no longer judge the tone and hesitations in a doctor's diagnosis while lying cold and naked on the examination table. It's like watching foreign cinema when their child screams, in someone else's voice, *CLOSE THE DOOR WHEN YOU LEAVE!*

The mothers give in easily, pressured to better communicate with their alien offspring. They take their cues from soap operas, then from each other. The fathers fall into deeper silences, growing weary in the hunt for the right word.

With languages, I've decided, it's best not to know anything at all. When a language is completely unknown to you, it's like a gleaming box on a table wrapped in black, festooned with a golden bow. It has edges, walls, contours. A solid shape—there are dimensions to it. You can pick up the box and carry it from one end of the room to the other. You can refer to it, point to it. Whatever is inside, fits. *That right there is French*, you can say. *I do not speak it.*

Then a day comes when you need something from the box. A tiny, insignificant item. A word. A phrase. Something to impress the Parisian boy in your seventh-grade geometry class. And you unlock it, and without understanding exactly what is happening or how it is possible, the box turns inside out. The walls are now not walls but something expanding perpetually, like the universe, say. You are in a shapeless world, with no beginning and no end. The hopelessness of parallel lines that will never intersect.

Aslı begs Bulut to consider the currents. "When it's man against nature, nature always wins. Every. Single. Time." She bangs her fist on the table with each of the last three words. "What if the weather turns? What if one of you gets a cramp, what then?" She tosses out each hypothetical with her hands. An unattended tea glass topples over, but she immediately rights it without losing a drop. "You're going to carry each other all the way back?"

"Hey, don't look at me," says Ozan, waving off Aslı's glare. "I never agreed to this. Keep me out of it."

"Ada," Bulut says, "in all your years of swimming, have you ever gotten a cramp?"

I shake my head no and bite into my *tost*. I have been waiting many years for someone to seriously decide on the swim, instead of just fantasizing about it as we've always done, but contain my excitement. I'd rather have Aslı keep her frustration directed at her brother than tire her out trying to convince both of us that it's a bad idea. I know it's a bad idea—that much is obvious. But if we were to do it, really make it all the way out there . . .

"And how many years, Ada, have you been swimming?"

"Since I was four. Competitively for ten."

"All right then, so what do you say?"

Throughout the years, the conversation about the islands had taken many forms, but it's always been driven by Bulut. The underlying idea is to do something wild enough to leave our mark on this town. Something our grandchildren, when they are breakfasting on the terraces of their inherited villas, could commemorate with pride. As long as I've known him, Bulut has been bothered by the seasonality of our presence here. He has a discomfort with the transitory, and a desire for a concrete conquest. He can claim no fame, no quality worthy of acclaim. Ozan has his intelligence, Aslı the magnificent luck of not caring what anyone may think of her, and I, I am a mysterious half foreigner whose life cannot be measured up against the lives of others. Bulut scored average on his college entrance exam, and wound up as an international relations major at a decent university in the capital. He's warm and friendly in order to compensate for the large swathes of acne across his face and his nearly skeletal frame. The worst of it is that he cares deeply what strangers think of him. Which is, to be honest, not all that much.

"I'll think about it," I say casually.

"Okay, okay," Bulut says, nodding rapidly. "Here's the plan. I'll head into the town center to look up the weather for the next couple weeks at the internet café. And maybe talk to that *lahmacun* kid again, if he has any tips—"

"He didn't swim there!" Aslı whips out a hand, ready to slap some sense into her brother. I laugh. Having the *lahmacun* maker's kid in your corner is almost worse than having no evidence at all. "When are you going to get it? The kid's a liar."

"And then we'll talk again and if you're in, which you will be, we'll pick a date. Okay?"

"Sounds like a plan," I say.

"So then . . ." Bulut leans back again into his plastic chair. Then he topples and falls to the floor in a tangle of limbs. "That settles that." He raises a fist, declaring his victory from the sandy tiles.

Aslı groans, and slides her elbows farther and farther along the table until her face falls into a pile of damp beach towels. I lean over to ruffle her hair. Ozan continues on with his book, and across the street, in response to something I cannot hear, my grandmother cries out in joy.

By the time I head home, it's early evening, and my mother and grandmother have already sat down for dinner on the front terrace. On my plate is the full body of a fish, one large eye dumbly staring at me.

"Oh, take your time getting ready," calls my grandmother as I head inside to change. "Your food's gone cold, anyway. Not that you care as much about eating with us as you do with your precious friends." Her voice booms over the footsteps and murmurs of beachgoers trickling out from the Small Club. My grandmother has a big, dramatic presence—everyone in town knows her—yet she is crafty, and can slip right through you when she wants. She is a large woman with large breasts, a former model and doctor's wife, a widow for many years. In her aged heaviness, her grace remains. She had perfected her light-footed, ethereal aura during her career on the catwalk, floating on the crowd's adoration.

After I've shoveled my body into jeans and a T-shirt, fidgeting as I reaccustom myself to proper clothing, I take my seat at the table next to my mother and begin to delicately explore my sea bream with a knife and fork. I try not to pay attention as my grandmother, from across the table, indulges in one of her favorite activities: running commentary on those coming and going from the Small Club.

"Did you see that?" my grandmother says. Eyes wide, she turns to my mother to confirm that she, too, has witnessed the scene. "Emine didn't wave hello back. I told you, she's losing her memory. You can tell by her expression, not to mention that she still comes all the way over to our beach instead of the one near her new villa. Her facial features are sliding, too, they're not where they used to be . . ."

A boy around my age in striped swim trunks passes by, one I'd never seen before. "Who was that, Ada? Do you know him?" my grandmother asks. I'm annoyed, sensing that she's trying to pair us up due to our similarity in age. Before I can make a snarky remark, she answers her own question. "Ah, but of course, of course," she sighs, her voice trailing off. "That's the diagonal neighbor's boy. He usually spends the summers sailing farther south. How nice that he came to visit his family, even though he already sees them all throughout the winter, unlike some people . . . Ada, you should meet him. Oh, don't sneer like that, it makes you look like a village donkey. Meltem, teach your child to control her unladylike impulses."

Just as my grandmother never really accepted my father as my mother's husband, she's also concerned about my potentially ending up with an American. Dating Ian is a positive mark in her book, since being single is unquestionably worse, but I know that she's constantly on the lookout for alternates. There are some things, she tells me, that are very important to share in a long-term relationship. Like where you come from. Whenever I remind her that I was born in California, she scoffs, "That's not what I mean, and you know it."

This fish hasn't been deboned, I say, pointing at it with my knife. My mother doesn't seem to hear me; her gaze is out toward the Small Club, but her eyes are clouded over, a haze blocking what's directly in front of her. Mo-o-o-m, I repeat. The fish.

"What?" She glances at my plate, at the detritus of an ineffective surgery. "Oh, but honey, you don't know how?"

"See, this is exactly what I've been telling you," my grandmother says. "Everyone born and raised along the coast knows the proper way to debone a fish, don't they? And yet, look at your daughter. Where you live now, does it even matter that you live by the water? Everything in America is handed to you from elsewhere, you don't know where it comes from. The connection is severed."

My mother nods and motions for me to pass along my plate, but my grandmother shoves her arm back down. "Ada should learn," she says.

"But I can do it so much fast—"

"Leave it, Meltem."

I make an ugly face at my grandmother. She gasps in mock shock, then laughs, acting as if this is all in good fun. My mother drifts back into her reverie, shifting her focus from time to time to check whether I am struggling. I want to ask her about the man, but I don't want to reveal our meeting earlier in the day, so I stay quiet. I wonder if she's thinking about him, about how he couldn't recognize her. From across the table, she mimes how, with my knife, I should lift the skeleton clean from the body. I concentrate on the extraction but listen in as my mother attempts to defend my cultural ineptitude.

"Our community in California tries to make sure that the kids retain Turkish values," she says. My grandmother cackles. She asks my mother to please elaborate, then settles into a more comfortable position on her chair, as if preparing to watch a film.

"We celebrate every *bayram*," my mother says, maintaining her composure. "Youth and Sports Day, for example—"

"Oh, yes, well, I remember a photo from the one last year. It was at the fast-food place, what was it? The Pizza Hut. Truly festive, Meltem. Congratulations, you are a model parent."

"Yes, a place where the youth can enjoy themselves." My mother cannot defy my grandmother, and ignores her sarcasm so they can continue along a thread of agreement. "And there's the Republic Day Ball," she adds, turning to my grandmother, triumphant. The Republic Day Ball is a dignified event, where the flags are ever-present, and the national anthem is the cornerstone of the evening. There is nothing my grandmother could say to suggest that, when it comes to celebrating the Republic appropriately, the Turkish-American community falls short.

I could, but I don't. I keep my mouth shut, my head down, and focus on my fish. The Republic Day Ball used to be the highlight of my California year, up until last year's event. Last year was the first time I saw it in a different light.

The ball was held on the peninsula, at the Redwood City DoubleTree on Friday, October 31. That was as close as the Board of the Turkish American Association could schedule it to the twenty-ninth. Though officially a celebration of secularism, nationalism, and Mustafa Kemal Atatürk, the ball served as an annual attempt for the cultural community to strengthen its fraying roots. The mothers and fathers celebrated the greatness of a

country in which they were no longer living, and the children longed after a glory they had never had, but had been promised ran through their
blood. It was a celebration of pretending that something that had been,
was once, could again be yours. In years past, I slurped up this illusion
like lentil soup from a ladle. I feasted off of it like I was breaking the fast
of a lonely American autumn.

A few weeks before last year's ball, my mother and I had gone shopping for evening gowns. Among the racks at Nordstrom, my mother
considered a lavender dress with sequins that shimmered down like a
rainstorm and gathered into a pool at the hemline. Its V-neck dipped low.
We bickered over whose skin tone best complemented its sunset hues
and compared the veins on the insides of our wrists, turning them over
in the fluorescent lighting. Green or blue? We couldn't tell.

"Ada," said my mother, checking the tag. "It's Jessica Macintosh. Like
your prom dress."

McClintock, I corrected. My mother stroked the chiffon fabric, dismissing what she considered mere detail. She held the gown up to her
body, even though it was several sizes too small, and pressed it to where
it hit her waist. In front of a mirrored column, she considered herself in
this way, shifting through angles while mentally adjusting all the areas the
years had reshaped or enlarged.

My mother lifted the dress off her body and held it out toward me.

"You try it on. It was clearly designed for someone like you."

We can just buy it, I said, taking the dress from her.

"You don't want to try it on first?"

I shrugged, checking the tag. It's my size, I said. I'm sure it will be fine.

Our new purchase in hand, we stopped at the food court for frozen
yogurt topped with mango cubes and mochi balls. "My favorite part of
the evening," my mother said, "is when they play the national anthem,
that's my true moment of connection to my past life. Everything before
and after, the speeches, the dinner, the dancing to popular music, it's just
ornamentation for the main event." But the truth was that my mother
loved every single second of the Republic Day Ball. Those evenings were
when she most closely resembled, I thought, the person that she used to

be. A social butterfly flitting among the tables, shaking her hips well past midnight. Seeing my mother in a whole new mood was one of the reasons I always looked forward to the Republic Day Ball.

"The thing is," she continued, searching with her spoon in the folds of her yogurt, "the younger generation, your generation, doesn't understand the connection we feel to our country. They see attending these types of events more or less as an obligation. Some parents are lucky, like I am with you, and the obligation brings with it a modicum of entertainment, making such things bearable."

I made a face at her. You sound like Grandma, I said.

"She's not wrong about absolutely everything, you know."

But what you said is not true at all, I countered. My Turkish-American friends feel just as strong a connection to the country as I do. It's not an emotion that can be qualified in a word as simple as "entertainment."

"No, no." My mother pressed a spoon against her mochi ball until it flattened. "The gulf between our experiences is too wide for us to have a similar perspective on this matter."

You can't just—

"Trust me, Ada. I know."

I didn't argue further, knowing that these were the types of beliefs that kept her grounded, kept her going. Back at home, with my bedroom door closed, I stepped into my new dress. I pulled the zipper up the side and admired how good I looked. My veins, as it turned out, were the correct ones.

Since my father had to work, my mother and I attended the ball by ourselves. I spent the first part of the evening nervously wandering the ground floor of the hotel, taking note of who had arrived, curious whether anyone of my generation had brought along their American partner. As more and more people streamed in through the revolving doors, I began to reconsider my decision not to invite Ian. He'd look out of place immediately, towering over everyone with an apologetic gaze. Cinnamon-colored hair so long it gets trapped in the hinges of his dark-rimmed glasses. Listening to the music in that condescendingly intellectual way of his— chin down, nodding slowly to the beat—that resembled anthropological analysis. Even though we had been dating for a few weeks by that point, the idea of bringing him filled me with dread. Rather than a substantive addition, it would be a detraction. Worse than coming alone. There were two opposing thoughts lodged firmly in my brain: one, that I was fascinated by and drawn to Ian for reasons beyond what he could offer me, and two, that his inability to provide any sort of stepping stone toward my culture was reason enough to shut him out of that part of my life completely.

I didn't explain it to him this deeply, of course. Over burritos at the dining hall, beans falling from the unfolding bottom of my tortilla, I simply told him, "It's not that much fun if you don't speak the language." Then I took a giant bite, buying time to answer follow-up questions that never came. Ian waited a few seconds, aware that there was something clearly left unsaid, but curious if I had the courage to say it. I chewed, gazing at him expectantly in turn. He conceded, realizing that it wasn't a battle he could win that day. Instead, he shifted the conversation to weekend plans, and asked if I wanted to hike Mount Tamalpais with him. I said sure, and felt relieved.

At the DoubleTree hotel, I wondered if I had made the wrong decision. Maybe I should have invited him. I went to the women's bathroom and locked the main door, then slid my body up onto the counter. Shifting my dress in various positions, I took several pictures of myself with my flip phone. I selected my three favorites and texted them to Ian. Thumbs whirring above the keyboard, I finally tapped out my message: *Next year!*

Next year, I thought, maybe I would be ready to introduce him to everyone, to explain why every corner of the ballroom was draped in prints of a blue-eyed blond, the founder of our Republic. I might even feel ready to witness Ian's attempts at dancing to *çiftetelli*, or, worse, watch him watch *me* try to move to that Middle Eastern beat. I almost always sat out the dancing portion of the evening, embarrassed at how my body refused to move to a rhythm that should, like all my ties to the homeland, already be flowing through my veins.

It wasn't long before I learned that not only had no one my age brought their significant other to the ball, but that none of my friends had even decided to attend in the first place. I weaved among the circular tables, each topped with a vase full of evil eye beads where an organizer had propped up two miniature flags, searching for someone, for anyone, under the age of fifty. For most of us, it was our first college Halloween weekend, and we were at a time in our lives where, apparently, that took precedence. Instead of celebrating their country, my friends were pouring orange juice and tequila shots into large red cups, spilling stale beer onto polyester outfits. I wondered where Ian was. I wondered where I should be.

Before dinner service, I spotted my mother deep in conversation with someone my age, a girl in a flowing golden tunic gesturing inelegantly with a glass of white wine in her hand. For a brief, beautiful moment, I was excited to have a friend in attendance, then recognized her as Deniz, daughter of the president of the Turkish American Association of California. A perpetual volunteer at cultural and charity events who proudly juggled multiple jobs at once: crouching by dinner tables to peddle the last of the raffle tickets, announcing items up for auction, and often handling the sound system while someone with more advanced Turkish led the group in the national anthem. In international circles, she introduced herself as something closer to "Denise," the name by which her American mother, Eliza, a Long Beach native, called her. As I walked toward Deniz and my mother, Deniz turned to face me, her eyes protruding and pink-rimmed, like the insides of seashells.

"Ada!" She opened herself up for a hug, which I allowed her to give. "Your mom and I were just talking about how you two have to plan your vacation with ours, align it in the same way. We're going to do the Blue Voyage on the boat and we're looking for more people to share the yacht with."

"It's called a *gulet*," I said, already annoyed. "Not a yacht." Deniz's Turkish, which she was speaking only due to my mother's presence, was overly formal and slathered over with a thick accent. She elongated words until the very fiber of the letters stretched itself thin, and mishandled her *r*'s, rendering them flat and lifeless where they should have been hot and quick, like peppers. She tried to make up for it by repeating the same message over and over, hoping that one of her renditions would catch.

"Sorry, I mean a *gulet*. What a funny word! It'll be a bit later in the summer, we're heading to İstanbul in August for a few days, then off to Fethiye from there. What do you think, can you make it work?"

"I don't know about that," I answered in English, doing her a favor. "We can't exactly plan that far in advance. My mom and I are a bit last-minute with our travel plans."

Deniz stubbornly insisted on her initial language. I winced as she continued. It could be possible that she received a twisted joy in hearing the mangled words fall lifelessly from her mouth, as if it somehow brought her closer to something just to have made the half-hearted attempt. "It's fascinating how it took me so long to love my summers there," she said, turning to address my mother. "When my dad forced me to vacation in Turkey as a child, oh, I was so bored, I hated it. All I could think about were those pool parties and bar mitzvahs that were going on without me. I'm so embarrassed about it now, of course. So ashamed. So . . . regretful."

One of the organizers called out for Deniz, and she snapped around and gave a sharp nod. "I have to go," she said, her tone suddenly official. "They need me, but please, enjoy the evening!" She tapped her chignon to check that her spray was still holding, and disappeared into the crowd.

Over dinner, Deniz and Eliza sat at our table, the men in both our families represented by the two empty seats. My father was on a business trip to Singapore, and hers was occupied as the master of ceremonies. I became intently focused on separating my grilled vegetables by color, and Deniz was forced to shift her attention to the adults.

"Right, your daughter mentioned something," my mother was telling Eliza in her stunted English. "Unfortunately, we always go straight from İstanbul to my mother's villa in Ayvalık. I don't think we can fit in a Blue Voyage."

"Does your daughter actually have any fun out there?" A heavily bejeweled woman on my mother's left leaned into their conversation, curiously blinking what had to have been a reconstructed set of eyelids. I arched an eyebrow toward her, indicating my presence and therefore capability to answer for myself, but she continued on. "Every summer, out of obligation, of course, we have to visit my in-laws in Ankara, and my poor boy just sits there all day, rereading comic books. He hates spending time in that country, has made no friends there. He doesn't speak Turkish and has zero interest in learning. And the way he speaks English . . . a mile a minute. I was educated with proper British schoolteachers, of course, but we don't understand each other at all. At all." At the end of the sentence, she fell despondent and closed her eyes to showcase her improved skin, fleshy and pert.

"Well, Ada loves Turkey," said my mother. "No wine for me, thank you," she told a waiter poised with a bottle behind her. My mother detests wine. She motioned toward the *rakı* that she was drinking instead.

The woman raised her eyebrows. "But of course, your daughter is just there during the summers, all she gets is a glorified glimpse. For kids like Ada and Deniz, the place is nothing more than a holiday country. Just comfortable enough to navigate at their language level. To enjoy the highlights of a secluded beach town, without all that impossible big-city chaos."

I had reached over to sample some of my mother's *rakı*, but when I heard this, I spat it right back into the glass. I stared at the woman, incredulous. Had she really just compared me to Deniz like that? Couldn't she see that we belonged to two different categories, two different worlds— that Deniz (*Denise!*) lay fathoms below me? It's true that I never feel completely at home while in Turkey, but here, among the Turks of California, I am one of the few of my generation who truly enjoys my summers there, one of the well-connected to the country. I even speak the language, for crying out loud. Deniz can barely string together a sentence, butchering every coincidentally correct word with that horrendous accent of hers.

"Totally!" said Deniz, taking a healthy sip of her mother's wine. "I mean, I love it, but like, I'd never be able to live there."

"What an idiot," I mumbled under my breath. Nobody heard me, though the bejeweled lady across the table smiled sweetly, as if my attempt to join an adult conversation was comical and cute. I scowled at her, and was pleased to notice that her eyelids could express only so much of her shock.

As dinner wound down, I slouched deeper into my chair, annoyed about the onset of the next part of the evening, the part I always avoided. The dancing. Dancing to old songs with lyrics I never knew, or to Turkish pop hits—but only from summers, never from now. Since nobody at this ball traveled to the country in any other season, nobody knew what songs played on the radio the rest of the year.

Those who gather and feel at home at events like the Republic Day Ball, I decided, are those who chase after lives that will always remain just out of reach. I made a promise to myself that I would never again attend one of these events. I did not want to be one of those people. I did not want to be like my mother.

"Ada, get up. Get up right now!" Deniz pulled at my arm, the edges of her gold bangles scraping against my wrists. "I hear they beat up those who stay seated," she laughed, mimicking a phrase she'd heard from parties past. "Come on, your mom is already on the dance floor, she's asking for you." I turned toward the stage, unsurprised. Yes, there she was, part of a circle of middle-aged women in rhinestone dresses. They were dancing to "Bambaşka Biri," a cover of "I Will Survive" by Ajda Pekkan, a pop star celebrated for her ability to look younger as the years went on. I watched my mother make her way to the stage while lifting her arms as if in prayer, eyes to God, to the DJ, to whoever was up there and would listen, telling them with violently shaking hands that she was stronger now, that everything would be different. All she had wanted, my mother screamed along with Ajda, was to take back the past that he had stolen from her. Then she laughed, winked at the DJ, and sauntered back to her place among the women. "Hey, hey!" they chanted at the chorus, fists in the air. "Hey, hey!"

I gave Deniz an apologetic look and put a hand to my stomach. A vague indication of indigestion, of cramps, of general fatigue. Food poisoning, maybe. She rolled her eyes and returned to the group of singing women, her body collapsing into a shimmy as soon as her stilettos sensed the transition from linoleum to hardwood.

Let them have their fun, I thought. Let them dance the night away. I flipped open my phone and smiled at Ian's response to my text. *Yes, next year!* But at that moment, I knew that there wouldn't be a next year. This would be my last Republic Day Ball. This was a place pretending to be elsewhere. All this, I thought, looking at the tiny flags in the evil eye vases, the beaded ball gowns, the broken words falling from Deniz's lips as she translated lyrics for her mother, all this just brought me closer to nowhere.

⚓

"For the dinner at the Big Club this week, you should wear your white dress," my grandmother says to my mother. She scrapes off the bones of her sea bream for a tabby cat meowing at her feet. "That one we got from Vakko, years ago. Now that you're no longer married, you can't afford to look like a hag. There will be a show, it's a proper event."

"Excuse me?" A shadow flashes across my mother's face.

"Though with your extra kilos, now it's a real gamble on whether it'll still fit."

"In what world are you living? I'm still married, aren't I?" She wiggles her left hand, the thin wedding band still on her finger. Minimalist jewelry has no chance of impressing my grandmother, who chuckles to herself. I slink out of my chair and join the cat on the floor, hoping no one asks for my opinion. There's no way that I'm letting my grandmother have the pleasure of knowing that I'm in agreement with her.

"It's just a rough patch, that's all," my mother continues. "We'll work through it once I get home. I'm sure of it. And besides"—she bobs her head side to side, as if considering some unpleasant evidence—"I wouldn't say that I'm entirely without blame."

"My dear darling daughter, how are you ever going to get over something as hideous as an *affair*? No self-respecting woman can. Take it from me. And what's your greatest fault? That you miss me, want to spend time here? Nothing that a man shouldn't be able to handle."

"Missing you . . . I suppose, yes," my mother says, but her eyes are on the sea.

My grandmother's dominance is what drove my mother away from Turkey in the first place. Ever since I was old enough to voice an opinion, my mother has gone out of her way to offer me options. *Carrots or peas?* she would ask at dinner. *Do you want the red dress or the blue overalls?* "I do this," she had once explained, "because my mom never did. And look where it got me. I never know what it is that I want, and every decision overwhelms me."

My mother increased her distance from my grandmother slowly, starting with a trip to Paris, where she met the American backpacker who became my father. She had had dreams to attend a prestigious music conservatory in France, but my grandmother had forbidden it. Instead, my mother had gone to a university in İstanbul and graduated with honors in mechanical engineering, a degree with which she did absolutely nothing.

"He said he's still working," my mother says, tossing the sentence out casually into the silence, like a stone into a still lake. "Going back and forth to İstanbul."

For a second, I wonder if it's my father who is coming to Turkey for work, but the softening in my mother's tone makes it clear that we are no longer talking about him. We are speaking, I am sure, of the man with the shark-tooth necklace. The man my mother once knew. I stroke the stray cat between her ears while she paws at the remains of the fish. The ripples from my mother's comment grow larger than expected, echoing out a heavy suggestion. My grandmother is swift to pick up on the unspoken.

Her eyes gleam from their small, wrinkled holds, reflecting the radiance of her sapphire necklace. "Wonderful!" She claps her hands, then shifts a bit in her seat. "You know, Meltem, you should absolutely go with him to the city one of these days. It would be good for you, to go back to where it all began. To start again."

"You can't be serious." My mother dismisses the possibility with a wave of her hand. "It's just a coincidence that he's here anyway. A strange, absurd coincidence. That's all. It means absolutely nothing. You know he took one of those villas behind the market?"

I lift myself back up to the table, moving closer to the conversation. I am intrigued by this man from İstanbul. İstanbul has always remained mysterious to me, a city I've never really gotten to know. It's only ever been a layover for us, just one or two nights in my grandmother's winter condo after the transatlantic flight, then onto that blue-and-white bus southward, family calling. The condo itself is unlivable during the summer months, the whole place draped in rose-colored bedsheets to shield the antique furniture from the dust. Halloween town, I used to call it. The İstanbul home as a living organism is a foreign concept to me. Never have I seen its furniture sparkling, its host present and welcoming, a kettle boiling on the stove. During our nights as boarders, my mother and I place a polyester tablecloth over the mother-of-pearl-studded dining room table. It's our tradition to order İnegöl-style meatballs and *mantı* from a restaurant on the Avenue, poking at our food with plastic cutlery and chewing quietly so as to not disturb the slumbering antiques, ignoring the incongruity of our modern reflections in the tall wall mirror.

"You saw him, too, didn't you, Ada? Today, on the beach, your mother's friend?" My grandmother loves asking questions she already knows the answer to. Her expression dares me to deviate from the truth.

"He seems nice," I lie. He seems forceful, like he could turn our lives upside down. I like that. I don't like nice. My father is nice. Nice can destroy you as you sit with it forever, content to never move again.

Ian is nice.

"Where do you two know him from, anyway?" I ask.

"Ohhhhhh," says my grandmother, diving into the thick of the answer. "From İstanbul, my husband and his father were dear friends from high school. Your mother and he were quite close, romantically, I mean, until they weren't." Here she looks at her daughter, but her daughter doesn't react. Instead, she smacks her lips.

"Wow, this sea bream is quite yummy," my mother says.

I make a face. It feels pathetic, this trite description of hers. I consider what it means that those are the only descriptive words she can summon after decades of experience. How easily language can slip away after years abroad, strategically leaving behind vague descriptors, widely applicable. Just one more thing my father has taken from her. It suddenly becomes very important to me that she fall in love with this man, that she reclaim the precision of her vocabulary. *This sea bream,* I want to hear my mother say in Turkish, *is fresh-caught, wild, and meaty. Look at it: the gelatinous eyeball, the sweetness of the cheek meat, the copper burns along its iridescent flakes.* A simple reconnection, a quick slip back into her old life. After graduation, I could come live here with her. Fall and winter and spring. In the summers, I would visit my father. I move the fish around my plate so it looks as though I've eaten more than I have, then get ready to meet my friends for our nightly beers.

3

THE BIG CLUB

On the evening of the dinner and show at the Big Club, my mother, grandmother, and I get ready as one would for a night in the city. We yank brushes down the tangles of our hair, fumble around the shoe racks for sandals with proper straps, and choose to be optimistic about the effectiveness of old tubs of moisturizer we find around the house. In the shower, I scrape the salt from my scalp with my fingernails, and scrub the sea out of my skin with a congealed, apricot-scented bodywash. There's a travel-sized blow-dryer at the bottom of a cabinet, but it sizzles and smells like ash. I wrap my hair in a towel instead and wander in and out of the upstairs rooms, killing time.

In the balcony off the master bedroom, my grandmother's room, I loop my wet bikini around the wooden railing and contemplate the islands. How far could they possibly be? Water transforms distance. It spreads and spreads, and then, after a certain point, a reasonable point, it folds onto itself and conceals the remaining miles. But even keeping this in mind, the islands still don't seem that far to me. Besides, it's just water; all you have to do is keep swimming until you get there.

I head back to the bathroom to poke around the cabinets. In one drawer I find a bottle of Tahitian vanilla body spray purchased years ago in Sunnyvale from a strip mall that's no longer in business. Likely left over from my middle school years. I press on the pump, and step into the mist just as my grandmother walks into the bathroom. She coughs, covering her mouth with one hand while waving away the smell with the other.

"What did you do, Ada, bathe in this?" She plucks the bottle from my hands and runs a thumb over its flashy gold logo. Though it's still three-quarters full, she tosses the spray into the trash bin next to the toilet. "You're a woman now. Maybe it's time for a more subtle aroma, no? For the love of God, let me help you." She scans the bottles atop the bath-room cabinet, but can't find what she's looking for. Then she opens and closes its drawers, snaking her hands around tubes and boxes and bottles until her fingers latch onto something with a twist-off cap. "Aha! Here it is. I bought this for your mother years ago. A rose oud. Try it." Before waiting for me to answer, she uncaps the bottle, grabs my right hand, and sprays along the curve of my wrist.

"Grandma!" I jerk my hand away from her. "Get out of here, this bath-room is too small for both of us." Placing my hands on her shoulders, I guide her backward down the corridor, into her room.

"You don't like it?" says my grandmother. "Then eat whatever shit you want to eat." This is her way of saying, *Suit yourself.* Her ankle hits the base of the bed, but she descends lightly on her way to sit down. She folds her hands upon crossed legs and inspects her fingernails. Chipped. I watch her lips purse in a mix of surprise and disgust, as if she's sampled an inferior lemon from a neighbor's yard. As I roll my eyes at her antics, I glimpse my mother in the periphery.

In front of my grandmother's vanity, my mother is applying her makeup. Though her own bedroom is the last down the hall, my grand-mother's is the only one with a mirror. Unzipped bags of lipsticks and powders, sachets of jewelry lie out open in front of her, like mouths yawn-ing. An eyelash curler glints in the evening sun. She must have found the kits in the bathroom cabinets, as they all flaunt the garish designs of the past. I can't remember the last time my mother attempted any sort of beautification with such effort, other than for the October ball. My annoyance at my grandmother disappears immediately, and I clasp my hands at my chest, hoping that this might be the beginning of something. My mother dips a hand into a mini canvas bag and pulls out a lipstick, staring resolutely at her reflection. I recognized the shade, Cabana Kiss. I had bought it at the Frankfurt duty-free several years ago.

She gives me a half smile by way of apology, but I don't mind at all when she takes my things without asking. Most of what we have, we share. I give her a full smile back, and watch her transformation. Its beginnings are grotesque. Her face has been smeared with primer, and there's a beige concealer across her lips ready for the tube of deep red she holds in her hand. All the pigmentation of her skin, the rose pink of her lips, and the fissures of age that crackle out from the eyes, curve along the mouth—all of them have been swallowed whole by the cosmetic liquid. What I see in the mirror is a woman with no face, no mouth, and no obvious age. Then she moves her hand and slowly bleeds the color back into herself.

After my mother heads back into her own room to change, I linger in front of the mirror to sift through my grandmother's jewelry. "Grandma, everything you own is clunky and turquoise," I complain, peering into the sachets. Whatever I try on drags my earlobes down, and I can glance for only a second at my reflection in the patina of the mirror before turning away. It's extraordinary to me that my grandmother can be interested in all this weight. I finally find a pair of stud earrings shaped like silver starfish, their convex design creating the illusion that they've suctioned onto my skin. I am a boulder in the middle of the ocean. Before heading out, I dab the smallest bit of rose oud on the inside of my left wrist to even out the scents of the dueling perfumes. I lift my hand to my nose. It smells ancient, like the bedsheets draped over the furniture of the İstanbul condo.

The gate of our villa closes gently behind us, and we step into the type of weather that we call lemonade. The most comfortable warmth, one you can't even tell that you're moving through, undercut with a slight breeze. Ice in the glass of your summer drink. Under a golden sky, my grandmother stops across from the Small Club and clicks her tongue in disappointment.

Her hands move to my mother's shoulders, each hung with a bow supporting a white eyelet dress, pulled so taut that the neckline is nearly up to her chin. It's only now that I get a good look at what she's wearing. The outfit seems outdated. In fact, there's a slight streak of yellow under the arms and along the hem. My grandmother must have fished it out of some old trunk. I breathe in deeply, searching for the scent of mothballs beyond the harsh notes of my own perfumes. My mother stares vacantly as my grandmother undoes the bows, loosening them so that the dress drops lower on each side, exposing the wilting crevice between her breasts.

"You should take care to look nice, Meltem," she begins, but a scream interrupts her. It's coming from the Small Club. The scream multiplies. My grandmother turns in to the oleanders and rushes down to the café, ravenous for gossip. My mother and I follow close behind.

There are only a few people in the café at this hour, evening swimmers who prefer quiet and stillness. But tonight all of them are on their feet, yelling and waving their hands. We weave through the tables to get closer, out of place in our city clothes. In the water, well beyond the wooden raft, there's a disturbance. Two arms reaching up out of the waves, the dark shadow of a head slowly sinking.

There is no lifeguard at the Small Club.

We are not doing anything, only standing in shock. Many continue to yell and wave, hoping that it may help, but why is no one getting into the water? My mind keeps wandering to how my lips are red and my elbows are moisturized and how the three of us do not belong here at the Small Club, dressed as we are. Then all our heads whip to the side as a flash of orange thunders down the pier and leaps into the water.

The man resurfaces from his dive and disappears into the whitewater of his urgency. The drowning swimmer's arms shorten, shorten, disappearing. The man passes the raft; he is nearly there. There is too much going on, but what I am most worried about is the awkwardness of wearing shoes in the Small Club. I try to tell myself that there are worse things; there is not knowing how to swim, for instance. The man reaches the swimmer—I can now see the thick shoulder straps of her suit. He takes her on his back, and together, slowly, they head toward the pier. At the base of the ladder, the two unspool, and the man gently guides the woman out of the sea. She is much older, with large thighs, a crooked back, and a trembling hand. When the man comes up on the pier beside her, he takes her arm and they walk down together toward the Small Club.

"Emine!" my grandmother gasps. Then she squints. "Is that Levent?"

My mother doesn't adjust her gaze; she's already seen him. "Yes, that's Levent." She nods. "He's the one who saved her."

"A hero," my grandmother says.

I recognize the man with the shark-tooth necklace. I can see the leather string around his neck as he turns toward the showers, seawater dripping from his orange swim trunks.

A-ah, I say to my mother. Look, it's your friend.

"Friend," she repeats sharply, as if correcting me.

My grandmother grabs my mother, who in turn grabs me, and we scurry to the showers. A few people are coming by and congratulating Levent as he rinses off, but most of the people and attention are focused on Emine. She sits on a sun bed, coddled in a towel and surrounded by waiters and neighbors.

"The family together," Levent says, giving a nod to each of us. He reaches for a striped cloth towel from the towel rack, holds it for a minute, then slings it around his neck. I don't know why he doesn't dry himself. There is water everywhere. His orange swim trunks cling to his thighs, translucent where they touch the skin. Water drips from the curled edges of his long black hair, from his eyelashes. I track one slipping down his cheek, falling, then sinking into the waistband of his trunks. It is different, seeing someone so naked in the evening, especially when I am properly dressed.

Levent's towel is a *peştemal*, in vogue the last several years for their light weight and absorbency. Us, we have too many towels collected over past summers to switch to anything new. The ones we drape around our shoulders are always heavy with water or hardened by the sun.

"Yes, all of us together, our little family. It doesn't happen often," says my grandmother. Her face is bright, and her pearl-pink lipstick shines.

A drop of water hesitates on the very edge of Levent's hooked nose. I have a sudden urge to place my hand underneath and capture it before the fall. To walk around with that droplet on my fingertip, protecting it. I imagine it holds the secret to his great adaptability, his audacity to already start saving us from ourselves when he has just arrived in town.

The droplet drips, then disappears onto the stone between his feet. I gasp.

"Ada?" My grandmother raises her eyebrows at me. She cannot stand when I act inappropriately in front of mixed company. "Is everything all right with you?"

I nod, unsure of what's come over me.

"Ada I had the pleasure of meeting only recently," says Levent. He smiles at me without showing his teeth. Then he opens up into a grin, a line of small yellowed squares. "Her Turkish is very good. Meltem, you've done an excellent job."

I know my Turkish isn't as good as it should be, and I know that you would never compliment someone on something that seems to come naturally to them. I want to say something in Turkish now, a sentence I have spoken over and over again that has developed the fluency of a local, but nothing comes to mind. I remain mute. My grandmother leaps in, sweeping away the attention.

"Meltem has never forgotten her roots, of course, but you! How are we standing here talking about something other than the fact that you saved a woman's life today? Oh, the event has messed with our minds. You are a hero, Levent!" Without invitation, she steps over and kisses him on his wet cheeks. When she retreats, Levent looks embarrassed.

"Emine!" My grandmother remembers, and rushes over to see her friend. My mother follows her, but I stay where I am. Levent lifts the end of the *peştemal* up to his face and gives it a cursory wipe.

"Ada, do you spend much time in İstanbul?" he asks.

"Sure," I say. "We fly into the city and stay on the Avenue."

"The Avenue." He pauses to consider this. Then he shuts his eyes so tightly his upper lip lifts, as if thinking of something he shouldn't. He opens them again. "Do you ever go to the European side? Do you know it well?"

"Yes." The lie surprises me. My mother and I almost never cross over, but I don't want him to know this. I don't want him to know that if I go to the European side and am no longer on the Avenue, which runs parallel to the Sea of Marmara, I won't know how to get to the water. To be lost in that way is embarrassing in this country.

"The European side is the best side, full of history," he says. "The other side, there's not that much there."

"No," I agree. "There isn't." I am suddenly very aware of my hands. I place them on top of my head, a daytime habit for when I want to assess the strength of the sun. My hair is cool from the evening and silken from the conditioner, and everything feels wrong. I drop my arms back to my sides, trying to act natural.

"You belong on the European side," he says. "A girl like you, you would turn that place inside out. You would wreck that city, do you know what I mean? As we say: İstanbul, cauldron; you, ladle. Cihangir, Çukurcuma, Bebek. All those neighborhoods are filled with girls like you. Color and laughter and energy. It's a pity you don't spend more time there."

"We have to see my grandmother," I say. "She moves down here in May, and she misses us too much." Spoken out loud, it does not sound like a good enough reason. Levent's expression, one raised eyebrow, reflects my own thoughts. *Not good enough, Ada.* His face is an echo, an amplification of my insufficient excuses. I look down at my feet and tell him that I should probably go check on Emine.

⚓

After leaving the Small Club, we arrive at the Big Club. We're shown to a table for four by the windows that overlook the abandoned dock of Sıfır, and wait for Neslihan, a friend of my mother's who will join us for dinner. The outdoor seating of the Big Club is tiered, and on the terrace above, grandparents in swimsuits play cooncan, ignoring the club's official transition to a fully clothed evening program. On our level, men fiddle with lighting equipment near a makeshift stage, where the kids of the town will put on a dance show, and then a woman will sing hits from decades past. Most of our *site* will be here tonight.

A waiter greets my grandmother, who immediately begins to inter-rogate him about this evening's selection of fish. "Ada," says my grand-mother, once the matter is settled to her satisfaction, "why don't you go inside and choose some appetizers for us from the kitchen display? Try not to get anything with too much garlic."

I pull out my chair and ask my mother if she has any preferences.

"Meltem shouldn't eat anything with cabbage, obviously," my grand-mother says. "It gives her terrific gas."

I walk inside the building, which houses the manager's desk and the kitchen, and where the appetizers are displayed in a refrigerated vitrine running along the hall. The restaurant manager is in a heated discussion with a waiter on how to remove the gambling grandmothers to free up space for the evening's guests. As I order, I keep one eye on the rotary landline on the manager's desk, wondering if I can squeeze in a long-distance call. There's never any privacy at home. I point at several cling-wrapped glass trays as another waiter scribbles down my order: sea beans with garlic, purslane with garlic yogurt, fried eggplant with tomato sauce and garlic yogurt. Can you add garlic to the squash blossoms? I ask. No? Well then, stuffed squash blossoms, arugula salad with pomegranate mo-lasses, and cockles drenched in white wine. I wonder which ingredients might give my grandmother gas. I add a spicy walnut paste and artichokes in olive oil to the order. It's probably not enough, but just as I'm about to place another three orders, the frustrated restaurant manager leaves his desk to see to the removal of the card players himself. "That's all, thank you!" I wrap up, and slide into the newly empty office chair. I twirl in the country code, then the number I know by heart. Ian picks up on the second ring.

"Hiya, it's me."

"Ah, we hear again from the ever-elusive Ada."

"Tough to catch a break," I say. In the kitchen behind me, the cooks whisper among themselves, but I know that they're too busy with or-ders to kick me off the phone. I have not been good about keeping in touch with Ian this summer. In all fairness, I had warned him about the potential drop in communication. I'm rarely indoors, and it's hard to ford the mental distance between here and there.

"I'm kidding, you know I'm honored. Tell me, where are you right now?"

"We're at a little event at the restaurant in our town. Small drama—someone nearly drowned. And my grandmother is eternally aggravating." I lower my voice, cognizant of the waiters listening in. "I feel so awful for my mom. I don't know how she puts up with it. Tell me something about you, how you're doing. Get my mind off my family."

"A drowning?" Ian sounds alarmed.

"She's safe," I say, and am annoyed with myself for having brought it up. There's something too intimate about the scenes from today; something stops me from sharing them in detail over the phone.

"All right, all right. I know just what you need," Ian says. "Hold on, I'm propping the phone on the keyboard, I won't be able to hear you, okay?" I recognize the opening notes to Chopin's *Fantaisie-Impromptu*. It's an electronic keyboard, but Ian's mastery brings its own authenticity to the music. One day, he will become one of the Greats. This is not because I know enough about piano to give a professional opinion, although I do, but because it's one of those things that you can see in his eyes and hear in his voice whenever he talks about his future. Ian holds a deep regard for the Greats, without bias to their domain, as long as it overlaps with beauty. He is fascinated by the men who devote themselves to one calling and one calling only—reads biographies of Dalí, of grand chess masters—and is terrified by the bleak lives of those who must supplement their genius with day jobs. Because he naturally excels at biology, he's been pressured his whole life to apply to medical school. I know he'll do it, too. I tell him his parents have him brainwashed, but he demurs. Stability is a common desire, and sometimes at night, he even dreams of his own artistic incisions. Though we've never addressed this commonality directly, one of the things that draws Ian and me together is our shared suspicion of whether it's possible to be two things at once.

I clap enthusiastically at the end of the *Fantaisie-Impromptu*, cradling the phone on my shoulder. Ian mumbles out a perfunctory thanks. I know that he is not blushing. He understands how good he is, but he also knows how long the road to genius will take. There is the shuffle of sheet music being put away; then he switches his tone to something gentler and describes the bedroom he's rented for his summer internship, in an Edwardian duplex in Russian Hill. It's one floor above the dry cleaners. "Every time I walk inside my apartment," he says, "I feel like I've been tossed into the washing machine and doused with a hot blast of Fresh Pine Air." Where I am, I tell him, the heat from the grill rises and spreads over my body; the smell of fish tangles itself into my hair. I giggle, imagining him as a tree and me as a fish, and then stop, concerned that I cannot find a suitable landscape upon which to superimpose the cartoonish image. Just then, the restaurant manager walks back through the doors with a look of professional satisfaction. I ramble off a goodbye-I-love-you and hang up. Back at our family's table, someone has taken my seat.

Despite being small and frail, Neslihan takes up a lot of space. She is the type of woman who drapes herself in bold coral jewelry and picks up pastry crumbs with the licked pad of her finger in our garden during teatimes. She speaks loudly, gestures freely, and has an unapologetic authenticity that I love being around. When I arrive, the three women are in the trenches of a heated discussion, so I smile my hello and take the remaining empty seat, which happens to be next to my grandmother.

Neslihan inches her palm closer to the middle of the table, in a series of failed attempts to interrupt my grandmother, who is dizzy with the passion of her own tirade. "Mukadder *teyze*—" Neslihan pleads, but my grandmother clips her short. "Mukadder *teyze*, will you please listen—"

"If she hadn't made that decision—" My grandmother's voice crescendos, and I flinch. "Maybe if you had talked some sense into her back then, if she hadn't decided that this was the time—of all times!—to make her own decision, then maybe I wouldn't have had to give up my entire family for—"

"Mukadder, that's enough!" Neslihan shouts, and the entire restaurant, all terrace tiers, trickle to a silence. Ceramic plates settle softly on the white tablecloth as a waiter arrives with our squash blossoms. My grandmother presses her lips together, her nostrils flaring at the show of disrespect from Neslihan, at the audacity to address her without "*teyze,*" her honorific.

My mother sits with her hands folded on her lap, looking torn. There are lipstick stains on all sides of her water glass. "What's done is done," she mutters. She places a napkin over her thumb and rubs it along the edge of her glass.

"Meltem has an incredible life in California," Neslihan says. The elegant clatter of silverware picks up again across the restaurant, though some diners still cast stares in our direction. "The husband she chose has been an excellent provider, a good father. How could you ever expect to control someone's life like that? Ever since I bought my villa here, it's been a decade of complaints from you, Mukadder *teyze*. All the ways that things could have been different. You know how much I respect you, but please leave my friend alone. Let her go back to the life that she built, by herself. Just let her go."

My mother, California, an incredible life? Ever since I've known her, my mother has been a shell of her former self. Always a bit lost. In our neighborhood of Palo Alto, miles and miles south of San Francisco, the architecture keeps a low profile, wary of attention. Neither the homes, nor the businesses, nor the rare government building is tall enough for my mother to position herself in relation to it. To find her way as one might navigate using the North Star or, say, the minarets of a neighborhood mosque. There are no hills along Palo Alto's suburban streets, no accessible promontory from which she can gaze out to the bay and think, *Toward the water, away from the water.*

"The streets aren't settled inside my head," she told me once. "They are constantly floating. Elevated, a bit. Elusive, ephemeral." The last two words she said in English. She beamed at her alliteration, at the great, geographical expanses of her lexical memory.

My mother never hesitated to hide her displeasure at the wide suburban streets upon which she was expected to construct a life. Streets devoid of pedestrians, of sound. "*İn cin top oynuyor!*" she would cry, gesturing violently out the window to emphasize the emptiness. A ghost town! To me, the city was plentiful, and her disappointment, confusing. Friends were everywhere. Reviewing Cornell notes with me at the Starbucks in the strip mall; chugging red Gatorade, swim-capped, in the next lane over. When I later realized that adults weren't meant to be so alone, so confined to empty circles of domesticity, my golden life suddenly seemed dull. If my mother was truly unhappy here, then something must be missing from the place itself. My illusion about the sparkle, the expansiveness of my life, crumbled. A quiet humiliation took hold.

The question hovered, settled, lingered: What are we missing?

There was no cure for my mother's California solitude, and nobody else seemed to care. My grandmother was too far away to do anything about it, my father too busy working, and all her Turkish-Californian friends seemed to find nothing unnatural about their shared, limited existence, interacting only with each other in their living rooms. In the rare moments my mother did cross paths with Americans, she preferred to remain silent unless communication was absolutely necessary. She paced the grocery store aisles alone, wandering aimlessly among myriad brands of olives, rows upon rows of pickle jars. When asked if there was anything she needed help with, she would smile kindly at the store clerk and shake her head no. It was only several years after the international move that the truth had finally set in that she was here to stay. It had been a gradual understanding, like slowly boiling water to kill the animal.

My grandmother calmly takes a sip of red wine, which she has ordered for the table. "California," she says, slowly pulling the reins of the conversation back to herself, "California is a lost island in the middle of the ocean, on the way to nowhere. There is no California blood that runs through any of us."

Neslihan puts a protective arm across my mother's shoulders.

"My apologies that you had to witness this, Ada," says my grandmother. She reaches over to the salad bowl and points its tongs at me. "You seem to have caught us at a particularly tense moment." I am used to the tension, as this argument occurs nearly every summer. Even after twenty-four years abroad, my grandmother still has trouble accepting the fact that my mother hasn't returned home for good. I, too, am tired of watching my mother live this way.

The restaurant manager appears on the stage and taps the microphone three times.

"Good evening, ladies and gentlemen, dear children," he announces, turning to address each end of the crowd. "Tonight we're very pleased to offer you an evening full of entertainment." The first act, he says, will be a short performance by the young girls of the town, who will enthrall us with a choreographed dance. Then a performer from central Balıkesir will sing classic Turkish ballads. As the girls set up for their dance, I spot Aslı, Bulut, and Ozan at a far table, among aunts and uncles I vaguely recognize out of their swimwear. Just as I'm waving hello, the lights dim.

A dozen preteens skip onto the stage in tank tops of various colors and matching denim shorts. Several are in sneakers, others still in beach sandals. I've known almost all of them since they were babies, back when they were throwing fistfuls of sand in each other's faces in their frilly bikini bottoms and sun bonnets. Now their bodies are long and lean, and their fight tactics more sophisticated, underhanded.

They take their places a few feet apart from each other in three haphazard rows, backs to the audience. They lower their heads, steady their arms out at their sides. Someone whoops loudly. One of the girls, Göksu, her hair in pigtailed French braids, stays to the side with the boom box and waits for the others to assume position. She gestures madly, a frantic semaphore. Then she presses play and scrambles to take her place at the front of the group.

The first notes of a Britney Spears single burst through the speakers between sparks of static. The girls cartwheel across the stage, bumping into each other and laughing as their legs crisscross in the air. They take a step toward us, twist around, move their hands like windshield wipers while shaking their hips. Two of them mouth along with the lyrics, which I find hilarious. A second behind on the entire rhythm, they strictly follow the moves one after the other, loyal to the order but not to the beat, yet seem carefree in a way that I don't think I have ever been able to manage. I watch carefully for mistakes and missteps. There are many, but no one lets on. When it's over, we all cheer. The girls take their bows and high-five over a job well done. None of them seems to be the least bit embarrassed.

When the singer takes the stage, my grandmother still has yet to surrender. "Exploration destroys a woman. There is no reason to *discover*," she is saying, underlining her words with a strike of her fish knife. She leans across the table toward my mother. "It's an endless game, Meltem. Pay attention to your own needs. You know exactly what they are. They have been the same all along. As your mother, I can promise you that. As my daughter, you should trust me."

My mother hunches over to smooth out the napkin on her lap, and fiddles with a bracelet on her wrist. When she raises her head again, she looks toward the distance, expectant, like one trying to make out the silhouette of a ship on the horizon. One by one, the three of us turn to follow her gaze. Standing by the restaurant entrance with a cigarette in one hand, waving it to the beat as he sings along, is Levent. My stomach lurches as he notices us. When he smiles, his whole face crinkles up like a street cat's. His hair is shaggy and clouds around his ears, a black smoking into grays. He's wearing a white linen shirt that's open at the collar. Now this is what my mother deserves—to be in İstanbul with a man like him. Someone local. A born and bred urbanite who knows his way around the city linings, can navigate both land and sea. A hero in all landscapes. He could take you by the hand and lead you across the hills of the metropolis, lightly stepping over its bridges, zigzagging down its strait. He'd know the timing of the sunset in all its seasons, could smooth talk the waiters into plucking off the metal "reserved" tents and offering him a table "zero to the sea," one of those right on the water. Uninitiated diners may lean carelessly in their chairs and topple into the Bosphorus, but that would never happen to him. He seems to be a man who can sense the millimeters of the city, know exactly where one thing ends and the other begins. A man who can stay inside the lines while maintaining an endless flirtation.

My mother, however, is in a position to fall. All she needs is a little nudge.

The right romance just might bring her back to her old self. The person she had been before I was born, the one I had never gotten a chance to know. Red lips, smiling, basking in the sun. Finally home. I might be able to meet her all over again. She will move back to İstanbul, where I will visit her in our house, because what's mine is hers and what's hers is mine. When I arrive in Turkey, she will no longer jolt at my unexpected presence, the city and her daughter peacefully coexisting in a single moment, the dividing line fully erased.

It's hard to focus. I think of color and laughter and energy. The mauve glow of bridges, laughter bouncing until it reaches the height of the Galata Tower, the wild look in a woman's eyes as she steps into a nightclub on the shores of the Bosphorus. I think of myself in İstanbul, surrounded by girls who look like me. I want to know what it means, to wreck a city. Then I realize that I am still staring at him and gently shift my gaze to the singer. She sways her hips, bellowing about a lover who didn't believe her when she had told him that they were doomed. *You never understood, you never understood, never had you believed in fate.* There is so much joy in her voice as she wishes him well. Why can't she give in to her sadness, like the Americans do? It's a cultural peculiarity, the ability to look upon a misfortune—especially one foretold—with such high spirits.

When my eyes flicker back up, he's looking right at me.

"Levent's ears must have been ringing," says my grandmother. She lifts her wineglass. "Cheers. To old friends."

Levent notices her gesture and raises his cigarette in response. The two salute to the memory of a shared point in time right before things, apparently, went wrong.

4

THE PARK

A few nights later, my friends and I take over the children's park. We bump down metal slides, balancing beers and bags of barbecue chips; we swing on the four-seater bench as one of us kicks all of us forward with sneakers gripping the backrest and hands steady on the parallel pole. I look up at the sky and connect the dots of constellations, a simple action delineating the present moment from my childhood. Back when my summer evenings revolved entirely around the park, my curfew had always been the sunset. I'd watch the horizon from the top of a slide until that thin arc of orange sank into a mainland silhouette. As the halo of light around the islands faded, I would scream goodbye to everyone and everyone would scream goodbye to me and I would race down to the water, veer left, and reach the gates of the villa panting and electric with adrenaline. A second later, my mother would come up behind me, hair dripping wet, back from her evening swim. What dictated, still dictates, our lives is the movement of the planet, rather than the measurement of that movement. Nobody ever watches the clock.

In this park in the dark, I swell with my own earned power, a child in an adult's body, or an adult in a child's body, or someone somewhere in between who has finally gained access to a world she has wanted while she still wants it. Aslı crouches over in the corner by the fountain, picking weeds, and tells us all to gather around. We have run out of beer already— already!—and someone needs to go to the market to get more alcohol and also, maybe, some Doritos. She brings her hands together, and we all look at the four weeds standing as straight as soldiers rising from the earth of her palms.

I pluck the shortest one, and everyone laughs and says that I got what I deserved, since I was the one who had gone through the most beers. Fair, fair, I say, and hop over the low wall behind the fountain and stumble my way along the side of the soccer field. The glow of the market pulses in front of me. The wind has picked up tonight, even though we are in the middle of summer. The name of this wind is the *poyraz,* and I am proud that I know this fact. People often prefer the Aegean over the Mediterranean coastline for its breeze. Another fact. I skip along the road, pleased with the wealth of information I have about this country. My country. I murmur, then start to sing a Turkish pop song I only half remember. I'm deep in the chorus when I hear a cluster of giggles.

The young dancing girls of the *site* are walking toward me, sucking Chupa Chups in crop tops bearing the names of places where I have been, but that they have not: MALIBU, NEW YORK, MIAMI. I have to remind myself that these are cities on a map, that they are possible to access. Here, they are nearly mythological.

"Is there something funny?" I ask, extra formal in my inebriation.

The preteens look at each other, daring someone else to say it first. "Something's wrong with the way you sing the words," Göksu blurts. Her name is a portmanteau of the Turkish words for sky and water, and already I feel swallowed up by her. "The way you say them, it sounds a bit stupid."

"It's because she's American," sighs a triangle-faced girl whose name I can't remember, though her absurd cartwheels from the other night are seared into my memory. Her stage presence earlier this week was enthusiastic and joyous, but she now stares at me with a fierce gaze under thick, slanted brows. "Sorry, Ada. But to be honest, it did sound a bit off.

Maybe lower your voice next time you go around singing. Have a good night. Come on, girls."

I watch them leave, dazed from the interaction and slightly sobered. They all look the same from behind, even the particular saunter of their walk sways to the same rhythm. I still have another verse to go and it feels rebellious to continue, so I do, but drop my voice to a hum. The song is about a scorned lover who walks around an upscale cove in İstanbul with the sole vengeful purpose of perhaps being glimpsed by her ex. *If you've got the time to dedicate to me . . .* I consider the passion and power of that relationship—a jealousy in its extremes. Not at all like my relationship with Ian, which is simple, straightforward. Predictable. Boring?

Ian's dorm at Stanford was ten minutes from mine with no slope no matter how you went about it. He arranged his schedule to be able to attend all my swim meets, both at home and away. Never once did he come to a race empty-handed, always equipped with bouquets of pink tulips, or boxes of dark chocolate with marzipan filling. The flowers went into a vase on my roommate's side of the dorm room, and I offered the chocolates to the smattering of homeless men who read secondhand books on the benches of University Avenue. He had first noticed me in introductory physics. I had signed up to earn the required science credit but found myself enthralled from the very first class. The theory of relativity haunted me; I wanted to understand its every nuance. It wasn't long before the professor began to ignore my raised hand to give others a chance to speak.

Ian and I were seated next to each other during our first exam. While sketching out a rocket ship to illustrate time dilation, I felt a hand on my back. A boy with hazy autumnal eyes full of concern tilted his head at me, giving my shoulder a gentle squeeze. I shrugged and shook him off, but when I looked back at my splotched exam paper, I realized that I had been crying.

He was waiting for me in the hallway after class, which surprised me.

I had taken a long time with my exam, poring over the philosophical implications of all the questions long after I had finished answering them. "Hey," I said, "I appreciate the support."

"I've never seen anyone be so emotionally affected by a test," he replied, placing his hand gently, carefully, again on my shoulder. "And I'm premed. I was starting to get worried about you. Ada, right?" I nodded. "I'm Ian. We gotta lighten you up. You can't take things too seriously, you know."

"I don't like it," I said, feeling a little stupid. "The relativity, the multiple frames of reference. Time should work the same for everyone." I kicked the ground, scuffing my sneakers. "Everyone!"

Ian laughed, startling me. His laugh was quiet and bright, and his way-farer glasses slipped down his nose when his head moved, which made me smile. He pushed them back up and peered at me through the lenses. Something shifted, and I relaxed. I breathed in, taking in the attention.

"Unfortunately, my anxiety about the laws of physics is at an all-time high," I said, suddenly coy. "I will definitely need to be soothed." Ian didn't miss a beat. He looked off in the direction of University Avenue, and said that there was nothing an ice cream sandwich couldn't fix. We went from there.

As cautious as I'd been about Ian's integration into my life, the ease at which he slipped right in left me with a bad taste in my mouth. Of course, this was impossible to explain to him. It was like blindingly white clouds in the sky you couldn't cup in the palms of your hands, couldn't bring to someone and say, See this? It shouldn't be this easy, I thought. Nothing good can ever come easily. I always kept an eye out for the cracks.

One thing we could never understand about each other was our cin-ematic interpretations. Like that time we had gone to an independent theater in Palo Alto to see a Danish film about a couple whose marriage unravels because the woman doesn't want children, though the husband thinks that they are still trying. She crafts all sorts of tricks to ensure that nothing from the man enters her. She slips kroner to gynecologists and fertility specialists to tell the couple that nothing is wrong so that the man will not leave her. They must keep trying, she whispers into his ear before orgasming. She cannot survive without him, but also cannot bear the thought of birthing a human being. The woman speaks with friends who have torn through tissue for a set of twins. Whose feet have permanently swelled up a size and who find themselves donating old stilettos from their old lives. They do not seem unhappy about it. The husband gazes wistfully after diaper bags, and the wife scowls at the decisions of the mothers, who have given up themselves for something ungrateful, something that will do little else but rob them of who they are.

We grabbed mushroom-and-olive slices at Pizza My Heart afterward to discuss what we had seen. Never once did it seem like Ian and I had watched the same film, and the men and women who worked the pizza counter on Saturday afternoons (we preferred matinees) were used to our presence by now. They would perk up one ear toward our argument as they prepared slices of pepperoni. When impressed, one of them would let out a low whistle, or bring us extra garlic bread. I liked that they enjoyed our repartee because I loved the thrill of fast-paced conversation. Even if what I said wasn't always correct, at least in English I could still be clever.

"She's clearly a miserable woman," said Ian, peeling off a mushroom from his own slice to add to mine.

"The film's Danish," I countered. "Aren't your great-grandparents Scandinavian or something? They have different views there, on women and the lives they're expected to lead."

"I didn't say everybody has to have children. I'm just saying that this particular woman, there was a sense that she could never be complete. Whether or not she becomes a mother isn't the issue, it won't solve whatever it is that's eating away at her."

Behind the counter, a chef with a hair net and a pregnant belly paused before placing dough in the wood-fire oven.

"It's a battle," I said. "You have to choose. Is it going to be your life for you or your life in the service of someone else's? The beginning of something implies an end," I added for emphasis.

"No, it's the self-hatred that drives her pity, not something inherent in her decision on whether or not to have a child." Ian placed three extra mushrooms on my slice. I grinned and took a large bite, pleased with the additional toppings.

"You're allowed to be spiteful if everyone's making a decision that you think detracts from their own lives."

"You're continuing on a different track than I am, Ada."

"But all the techniques of the directorial eye point to my point. Didn't you see? There was dichotomy everywhere." I note the duality of light and darkness in moments alone and in the company of children, the melancholy of the melody when the woman briefly considered hosting another life in order to keep her husband, the vivace of the score when the two of them fucked while the woman knew that barriers to the swim had been put up inside her. "Can't you see all the signs," I said at the end of my monologue, "that support my version of the story?" I can read between the lines, I claimed. I can interpret the mood from the props and the lighting.

The pregnant woman came to our table with a macadamia nut cookie and placed it in front of me. I beamed, considering it a reward. "It's because I'm right, isn't it? You saw the movie?" I said. The woman shrugged and turned toward Ian, wiping her hands on her red apron.

"Doesn't quite matter who's right these days, does it?" she asked. Ian blinked at her questioningly from behind his glasses. "But you hear the belief in her voice? It's like music, my friend. She's going to keep on seeing whatever she wants to see. Enjoy your cookie," she said, and took her leave.

I pushed the dessert plate over to my boyfriend's side of the table. "It's only fair," I said. "You let me have all the mushrooms."

⚓

As I walk to the market, I feel a pull of nostalgia for my days in English. When I could speak without stuttering over the words, my eloquence so proud and clear that whether I was right or wrong was nearly irrelevant. In English, there are no girls in crop tops and long hair correcting my lyrical missteps. I head into the market from the rear entrance and turn left into the grocer's. Every morning, my mother or grandmother goes to the grocer's to pick up the morning's newspaper and often, a loaf of bread. They always try to get me, as the young woman of the house, to do it instead, but any battle here is futile. No one can stop me from sleeping in.

The market's a two-story, open-air building, with gaping entrances on the north and south sides. On the ground floor, there's the baker, the doctor, the *lahmacun* restaurant, and, of course, the grocer. And tonight, at the register of the grocer, packing up his purchases, is Levent. I step behind a tall rack of newspapers just outside the grocer's door, pretending to consider the very large headlines.

In one of Levent's plastic bags, I spy the metallic blue cap of a *rakı* bottle. I expect him to reach into the pocket of his jeans and pull out his wallet, handing over a credit card to the grocer's boy, who always mans his father's till. Or—still wrong, though acceptable—leave a few bills on the counter. Nobody pays in the middle of the season. As everyone is always in their bikinis and there is nowhere to put your money, nearly all transactions in our *site* are IOUs. Instead, the boy opens a large book that resembles a town directory and carefully writes your name in all capital letters, along with the updated owed amount. At the end of the summer, everyone must settle their accounts.

But Levent, it seems, has already fallen into step with the rhythm of this town. All he does is pat the young boy on the back and turn to leave. This fluidity surprises me. I recall his perfect dive on the dock. Hadn't he just arrived here? It's taken me years to find my footing, and I still stumble. It's completely unfair. When he walks out the door, he notices me behind the newspapers and cocks his head. Again, that gaze of curious familiarity, the one that had stunned me on the day we met. There is something in his expression that welcomes me back home.

Levent doesn't lower his gaze. Unsure what to do, I start to play with the edges of my clothing. The cutoff of my shorts, the neckline of my blouse, then its scalloped hem. My fingers graze over my body quickly, like a spider, checking. I no longer feel adequately covered. I feel open and accidentally inviting.

The grocer's boy mocks my loitering. "You read through every newspaper yet?" he asks.

"I am a little drunk," I say, grateful for the interruption. "Don't worry, I didn't understand a single word I read. I took no value from your papers." Levent steps toward me, leaving barely any space between us.

"Steady now," he says, and winks. He smells like the hot skin of the tomatoes in my grandmother's garden. I try to focus on his eyes, understand what color they are, and are they a color my mother might like? But they keep blurring and moving and I lose my balance and stumble into the racks. He laughs and helps me gather myself back up. By the time I'm on my feet again, we are slightly farther apart.

"Do you need help finding something?" The grocer's boy cuts in, annoyed that we're still there. I get a hold of myself and walk straight into the store, sensing Levent following me. I announce my two items, beer and Doritos, as if I have not come to the grocer's every day of every summer, as if I am a first-time customer and have no idea where anything is in this tiny space that is barely larger than our living room.

"This is better, no?" says Levent, pulling out a bottle of wine. He turns the label toward the boy, who writes down the name—Kalecik Karası—and price in his notebook. I take the bottle from him, nodding aggressively: Yes, it would be nice to have something different to drink tonight, yes, yes. My friends will love it. "Doritos Doritos Doritos," I mutter, crouching in front of the chips and rummaging through them like something feral.

On the floor, pulling down bags of chips, I begin to wonder what Levent is even doing here at this time of night. The older men visiting their families often leave the *site* in the evenings for the town center, with its bars and restaurants and jazz clubs, or head to the nightlife of Cunda Island. The only options for entertainment here are card games with octogenarians or a quiet drink at the Small Club. I turn around to ask him this, but Levent's already gone, heading out the front entrance of the market, toward the basketball courts. He did not say goodbye. I show the boy the chips I want and walk out from the back, into the moonlight and toward the park.

≈⚓≈

I return home much later in the night and unlatch the gate. My grand-mother and mother aren't in their usual positions waiting for me, sipping turnip juice in their floral muumuus as they rest their feet on the railing or lounge on our creaky porch swing and gossip. Instead, my mother sits upright at the end of the table in a tangerine-colored dress with golden straps, a determined look on her face. I like the way she looks and go over to kiss her on the cheek. "Pretty-pretty," I say, running a finger along a braided strap. My grandmother is halfway across the threshold, propping the screen door open with her hip while she balances a tray with plates covered in scraps of fig skin and three tall *rakı* glasses. The scent of anise hangs in the air.

"You just missed him," my grandmother sighs. There is no regret in her voice, but rather, a thinly veiled pride. "We had such a nice visitor come by this evening. Didn't we, Meltem?"

"It felt like old times," says my mother. "Look," she adds, turning toward me. "I have a darling daughter." She puts her arms around me, and I lean in closer, resting my head on top of hers. Her hair has been washed and smells like grapefruit. I feel strangely electric, like I have been struck by lightning in a field of citrus.

Levent had not gone to Cunda, to the jazz clubs or the island bars, but had come here, to our villa. It's extraordinary to see my mother like this, the life trickling back inside her. It's a far cry from her California self, where she is like the roads she could never quite get a handle on. Elusive, ephemeral. My mother will be with a handsome man who knows the city like the back of his hand. Turkey turns a shade more foreign each year she is away, and America remains an impenetrable fortress. But Levent can root her back to where she might blossom: in the city and relationships of her past. I will make sure of it. In her absence, my father can dine alone at Greek restaurants and think about what he has done.

5

THE OLIVE GROVES

M iss Island!"

The literal translation of my Turkish name, croaked out in English with a slight British accent frosting the words. I pause on the path from the dock to the Small Club café and squint around for who it was that called out to me. The day is too bright, last night's drinks in the park amplifying all of today's sensations. From one of the sun beds, an old man lets out a sharp whistle, motioning for me to join him and his friends. His ears stick out like soup ladles, and his stomach, mottled with liver spots, hangs over the elastic of his swim trunks. Though the man's voice betrays his age, his whistle holds an ageless power. I walk toward the group of two grandfathers and a younger, freckled boy who nods a hello.

I recognize the old men from their daily walks past our terrace, doffing their boyish baseball caps as a good-morning salute to my grandmother. The younger one I have definitely seen before, but can't remember from where.

"How are you, Miss Island?"

"I'm fine, thank you very much." I respond to the old man in English. Seawater trickles down my face. "And how might you be?"

"Oh, you know us," he says, laughing. "Every day is a gift." Then he turns to his friends. "This is Mukadder's granddaughter, Ada. She comes here every summer from Los Angeles. Movie star!"

The younger man lifts his chin in a welcome, as if we're already acquainted. I notice his striped swim trunks and remember—he's the son of the bank manager who's our diagonal neighbor. The boy who spends most of the summer on the southern coast, sailing. The other grandfather must be his.

"Palo Alto," I correct. The sailor's grandfather nods knowingly.

"In Mexico?" The man places a hand behind his soup-ladle ear, confirming that he's heard correctly.

"San Francisco," I say. I bend my body to resemble a crooked California, and point at my chest.

"Yes, in the northern part," the sailor's grandfather clarifies. "And when she grows up, she's going to be in the technology business, just like her father." His grandson gently elbows him in the ribs, but it takes a moment for the man to realize his faux pas.

"Oh," he says softly, and turns away from me, embarrassed. News of my mother's dilemma has already made its way around town, it seems.

"I don't have any intention of going into business," I say, letting the reference to my father slide.

"Oh, your father, your father!" Ladle Ears straightens up, but it's of no use; his belly still hangs. "Did you know," he continues, addressing the young sailor now. "Did you know that Miss Island's father will soon be a famous man? He invented . . . a sort of chip . . . something. A lot of money. Your mother is lucky," he says, grinning. "Your mother is a very lucky woman to have found a man like that."

The other two men look uncomfortable at the second mention of my father, so I change the subject. "For the record," I say, "I actually haven't chosen my major yet."

The sailor speaks his first words to me. "You're not going to study business?"

"Probably not."

"Computer science, then?"

"I'm thinking ethnomusicology."

"What?" asks the sailor.

"Music," I simplify. There's a forced murmur of appreciation, and they then, inevitably, ask me what I play.

The fact that I don't play anything or, rather, play a little bit of everything, has never been the answer that anyone is looking for. I took piano lessons when I was younger, then a few months of violin before I realized I hated the feeling of the chin rest, though I enjoyed the forced bow to the music. There was no instrument that captivated me as a player more than any other, and I had no interest in composing. It took me a while to work up the courage to decide that I wanted to study music without any desire to become a musician myself. The idea of enjoying something so fully without stepping completely into it, without a desire for conquest, was an argument that I was tired of defending.

"The guitar," I say, making things easy for everyone.

The sailor nods knowingly but is unsure how to continue the conversation. The idea of a businessman's daughter being a music major is too outlandish for them to handle.

"But now, but now," prompts the sailor's grandfather, and I can tell that he is attempting to build a structure around my whims, "you are at university, it's time to be serious. Do you have a summer job that you'll be returning to? Maybe some research on . . . music? Surely you are not spending the whole three months here anymore."

I don't know how to answer him. I tell him that I am, and that university works differently in the United States. "Work starts when you graduate," I say. I can't explain to him that if I were to stay and work over the summer, I would be wasting time. Not that Ian was wasting time, of course. But I would have been.

After I politely take my leave and am walking back to our café table, I overhear the sailor's grandfather tie up the gossip in a neat little bow. "The family doesn't discuss it," he says. "But it's because the woman spends too much time here. He may be a genius, but he is also an American. Works year-round, spends his summers in . . . San Francisco."

I want to tell them: My father is not so much an American as he is a man who believes in himself more than he believes in the divine order of the universe. I want to tell them that he is a man who does not use phrases like "God willing" or "That's the fate it was given." He is not a man who knocks on wood at the mere mention of a tragedy. *Just look at the fortune I'm making for my family,* my father would say to me. *And tell me that it's because it's been written on my face. Does it say it here?* he would ask, pointing at his forehead as he bent down to my height. *Do you see it? Ada, do you see it? That's right. You go out,* he would instruct. *You make your own destiny.*

When I think of it now, in light of everything, it seems to be his greatest failing.

In the early evening, as I leave the Small Club to get dressed for dinner, someone calls my name. My real name, Ada. There, in the olive groves to the south of the Small Club, is Levent in his orange swim trunks. His feet are bare as he stands atop the flattened reeds, and his hair's in a short ponytail. This clearing in the groves is used as a makeshift parking lot for the beach, and he looks like a time traveler among the Fords and the Renaults, between whose hoods and windshields lie smatterings of hard green olives. "You up for a walk?" he asks. I stand frozen in the middle of the road, and slowly, feeling every tiny movement, check the terrace of my villa.

Nobody. I turn on my heels and head toward him. In an effort at nonchalance, I pick up a couple fallen olives from the crevice of the car hoods and offer him one as I pop another into my mouth. My face contorts at its bitterness.

"It's not yet the season," says Levent, cracking a smile.

"So I see." I spit it out on the ground.

"Coming? This way."

I tighten the sarong around my waist and follow him southward, pausing from time to time to shake out the weeds that have gotten caught in my Adidas slides. My grandmother hates my slides, says they make me look like a peasant. I pad along, wondering what he wants to talk to me about, though I can think of no other possibility than insider information on my mother. I prepare my argument: *You can see it on her face, she's been so unhappy. Do you know the English phrase "fish out of water"?*

After a while, I ask him point-blank. "What's going on between you and my mom?"

Levent stops. He tenses a bit, the shoulder bones protruding in deep lines, the muscles twitching. Then he releases his breath, and the canvas goes blank. I imagine all the untold stories wrestling inside him, all the scenes playing upon his body that he can never face.

"You know," he says as he moves forward again in that elegant, purposeful stride of his, "your mom and I are very old friends, but just because we share a past doesn't mean that we have that much to talk about. I thought that maybe, perhaps we might. We might, uh, pick up where we left off, I guess you could say." His voice is hesitant, and I can't tell if he's lying, or trying himself to believe what he's telling me.

I'm confused. He's so dismissive of my mother, so uninterested. It would mean a lot for my mother to be wanted again by a man like him. It would mean that she hadn't lost the connection that held her here, that there was an easy way for her to come back and belong. It wouldn't matter that she had forgotten to integrate the evolving vocabulary of the past two decades into her speech. You don't have to know the politics of a place, its cultural mores, or smooth out your accent if you're desired. Desire by itself is a strong enough root.

"The two of us, we've had a few chats . . ." he says, and his shoulders drop. "What drew me to her while we were friends is no longer there."

What was it, I wonder, that my mother had when she was young? Maybe it was her youth. I'm young, I suddenly think. I have something she no longer has. When I look up at Levent with this realization, he is staring right back at me. I lower my head and focus on walking.

We follow the coastline, but it's not an easy trek. The groves stretch out toward the sea until a low and unstable drop-off to a tangle of seaweed on a pebble beach. Eventually, the groves should give way to the next town over, which surely has its own Small Club and private beach, but

Levent leads us inland, at times even uphill. To my right, the water spar-
kles in patches through the trees. The blood in my limbs begins to run
slightly cooler. We are quite alone here. For the first time, I feel a small
tinge of fear in the heat of summer. But just as I take a deep breath and
open my mouth to ask exactly what it is we're doing, where we're going,
he turns around and takes a good, long look at me.

"I realize this is strange," he admits, and pauses. "I'd like to spend some
time with you, but there are very few places in this town where we can
be alone. I never really understood why people had kids until I met you."

I release a breath I didn't know I had been holding. "What do you
mean?"

"The first day, on the dock, when I saw you swimming. You're so much
like her. Bolder, though. More decisive. Or at least that's my impression,"
he adds. "Can't say I know you well enough."

"I thought you said we didn't look like each other at all?"

"Mirror image of the movements," says Levent. "It's like I'm seventeen
again, seeing you there in front of me. Walk over there," he says. He points
west, toward the water.

"You want me just to . . ."

"Just to see the movement. Walk."

I do as he says, but I notice that he's not watching me, exactly. He
tracks my shadow.

"And there's the voice, of course," he says. "The intonations, the vocabulary. You're an echo." He stops to consider the direction. Then he points
eastward and carries on, nodding at me to follow. "Either it's because she
has kept the cadence of her youth and passed it on to you, or because you
yourself have wandered backward into the 1980s."

I can't decide whether this is a compliment or an insult. I decide to let
it lie flat and undisturbed, as fact. "That makes sense," I say. "I guess she
still speaks in the way she used to." The thread snapped when she left, and
the language evolved without her there to sop it up. I think of the man
with the soup-ladle ears and the sad mottled belly, of the pitch and acuity
of his whistle. Not every part of a person is ravaged by time.

"Almost exactly," says Levent. "Almost exactly. Everything else, the body, it changes. But when she speaks . . . it's as if her sentences are preserved in ice, congealed in the American years."

"You call them that like they're over." I am hopeful, still.

"On the contrary, Ada," he laughs. His laugh is loud and throaty, but it doesn't carry itself far in the silence. It stays right here, pooling into a sense of something shared between us. I walk through it. "They're only just beginning."

"My dad doesn't want her anymore." The words come out before I can stop them, and I clap my hand over my mouth. Levent acts as though he didn't hear and moves deeper into the grove. I raise my voice and try again. "She's not who she was before, and that kills him, that he didn't get the real part of her. The real part of her is here, somewhere, and every summer she comes back to find it, but each summer it fades away just a little bit more. To fully step back into it, she needs to move here and start again. You could help her."

It's then that Levent turns. But his face is not open as I thought it would be. All I can see are shadows of pity. He looks awhile at the olive trees, which have thickened and blocked out any mention of the water beyond. It's the first time this summer that I haven't been able to spot the sea; the slope of our *site* makes it so no matter what street you're on, you'll always see a flash of blue.

"You can't pin your hopes on a single person," Levent says. "You just can't. That was her mistake." He continues on among the fallen olives and motions for me to follow. The idea that he might know something about my mother that I don't know, that he had seen where the break emerged, been there for her undoing, stood there right on the border between the before and the after—his proximity to the faultline draws me closer to him.

I am unprepared for my next thought, which pounds into my head like a sudden rain: If a man like him desired a woman like my mother, it would mean that my mother hadn't lost anything in the intervening years. But if a man like him desired a woman like me, what would that say about me?

No. There is no use thinking about such things. I nod to myself, a small commitment, and keep walking.

Soon, a hint of civilization emerges. I start to make out the rust-colored brick of what appears to be a building. Another few steps to the top of the hill, and an entire neighborhood of half-built villas splays open at our feet, in a space where olive trees have been rooted up and razed. For most of the villas, the structure for both stories has been built, but the pathway between the floors is nonexistent, as if one could simply float up to the bedrooms from the kitchen. In one of the villas, there's a wooden ladder leading from the first floor to the ledge of the second-floor landing, a crude approximation of where the staircase will eventually be built. Many of the homes are missing several walls, like scientific dissections showcasing their insides. I make my way through the abandoned construction site, keeping an eye out for scattered, loose nails. The unfinished windows are holes into the interior instead of spaces for reflection. Running a hand along the concrete foundations, I imagine the types of lives that might inhabit these places once they're ready. Families, newlyweds. But when? Maybe it's too hot to work during the summer, I think. Maybe there are seasons for building homes.

Ian saw summer as the season to make our first home together. He'd found a place in Potrero Hill with the master bedroom available, and took me up to San Francisco in late spring, thinking I might change my mind about summer abroad once I saw those orange walls, those adorable green shutters. "The colors immediately made me think of you," he had said. Quick commute for him to his internship at UCSF Medical. In his mind, there was the possibility that my plans would change.

When Ian and I got to the city that night, the winds were high. They swooped down the hills as if to carry away all the debris and lives that weren't meant to live there. We pushed against it for a few yards as we trudged up to the house that could have been a home had it not been for my selfishness. Down behind us glimmered the low buildings of the small city.

It all seemed too straightforward for two kids who were in the beginning of what could be nothing. We'd just slide right in, in much the same way we gravitated toward each other between the buildings of our college campus.

"I'm climbing up to the second floor," I announce to Levent. What I need now is distance from him, from these thoughts that I'm having about him, across as many dimensions as possible: up and away. I walk to one of the terrace-less houses and shimmy my body onto the first floor. Then I tighten the Velcro on my slides, and put some pressure on the ladder to test that it's sturdy.

The San Francisco apartment had been on 18th and Arkansas, and the first thing I said to Ian when we crested the hill and came upon it was that never would I ever live on a street named Arkansas because landlocked states make me think of imprisonment and resignation. "Forget about any past associations you have," he'd replied. "You'd make it your own. Once Ada lives on Arkansas, the word itself will take on a whole different meaning." From the sidewalk pockmarked by chewed gum, sullied by names written with sticks in wet concrete and bicycle halves wrapped around stop signs, sprouted a proud orange building with olive green shutters. It was flanked by two large palm trees emerging from slim rectangular pots. The plants curved as they sloped up, as if wanting to grow to the sky while avoiding any contact with the building. *We are not the trees of this house*, they seemed to say. *We just happen to be planted here, that's all.*

We walked around the block, pretending. *Here is where we would get Colombian coffee before work, here is where we would buy secondhand books, here is where we would eat tuna tataki on a Saturday night before heading to a comedy club in the Mission.* Ian wanted to take a photo of me between the palms. I posed with my neck stuck out, imitating the trees in their desire to flee. I did not like Ian's insinuation that this was where I was meant to be.

Levent watches me with a bemused expression, certain that I've chickened out on the climb. But as soon as the memories fade and I set one foot on a ladder rung, he instinctively reaches out a hand from the ground below. "Ada!" he cries.

"Yes?" I don't want to turn to look at him, because I am afraid of having the same thoughts again, but I do. He looks genuinely frightened.

"Don't be a fool, now."

I count the steps. Seven. "It's just a ladder. The construction workers use it all the time." I take a quick, sharp breath to collect myself, and scramble up the ladder with ease. Then I sit on the scratchy landing and swing my feet in victory. Levent sighs. He claps his hands twice, preparing for the ascent himself. I sneeze. It's dusty up here.

"May you live long," he says.

"May you live to see it," I reply. I sneeze again, but he stays quiet this time.

He tests the strength of the ladder with one foot, then the other, then climbs in slow, measured steps. Once at the landing, he sits next to me and leans back onto his elbows, letting his legs dangle. Together we look out toward the smattering of homes. Half-realized dreams that people have been waiting for, the summer lives that have not yet been opened up to them. The apathetic attempts of constructors to build a dream, but what does it mean, they might have asked themselves, to work on the dreams of others? Maybe that's when they dropped their hammers, left their ladders, and headed on home.

Once Ian understood that I would never swap a summer in Turkey for the Arkansas apartment, or for any American apartment, we walked side-ways down the hill like crabs and I fell over because the laces to my sneakers had gotten undone. I asked Ian why he hadn't told me, and he shrugged, saying he hadn't noticed, but I could tell by the way he strummed his fin-gers on the sides of his thighs when he said it that he was lying, and that I had hurt him. Then I accidentally opened the passenger-side door of the Subaru too wide and scratched it against the pole of a stop sign. Ian and I locked eyes from above the car, but neither of us spoke. On the way to the Richmond for Burmese food, he missed a critical left and refused to make it until five lights later when the U-turn sign appeared. Satie's *Gymnopédie* no. 1 was playing on the car CD player. I switched to the radio. I felt that he had been playing it on purpose to make me believe that I had really missed out on something good. Ian carefully assessed the gradients of the slopes, the correct accompanying speeds. We inched slowly down the descents, which gave me enough time to look out beyond the landmarks and the hills, to focus on the bridges over the water, and to pretend that I was someplace else.

"This is nice," says Levent, peeking at me from the corner of his eye. I sit very still. I can't stand being so close to him, the implications of what it would mean if he were to get closer, so I get up and wander through the other rooms of the house. I walk into what must be the master bedroom. If we lived here, this is where we would wake up. I plod over to the bathroom with no sink, and imagine washing my face to start the day. I hear Levent's footsteps down the ladder. From the unglazed window, I can see the groves beyond, and consider the unimportance of views that do not look out toward the sea. What next? I'd go downstairs, have some breakfast. Levent would be in the kitchen below, frying up some eggs. No tuna tataki for miles. I head back to the main landing.

I turn around and place my foot on the first rung, but instead of securing the foothold, I accidentally kick the ladder over. It totters for a few seconds, then falls backward. When it hits the edge of the first floor, it splits in two and tumbles down into the weeds. My left shoe follows the fall, a second behind.

"Whoops."

Levent rushes out from the inside of the house, sees the ladder, then looks up at me. I sit cross-legged on the landing, fixated on the space between me and the ground. Only now do I understand how risky the ascent had been.

"Ada . . ." he says.

"I can't stay here forever," I say, looking around. "There is no view of the sea, and the summer olives aren't any good."

He doesn't laugh, but glances over at the other houses. "We looked already, this is the only one with a ladder," I remind him. He leaps off the first floor onto the ground anyway, and I wait while he scours the villas, checking for ladders, for stepping stools, for anything that might help. But he returns empty-handed and pulls his body back up to the first floor. "You're just going to have to jump," he says, not meeting my gaze, still hoping an alternate solution might materialize. But when nothing turns up in the next few seconds, he holds out his arms. "Drop down slowly," he warns. "And I'll catch you." He stands strong and steady below me, and this time there is no fear in his expression. I trust him fully. Ian would have gone for help. Ian would have left it to somebody else, to somebody stronger, to save me.

I lie on my stomach and slowly shuffle my body off the landing. One leg goes down first as I keep the other bent, but as I bring my second leg down, I feel the full extent of my weight. As soon as I attempt to inch my elbows off the concrete floor, I'm going to fall. "One," I say, clamping my eyes closed. "Two . . . three!" I squirm on my elbows toward the edge and let go. Halfway down, he catches me.

He holds me like that for a moment, then a moment longer. His fingers spill out from underneath my arms and splay across the curve of my chest, as if hesitantly displaying me like something he has won. The warmth of his breath spreads across my back, starting from where my bikini ties together in a single knot, then emanating outward. And this is when I know for sure. Despite all the hopes that I had pinned on her, it was not my mother who had been in a position to fall.

It was me.

6

THE BOAT

Every summer for a single day, our table at the Small Club lies
bare of our belongings. Naked in its cracked plastic, we suppose,
though we've never been able to confirm whether someone else
takes over for those unattended hours. The day for our annual boat trip is
never planned in advance, but is suggested sometime around midsummer,
when the days truly begin to tumble into each other, and each of us tilts,
somewhat shamefully, toward a desire for something different. A blasphe-
mous yearning that we all fight against until one of us breaks. Until the
children's cries at the Small Club begin to grate at our ears, until we've ro-
tated through all the ice cream brands in the Algida freezer several times
over and the idea of another strawberry Cornetto has us pointing at our
mouths with our tongues slung out, until we've just about had it with the
daily interceptions and interrogations by someone's grandparents as we
walk to and from the sea. The first one to tip over the edge brings it up
casually, during a game of cards, a round of Okey, or, as it happened this
year, while we're all tanning out on the raft, drying slowly in our salted
crusts.

"Should we do our boat trip tomorrow?" asks Aslı, resting her head on her arm as she lies supine under the sun.

"Ohhh," I murmur, easing out of my nap. "Sure."

"Yes!" says Ozan, and dives off the edge.

"Yes!" says Bulut, and tries to do a flip off the edge. But the raft isn't long enough to provide him with the running start he needs, and he falls horizontally into the water on his back. We spend the rest of the day pressing our fingers into his skin and laughing, creating clean white dots in the blood-rushed red.

That night we eat dinner with our families and spit out sunflower seed shells by the basketball courts for only an hour, returning home at midnight to prepare for an early rise. We meet by the minibus stop in the direction of the town center, beach bags bulging. Mine holds four cheese *poğaças* that I bought from the baker last night. When we stumble out from the minibus onto the main square, blinking in sunlight that attacks us bluntly from the sky and piercingly from the thin folds of the morning sea, I gather everyone around the Atatürk statue and pass out our surprise breakfast. We eat, then buy our tickets.

The day-tripper boats depart at eleven a.m. from Ayvalık's marina, schlepping thirty to forty people on a double-decker. It's a full day of tanning and games, of dropping anchor near uninhabited islands for snorkeling and swimming in crystalline waters, and of dancing to Top 40 Turkish hits as the sun goes down and the boat returns to the mainland.

Among the many boats in the marina, ours is, and always has been, *Eftalya II*. We chose it many years ago back when its giant blue waterslide weighed heavy in our decision-making, though now that type of thrill has been replaced by diving off the top deck's railing. *Eftalya II* is easy to spot in the row of boats lined up on the mirrored seawater of the marina. As we waddle up the gangplank with our perforated tickets, I notice the captain has scrawled the date in pen: 25/7. I stick my thumb in my mouth and smudge the numbers clean.

The boys claim a corner booth on the lower deck while I go upstairs and drape our towels over beanbags, which we call *armut* for their pear-like shape. Inside my beach bag I have tanning oil, a deck of cards, a Turkish book I picked up at the airport and have yet to read, and several changes of swimsuit. I hate sitting wet, and plan to swim at every stop. Currently I'm wearing my most ill-fitting swimsuit that I have to continually adjust, a pink bikini with a large frangipani on the left triangle. I'll swap it for another as soon as the first swim of the day is over. More and more people board our boat, and the volume of the morning starts to rise: a group of older women—much older—in sequined cover-ups, bleary-eyed parents holding babies in tiny jelly sandals and floppy cloth hats, some co-ed groups around our age, and an American couple whose voices cut through the din of all the others. When I hear them, I shuffle around on my knees and lean over the rail, watching the boy and girl walk the gangplank hand in hand. The boy's braces flash as he smiles, bright yellow bands on each tooth. The girl wears a mesh tunic that offers no sun protection at all, and I can see the glint of a belly chain, jewelry that's more appropriate in an upscale resort town. Why are they here, instead of in Çeşme, or Antalya, or Bodrum? Our small town is nowhere on the tourist radar, and its historical trivia is much less prominent than those of other cities strung along the coast. But my curiosity is overpowered by my desire to blend in, to be no more than the background of their postcard. I nestle into my camouflage. Their foreign ears wouldn't be attuned enough to the Turkish language to understand that I am different, anyway. They will simply consider me part of the larger crowd, of people who are not them.

I shove an *armut* under the shadow of the bench that runs the perimeter of the top deck, get comfortable, and drift off to sleep.

In my dream, I am in İstanbul in sepia, like in my mother's photographs. I am with someone—who is it? I'm with Levent, in the backstreets of Beyoğlu. I want a kebab, and he turns to me and laughs, saying, *Kebabs are for tourists.* He takes me into a nondescript building where he rings an unnamed buzzer and a wooden door with a golden handle clicks open.

We walk up and up the spiral stone staircase as if we're on our way to somebody's—a friend's—apartment, but the final door opens up onto a rooftop bar, and beneath us lies the thick, twisting strand of the Bosphorus, its sparkling bridges like jeweled combs tucked into her hair. I signal to a waiter for a shawl; the weather is cold.

"Ada," someone's voice wakes me. "Ada, get up." Icicles fall onto my stomach. Ozan towers over me, water dripping from his beard. "We've dropped anchor. Get up so you can swim."

I shake the remnants of the dream out of my head. Ever since our encounter in the olive groves a couple days ago, I have been unable to stop thinking about Levent. It frightens me, what this thought might mean for my mother. No one can find out about my desire to get closer to him.

I look out over the railing at the small, scattered islands. Several people have already jumped in, and their refracted bodies shimmer as they circumnavigate the rocky shores. The splashes, the smooth patter of sleek fins, the soprano laughter of the kids as they twirl around in their burnt-orange flotation vests. The sun shines over it all.

Turkey is, without a doubt, the most beautiful country in the world. "We're so lucky to be here," I say.

"Everyone's lucky," Ozan says, scanning the sea for swimmers. "We're on holiday." Then he curls his toes over the railing, leaps into the air, and slips into the water in a quiet dive.

I don't want to jump in because of my awkward swimsuit, so I head to the lower deck, where Aslı and Bulut are laughing their heads off at something. Aslı is speaking with an exaggerated drawl, her mouth drooped to the side, and moving her hands as if they're a waterfall of words tumbling out of her. But she keeps bursting into giggles, breaking character. I can't catch what she's saying; she's going too fast. There's a newspaper with its first page unfolded out in front of them, a full-body photo of a businessman in a gray suit and red tie. In a smaller rectangle to the side is a photo of a woman with very high cheekbones.

"Oh, Ada!" says Aslı. "Please tell me you saw the talk show last night."
I give her a blank look.

"The one about the CEO of the media conglomerate?" Bulut taps the front page of the paper. "Doesn't your family watch the talk show?" He says the name of the host. It's a name I haven't heard before, and I can't split the first name from the last name correctly. All I end up with is a jumble of sounds that I immediately forget. We never watch television during the summers. In fact, there is no television in our villa, I tell them. It seems strange to sit inside and watch programs or the news, because that's akin to taking the pulse of the world. There is the cultural zeitgeist, the political scene. And all that fades away for me between June and August. Nothing ever happens here during the hot months.

Aslı stares at me, disbelieving. "Are you serious? You don't have a television in your house?" Though we've been friends for years, we've rarely been indoors together.

"My grandmother just reads the newspaper," I say, staying silent on what my mother and I do. We do nothing. "So what happened on the talk show?"

The twins look at each other, at a loss. Bulut rotates the paper my way. "You know who this guy is, though, right?" Gray suit, red tie.

"No."

"Oh, it will take so long to explain," sighs Aslı. "Because I can't just tell you the joke, you know? You would have to know the context. Well— fine. You know how there's a big trial going on right now? Three years ago, this guy's son married a woman whose father was imprisoned for embezzlement, but no one knew until . . . Oh, dear God, would you look at that idiot with the life vest! Why come all the way over here if you don't even know how to swim?" Bulut and I follow her gaze over the railing to the sea, where the boy in the braces is engulfed in a puffy orange vest. His girlfriend swims clumsily around him, kicking her legs out like a spasmodic frog.

Aslı only switched topics because they both know how embarrassed I get when I'm unaware of something that the whole country is talking about. This happens from time to time. About a few minutes into a conversation like this, one of them usually catches a glimpse of my blank face, or my sudden interest in the coffee stains on the table, or my tracking the flight path of a mosquito I have suddenly decided to kill. The topic then segues so neatly into a trivial matter that the other listeners are visibly shaken by cognitive disconnect. But then they follow the speaker's concerned gaze toward me and understand. I always notice a brief look of sympathy before everyone delves with a strong facade of enthusiasm into something innocent and accessible, like the weather.

But this time, Aslı was too taken aback by the fact that we don't even own a television to gracefully change the topic. *She's not even trying,* I could sense them signaling to each other in some sort of twin telepathy. *She's not even trying to keep up with what's going on in this mixed-up country of ours.* I focus fully on the floating boy, and direct all my shame and hatred toward him. Levent probably has a television, I think. He probably watches the talk show every night.

The water is as blue as Kool-Aid and absolutely clear; you can see a school of small silver fish flicker to avoid the newcomers. But I don't feel like going for a swim anymore. I watch the twins take out their goggles and head down the collapsible staircase at the edge of boat, Aslı taking forever as she yelps that it's too cold, too cold. Bulut places his foot on her back and shoves her in. I don't want them to see me waiting out the swim. I climb back up to the top deck and try to dream again.

The boat docks twice more prior to lunch, and I don't go in the water at all. I mostly keep busy on the top deck, watching the Americans exaggeratedly enunciate their desire to have photographs taken of themselves, handing their cameras to strangers they deem trustworthy, those unlikely to drop electronics into the sea. They pose on the stern of the boat, worm their way into the captain's cabin and grasp the wheel, eyes on the horizon and hands at their foreheads, shielding off the sun. The girl tans in various positions and bites her lower lip while reviewing the shots on the LCD. When their gaze drifts in my direction, I pretend to be asleep. As the motor putters off in search of new shores, wet swimsuits tied to the railings flutter like national flags.

For a late lunch, we reconvene in our booth downstairs, our mouths watering in anticipation of the fried sprat eaten whole—tails, bones, head, eyeballs—which is served with penne pasta and a salad with red onions, walnuts, kidney beans, white cheese, arugula, and pomegranate molasses. I check to see how the Americans are reacting to the meal, wondering if they're focusing solely on the pasta, kindly declining the all-too-realistic seafood. But in the booth behind us the girl holds up the fish by their tails and drops them one by one into the boy's mouth, laughing as he washes it all down with a cup of orange Fanta.

After lunch, we head to the top deck, where a man with a peeling nose tinkers on a keyboard as he announces game rules and sputters out commentary into a microphone. Ozan and Bulut eagerly volunteer for "Pop the Balloon," and I cheer them on half-heartedly while pulling out the cards from my beach bag. I cut the deck, make my wish. The boys win. Then Aslı and Ozan race back and forth as part of the next game, keeping their bodies still as their bare feet skid along the hot surface, trying to prevent water from spilling out of plastic cups. They lose the relay to two older women who are part of the group in the sequined caftans, and come back chittering with adrenaline. I flip over my last king, too early again, but by now I'm getting used to not getting what I want. My future seems set, closed for revision. Levent won't change anything; my life could never go down a path like that—could it? His presence has already helped me conjure up those backstreets of Beyoğlu in my subconscious. Were they real? I try to map out the journey we had taken in the dream. Perhaps those short stays in İstanbul with my mother have seared the city's layout into my mind. If only I could remember the visual cues. If only I could make out the colors and the shapes of the buildings I had created from nothing (but, really, from something!). Is it possible that I could find my own way around İstanbul, without a guide? It's a strange thought, that I might be able to navigate the city without my mother.

"Gotcha!"

Two cold hands grip my ankles, another two like handcuffs on my wrists. My body jolts to escape the clutch, but Ozan and Bulut hold on tight.

"Let me go!" I yell. Then I pause, considering the options. "Do not," I shriek, trying to kick them off me, "do not do not do not *altı okka* me in the water." It's one thing to dive from the railings, but it's another to be tossed from the top deck *altı okka*, in which the two people in charge of your body swing you several times, then fling you into the sea. I remember Bulut's back from yesterday, its deep red fragility after hitting the water in a way that turned the sea solid. "Please, please don't." The boys laugh.

"Don't worry, Ada," Ozan says. "We're not going to *altı okka* you." With tiny side steps, they bring me up to the man on the keyboard.

"Captain, wait!" calls Bulut. "We've got another contestant for you."

They don't ease their grip until the man runs his fingers along the keys from the low to the high octaves, acknowledging our arrival. Once he presses his lips back to the microphone, I am gently released onto the floor and totter upon my legs like a newborn lamb.

"Our final contestant! Young lady, tell us your name and where you're from."

"Yes, hello, my name is Ada," I say, unnecessarily giving a full-sentence response. I wait for Ozan and Bulut to introduce themselves, but they're standing quietly to the side, grinning and nudging each other. Aren't they on my team? What type of competition is this? I hope it's something I'm good at.

"All right, Miss Ada, and where in our beautiful country are you from?"

"Um." The Americans are in the back corner, rearranging their *armuts* for maximum comfort, settling in for whatever show we're about to put on. The girl loops her hair through a baseball cap that says *UNLV*. "I'm from İstanbul."

"The great metropolis of İstanbul! Whereabouts? Europe? Anatolia? Looks like we've got a couple of ladies from İstanbul here today."

I hesitate before giving the neighborhood of my grandmother's winter home, then glance at the rest of the contestants. Sure enough, they're all women. I consider the coincidence.

"Yes, ladies and gentlemen, there you have it. Ada from İstanbul." The man plays a few more notes on his keyboard, reviewing the women and their origins as each of us takes a step forward to generous applause. Three from İstanbul, one Ankara, one İzmir, one Kütahya. Another short jingle, this one ominous yet inviting. Then he welcomes the audience to the one and only *Eftalya II* Oriental Dance Competition. I am Contestant Number Six.

The beginning of a *çiftetelli* piece wails out from a speaker from somewhere behind me. Contestant Number One steps out in front of the keyboard, and her body immediately commands the space into a stage. All eyes are on her. She bends backward and lifts her arms up and down like a bird in flight. Her hips slowly draw a circle around her, claiming space. Then the drums start and her movements lock into place. She becomes all the instruments at once. There is no beat unaccompanied by a movement of her body—a twist of the foot, a turn of the head, a shimmy from the hips, the shoulders.

"Contestant Number Two!"

One woman's movements slide into the next, the energy transferring from Miss İzmir to Miss Ankara, the sun glinting off the metallic clasps of her leopard-print bikini, a diaphanous sarong thinly veiling her curves. Her almond-shaped eyes are half closed in ecstasy, coming alive for a wink at the pause. Her hips are in a violent flirtation with the air around her, which condenses as it awaits their tap before releasing the drumbeat.

I want to throw myself over the railing. Sink down into the water, deeper and deeper until my body is punctured by the sea urchins. But I'm pinned to the deck, mesmerized by the women. One after the other they dance, each picking up from where the woman before her has left off. These are not the rhythms to which my body has been accustomed throughout the years. Every time I have heard the beat of the goblet drum, I have immediately retreated into the shadows and waited for the hot shame to pass. I have hidden in corners as blood pumped quicker and quicker through my extremities, every panicked cell scrambling for an exit.

I consider the dimly lit places where my body has moved before. To the songs on the radio as I drove down Highway 280, the slow dances in multipurpose rooms as parents of friends checked the distance between the sexes. A disco ball flaring, lighting up the glitter on the chests of pre-pubescent girls like a star shower.

"Contestant Number Six!"

I step out in front of the keyboard, but for me the transformation does not occur. The deck refuses to become my stage. Expectant faces blink up at me. In the corner, Ozan stifles a laugh, and I turn to glare, but the expression reflected back at me in his sunglasses is only one of helplessness. Is there something in my blood, I wonder, that will take over if I surrender, that will help me move to this music? I let go, I trust, and I wait.

The sound of the goblet drums. *Dum-tek-teke-tek, dum-teke-tek.* I stay exactly as I am. Nothing penetrates; nothing snakes into me and lights me up with the energy that I should already have stored in the depths of my body. My feet burn, stationary as they are, but I take it as punishment. So it's up to me now. I try to think of a movement, of any movement. Of any way that anyone has moved in the history of the entire world.

"Dance, girl!" someone yells from the back.

When was the last time I danced? I think of red Solo cups, of musty fraternities, of rap so rushed that I'm left breathless keeping up with the words. I pick a song from another evening, far away. I play it in my mind, and my body slowly but surely starts to move. That melody stops; I switch again. Back to middle school, back to being thirteen under a balloon arch, soaked in the scent of Tahitian vanilla. A French boy jumps in the air, his coral necklace flying so high it hits his teeth. I run my tongue along my braces, feeling for traces of olive from an earlier pizza party. Another boy with a dimpled smile comes up to me, holding a plastic lei to place around my neck, speaking in innuendos.

The MC clears his throat. "The rhythm seems obvious to me," he says, and a trombone sound effect booms from the keyboard: *womp womp.* "But this young lady's dancing to the beat of her own drum."

Someone boos the MC for his comment, or maybe boos me, and one person claps along to the beat for emphasis, to try to get me back on track. *I am so sorry,* I want to say. *This is the only way my body knows how to move.* In the back, the American girl in the baseball cap shakes her shoulders in a shimmy, which I realize I know how to do. I can do that move; it's easy. The upper half of my body takes up the beat now, though my hips and legs are still moving to my off-season life. And I am there, I am almost there, and I can feel myself getting there, but then I realize that the clapping has stopped, and a murmur is rippling through the audience. I look down at myself and see that my frangipani flower has shifted, it is folded up, and I am coming out of it, exposed. I yank down the fabric to flatten the flower, and the string snaps. The music stops. All I can hear is the gentle sound of the waves lapping at the boat.

"And that was Contestant Number Six!" yells the MC, wrapping up another contest on the *Eftalya II*. The applause is too loud. With my hands pressed to my chest, I walk through the parting crowd, a crowd afraid to accidentally touch any part of me, and down to the lower deck. I sink into our booth, fix my bikini, then order a giant plate of sprat. Over the dead fish, I drain the juice of two lemon halves, sticking my fork in the citrus to carve out the flesh. One by one, I pop their fried bodies whole into my mouth and crush the weak bones with my teeth. When I'm done, I order another plate.

Aslı comes down to talk to me and attempts to make light of the situation. I give her a stony stare, and she pivots immediately, hair whooshing behind her, and climbs back up.

"She wants to be left alone," I hear her say. Someone laughs, then stops.

A few minutes later, the American couple passes by. The girl pauses to lean over to me, letting her boyfriend walk on. "I thought you did pretty well," she says. "Sorry about what happened." Her mouth is wide with the enunciations, and the spaces between her words fall lifelessly into black holes. As if I would have any trouble understanding what she was saying. As if she did not know, from everything that had happened, that I had more in common with her than I did with anyone else, out here at sea.

7

THE MOVIE

The day after the horrendous boat trip, I want to spend time with my mother, but she has plans to dine with Neslihan at the last restaurant in the row of restaurants on Cunda Island. It's the most expensive one, and my mother knows that Neslihan will pay for the meal. "She will throw me into the sea if she has to," my mother says. "Or tie me up in one of those fishing nets they leave on the boats." Never has Neslihan let my mother pay for dinner. Not in high school, not in college, not in the years after. It's a tradition that began long ago because Neslihan's family owned a major home appliances brand and so it was expected. But then my mother had married my father, and if we are comparing bills to bills, technically my mother should be paying for seafood dinners, kebab dinners, ice cream cones, and, really, any and all outings. But once the tradition had continued for long enough to be called a tradition, it could not be stopped. Neslihan has gone to great measures to prevent my mother from pulling out her wallet at the end of a meal. Once, she arrived at the restaurant earlier than scheduled and demanded to speak to the waiter who would be serving them. Under no circumstances, she warned him, was he to accept her guest's payment. She

had slipped him fifty lira to make sure. My mother only understood the scheme once she was met with side profiles and scattering waiters as she offered up her card. "I have never been ignored like that, so completely," said my mother. Of course Neslihan should have just paid for the full meal up front, along with the bribe, instead of causing an unpleasant scene. But she revels so deeply in taking care of others that the simple act of saying *Don't you dare, this one is on me* while closing the server book atop a set of colorful bills is, for her, the entire point of a meal.

"So you see," says my mother, "why it must just be Neslihan and me tonight, at the restaurant at the end of the row. I cannot have her paying for your food as well."

Fine, I say. But let's go out the two of us to Cunda another night, maybe?

My mother pulls a face. "Grandma would need to come along, though. She'd give us hell if we both left her behind. I don't think we can do it."

Propriety, propriety, propriety, I mumble. Then I say: Forget it.

"We'll get back to our mother-daughter dates in California," she says, and kisses me on the forehead because I am sulking like a child. "I will bring you back a cockle in my purse."

You better, I say.

My grandmother and I eat dinner alone on the terrace, but we are having trouble finding things to talk about. She cuts her *börek* so lightly that the knife takes forever to make its way through the layers of thin dough. She just keeps sawing back and forth, back and forth, as if stroking it with a feather. I watch her in amazement. I pick up my own square of *börek* like a slice of pizza and shove it in my mouth.

"Propriety, Ada!" My grandmother's head snaps up as soon as she notices the infringement on etiquette under her own roof. Her small eyes bulge and she juts out her chin toward my silverware. "You have a knife," she says. "You are capable of using it, I presume?" I have already eaten everything there is to potentially cut, so I grab a lumpy purple fig. I tear it open with my fingernail.

"Why are you so on edge tonight, *anneannecik?*" I ask, juice dribbling down my chin. I use a diminutive to make her smile, but she just gazes helplessly at my face.

"I am not on edge," she states plainly. Her knife has still not made contact with the plate. I am thinking of sly questions I can ask to get it out of
her, because clearly there is something wrong. Perhaps she is mad at my
mother for taking a night off and going out with her friend. But then she
would actually be mad, not weirdly petrified as she seems to be now, as
if faced with a conundrum even her great octopus arms cannot reach far
enough to solve. As I'm musing over all this, the phone rings from inside
the house, and I go into the living room to pick it up. It's Aslı. She tells me
that tonight instead of meeting outside I should come over to her house
because there's a movie on Channel D that everyone's planning to watch.

"Since you don't have a television," she says, "I thought you'd like to
watch it here." I realize that I have no idea where her house is, because
all these years we have met only by the sea, by the basketball courts, at
the market, or in the park. Her villa, she explains, is up past the back of
the market, fourth left. There are three pomegranate trees in her garden
and a Peugeot under the pergola. I write all this down on my hand with
a pen I find by the telephone, then head back to the table to annoy my
grandmother out of her secret.

"Why don't our pomegranate trees have any pomegranates?" I ask,
knowing I will hit a nerve.

My grandmother heaves a huge sigh. "They're an autumnal fruit, you
Palo Alto princess. God help us. I told your mother not to raise any children in that uninhabitable suburban town. Look at you, with a complete
and utter lack of any common sense. Where is your connection to the
land?"

I tell her that no pomegranates grow in California and I can't possibly
be expected to know these things. She raises an eyebrow at my outlandish
lie as I reach across the table for another fig. "Does your boyfriend enjoy
it, Ada, watching you eat like an animal?" I wish my mother were here
to say something instead of toasting with *rakı* to being child-free by the
sea with her high school friend. I suddenly become very angry that she
has left me alone tonight. I should have just gone to Aslı's early and eaten
with her family.

"Actually," I say, "he finds it unbelievably sexy."

My grandmother slams down the napkin holder on my side of the table. I take one and wipe my entire face, save for where I can feel the stickiness of the fig juice. It's when I set down the napkin that I break her, because she reveals a glimpse of the smallest smile, shaking her head at me. "You little snake," she says, her grin now wide and bursting. "You little dinky donkey, what would I do without you and your mother? You two are my light, my light, my light." She gets up to clear off the table, and her body moves faintly to the rhythm of her last words. *My light, my light, my light.*

⁓⚓⁓

Although nobody's house is as easy to find as ours, I don't have any trouble locating Bulut and Aslı's villa. What I immediately notice, and what she had forgotten to mention to me, is that they have combined the two attached villas into one, theirs with Ozan's family's, so the two families can summer in one big home. It's bizarre to see the balcony wrap all the way around without the dividing half-wall between them, for the dividing half-wall is a key feature of the *site*. It's the area behind which a family can sit quietly and listen to the gossip of the neighbor, silent and unseen. That's how the gossip spreads so quickly here, because whatever one family knows, the family living in the attached villa will know come dinnertime.

When I get there, I find the three of them in the living room sprawled upon couches, and it makes me smile, this never-before-seen vision of them lounging in an interior. There's a bowl of popcorn, an array of beers, and a plate of cut peaches on the coffee table in front of them. "Moooom!" Aslı yells. "Ada's here!" A very slim woman with luscious dark hair skitters into the room, holding a large plate of watermelon slices.

"Hello, dear," she says. I have already forgotten her name, and I shoot a helpless look at Ozan, who is sitting behind her. He understands my distress, and tries to mouth the name at me. I'm not getting it. Then he raises an index finger and draws a line across the sky, then places his hands together as if he is begging. No. As if he is wishing on a star. Aunt Wish! That's it.

"Hello, Dilek *teyze*," I say. My own mother's name, Meltem, means "zephyr." I helpfully rescue the heavy watermelon plate from Dilek and set it beside the other snacks. She is looking at the two plates of fruit, furrowing her brow. She does not think that there is enough.

"All of you are going to fill up on that popcorn, and then no one is going to eat this healthy fruit that is filled with vitamins. Then all my children will become fat. Do you like Kemal Sunal?"

It takes me a minute to realize that the question is directed at me. Ozan helps out again. "Kemal Sunal stars in this movie," he says.

"Ah," I say. "I actually don't know who he is. But if these guys are staying in on a summer night to watch his movie, I bet he's pretty good!" My pleasant smile has zero effect on Dilek. She frowns, turning back to her family, and starts speaking as if I'm not there.

"It's strange," says Dilek to her own children, "because she speaks Turkish, doesn't she? I mean, it's almost there. But it's quite bizarre, to hear someone speak like this who does not know of Kemal Sunal. Huh!" She takes another look at me and flutters back out into the kitchen, beyond which she will sit at a table on the terrace, and smoke and gossip freely with her family, with no observers behind no walls. *It might perhaps be better*, I could imagine her saying, *if she were fat. Then you would know, of course, that she is an American, and it is not strange that she does not know our movie stars.*

We sit through the movie, and I think it's funny, even though I don't get all the jokes. I try to laugh when Ozan and Aslı laugh, and I don't laugh when Bulut laughs, because I know that our humor is less aligned. This strategy is tiring, but not impossible. About halfway through the movie, I finally admit to myself that I'm not enjoying this at all. Every muscle in my body is clenched, on edge. Nobody asked if they should put on subtitles, and I didn't suggest them. But there is a difference between understanding the fluid Turkish of today and the fluid Turkish of two decades ago. When the conversation strays from beaches or kitchens or the quotidian matters of a summer day, I find myself in a different land altogether. I let the words go and focus instead on examining Kemal Sunal's face from every angle, aging it backward and forward in my mind so

I will be able to, after the credits roll, recognize him anywhere. I will be able to see an ad for a different movie and say, *Oh, Kemal Sunal's in this, we should watch it!* I might run into him at a rooftop bar in Taksim and approach him for his autograph. I'd tell him that I'm a fan.

"It's really so sad that he passed away," sighs Aslı, spitting out a watermelon seed into her fist.

I will not see him in Taksim, but I will still see him on the movie posters. Recognizably so.

Every second of this summer is about adding and subtracting to the equation that is me. The more I learn, the more I know that there is more to know, that I will never be able to make up for the years spent abroad. My mother would understand these jokes, but there would be a tear for her, too. What year would it be, the year after which a movie would no longer have the comforting quality of home? How many years does it take for customs to change, for the obscure slang of today to become the default vocabulary of tomorrow, for a woman to feel a disconnect as a day in her old country plays out in film? Ten years post-departure? Twenty? From time to time, Aslı and Ozan flicker their eyes over at me to check if they need to pause the movie for any explanation, but I am so focused on the screen that I would not be surprised if my glare set the television on fire.

It's a real relief when Dilek *teyze* jumps back into the living room and asks if one of us could please go down to the market. She is out of cigarettes.

I tumble out of my chair so fast that initially everyone mistakes my volunteer spirit for an accident. Because it is completely inappropriate for a guest to wander off by herself, Aslı begrudgingly offers to accompany me under the death stare of her mother. Bulut kicks his sister in the back of her knee and, as she collapses, tells her to get some ice cream, too, while we're at it. Dilek *teyze* is shocked to see that all the popcorn has been consumed, mostly by me. "Oh my!" she exclaims, hand on her heart. But she catches herself and shows great restraint by not making any further comments.

When we step into the market, Aslı heads to the bakery for its ice cream selection, and I go to the grocer to get two packs of Camels. As the grocer's boy reaches for them in the shelves behind the register, I suddenly think of something.

"You're friends with the *lahmacun* maker's son, aren't you?" I ask. I can't remember his name, but it doesn't matter. He probably doesn't know mine, either—just thinks of me the same way everybody else in this town does, as Mukadder's granddaughter.

"Friends . . ." He considers the definition, scanning for meaning along the cracks of the market ceiling. "We ride our bikes together sometimes, down to the town center."

That should be sufficient. "What do you make of the fact that he says he swam all by himself to Barren Island?"

The boy shrugs, and one of the thick straps of his yellow tank top slips down his shoulder. On his shirt is a screen print of the Tasmanian Devil, the knockoff illustration uncannily similar to the actual Looney Tune. But the color's faded, and the edges of the animal's mouth are slightly misshapen.

"Well, did he?"

"I don't know," the boy mumbles, fiddling with a pen. "He says he did. But he says a lot of things, and some of them I know for sure aren't true."

"Okay, like what?"

"Like . . ." The boy digs his chin into his collarbone and drags it back and forth in a semicircle. "Like he says that Barren Island is cursed, but obviously curses aren't real, so, for example, that's one thing he lies about."

This immediately piques my interest. "There's a curse?" I ask. "What's the curse?"

"It doesn't matter because it's not real."

I wonder if Bulut knows, but hasn't told me because he thinks I'd back out if I knew. Everyone in this town has seen me at the Small Club, my cards spread in a circle around the table, my coffee always upside down to cool. "Just tell me what it is."

"I don't want to say it out loud," the boy says.

"Because then you'll be cursed?"

"I just told you, I don't believe in curses." He narrows his gaze at me, and his tone drops its fear, taking a turn for the serious. "Do you?" He doesn't seem to be testing me, not exactly. It seems like a genuine question.

"Of course not," I say, not quite believing myself. "Why don't you want to tell me?"

"Because it might matter to you."

"What, just because I like card fortunes? They're different, you know. One's an omen, a story you tell yourself. The other is a story someone else tells you. Why wouldn't it matter to the *lahmacun* maker's boy, but matter to me? This makes no sense."

"It's not because of your card fortunes."

I stare at him.

He looks down, picking out a scab on his arm, and mutters something I can't catch. I prod him again. "I don't want to say," he repeats, and then gathers up the courage to look me in the eye. The conversation is over.

"Fine then," I say, heading out the door. "Eat whatever shit you want to eat."

"Have a nice day, Ada."

Surprised, I turn around. "What's your name?" I ask.

"Efe," the boy says. "Same as the *lahmacun* maker's kid."

I walk quickly to the other end of the market to peek inside the *lahmacun* restaurant, where the wife is kneading the dough on the counter. She notices me and waves. If something terrible had happened to her son, she wouldn't have been here. There is no curse, I tell myself. There can't be because everything is fine. I have inherited my mother's healthy acceptance of fate and superstition, though the American in me works hard to stifle the more questionable philosophies. The American does not always succeed.

Take, for example, that night in high school when my car overheated driving back from a dinner in San Francisco. I had groggily pulled over on the 280 at one in the morning and called the house for help. My mother picked up, answering in Turkish. My father quickly arranged a cab and went back to sleep, but my mother was waiting for me when I got home, brewing sachets of peppermint tea she had bought from an organic foods store in Palo Alto. I asked her why she had answered the call in Turkish. I thought maybe I had woken her up from a dream by the sea.

"Whenever the phone rings in the middle of the night," she said, "my first thought is that someone is calling to tell me that my mother is dead." Her hand curled into a fist under the sleeve of her sweater, and I waited, now highly alert, for that superstitious knock on the oak kitchen table. A tiny, perfunctory action to mitigate the potentially damning effect of her words. But she released her palm without touching anything. Five tense, distinct fingers hovering over the table. Then she handed me a cup of tea. "Here you go," she said, but I was too stunned to reach for it. "Ada?" my mother asked, looking concerned. "Take your tea."

Why didn't she do it? The scene horrified me, playing out over and over again in my mind's eye. The tap should have been instinctive for her. It was the drumbeat to her life, trailing comments tinged with even the slightest hint of a disastrous fate. As we walked upstairs to our respective bedrooms, I knocked on the wooden banister. Just lightly enough so that my mother wouldn't hear and understand that I'd noticed what had transpired, but loudly enough that the underworld would. I couldn't get the image out of my mind: the ominous steam emanating from our mugs; that dark, unmoving fist. I could never figure out what it meant, her unexpected stillness.

I hear Aslı call out my name by the market's rear exit. She tells me to hurry, that the ice cream is melting, and I skip over to the back of the building. I wonder if I should ask her about the island's curse, but decide against it. I don't want her to know that I'm still considering the swim. She's just going to get frustrated with me and try to talk me out of it. I ask her which flavors of ice cream she bought, and she says vanilla, pistachio—and just then, out of the corner of my eye, I see a graceful movement that I recognize all too well.

"Grandma?"

My grandmother is walking down the slope toward the sea. When she sees me, she recoils, as if to disappear back into the second before I spotted her. "What are you doing out here?" I ask.

"Oh," she says, and I notice that she's changed from dinner; she is wearing slacks and a silk blouse, her sapphire necklace around her neck again. She brings her hands to the stones and touches them lightly, one by one. "Emine is ill, so I brought her some yogurt soup. What are *you* doing?"

I tell her that we're getting ice cream and cigarettes from the market, and she receives this information quite naturally without asking whether I have taken up smoking. Under normal circumstances, there would have been a dramatic interrogation. When we say goodbye and let each other go, I tell Aslı that my grandmother has been acting strange all night.

"She was definitely lying about where she was," Aslı says. "Anyway, the third flavor is mastic. So it's vanilla, pistachio, and mastic. Do those work for you?"

I am stunned but not surprised by Aslı's powers of perception. She seems confident in her assessment. "What makes you think she's lying?" I ask.

For the first time in all my fumbling years here, Aslı looks at me like I'm an idiot. "We-e-e-ll," she says, "she's your grandma, can't you tell? She got all fidgety. And besides, Emine is my mother's friend, and one, they were playing cooncan at the Small Club all day, that woman's healthy as a donkey. And two, you know she moved and she actually lives in the next *site* over now, so we are actually nowhere near her house." I consider this. Then I hand Aslı the cigarettes and tell her to go on without me.

"I just need a couple minutes," I say.

"For what?"

"A secret mission."

Aslı nods knowingly and turns to head back up the hill. She is serene, secure in the knowledge that everything will soon come to light. The inability of a secret to survive in this town is incredible. I try to remember what my mother said that evening when we were eating sea bream delivered from the Small Club. *You know he took one of those villas behind the market?* I loop through all the streets, searching. I know that my grand-mother has gone to see Levent, I just know it. Why is she so attached to this idea? Levent isn't interested in my mother! There is no reason to give her false hope. I weave in and out of the short summer streets until I find him.

He is on the terrace of the third street behind the market, sixth house down. I think fast, ducking into a set of hanging leaves that belongs to a neighbor's mulberry bush, a little alcove that shields me from his view. Under the pergola to the side of the yard is a black SUV, a license plate beginning with 34. An İstanbul plate. I watch him through the outlines of the leaves. He seems to be participating in an imaginary conversation. His hand circles around his wrist, moving down a list of arguments, and his face contorts into something resembling empathy. Is he letting some-one down? He relaxes his face, shaking his head. The scenario he had just conjured is no good. He is telling my grandmother, I decide, that it will not work. I understand the rehearsal, but we don't have all the time in the world. When the weather turns, we leave for California. Surrounded in the darkness by the fat ripe berries, I make a small wish that he will help me find what my mother could not.

The attached neighbor calls out to Levent, and as his head turns toward the dividing wall, I emerge from my mulberry bush and run as lightly, as softly as I can in the night, back to Aunt Dilek's.

8

THE GOSSIP

When I come down for breakfast the next morning, my mother is wearing a hot-pink bikini top that I bought for myself in San Francisco over a pair of denim shorts.

"It fits," my mother says, by way of explanation. The color flashes against her loose, dark skin. "And aren't you up early today?"

It's true, I am up very early. But I shrug off her comment and pretend that this is quite normal.

"Your mother is starting to look chipper, isn't she?" says my grandmother. "See this? Now this is the daughter I raised."

We all look around the table and smile at each other. Then I clear my throat and tell them that since I am already up and energized, I can buy today's bread and newspaper from the market.

"We don't need bread right now," says my grandmother. "We have some left over from yesterday. To what do we owe this sudden generosity?"

I hurry out before she can ask me anything else. In the air hangs the thin chill of the early hours, soon to be overtaken by the burn of morning. First, to be safe, I walk the entirety of the neighborhood, up and down every street, so that I can be seen everywhere all at once. *I saw Ada standing there,* someone in the *site* would say. *Well, I saw her elsewhere*, another would counter, and neither my true location nor my intention would ever be revealed. Once I've covered sufficient ground, I circle back to the beginning of the street that bisects the shoreline promenade and continue toward the market. The street soon narrows into the rosemary footpath that runs between the two basketball courts, and I hold out my hands to graze the bushes on both sides.

I pass straight through the market, take a right after the rear exit, and head up the hill a bit before turning left. As I walk down the street, the terraces come alive; I am the ticking morning hour. A baby in a high chair pours a glass of milk over his older sister at the breakfast table, shocking her into silence; a grandfather with paper-thin lips kisses his granddaughter, who breaks off a piece of *simit* for him that then hangs in his mouth like a crescent moon; a woman is so mesmerized by her book that she cannot hear the cries of her child, reading on as her hand blindly jumps around the table, seeking contact with her tea glass. But the scene I am heading toward is something else entirely—a single person with an attachment to no one.

Not yet, anyway.

When I get to his villa, I slip back inside the mulberry bush.

This morning, Levent sifts through a newspaper, a mug of coffee with the image of London's Big Ben on the table next to him. I am disappointed to see that he's absorbed only by the paper's last few pages, those summarizing questionable advances in medicine. And, of course, the sports highlights. The seismic shifts of the country and its political movements chronicled on the front pages fail to capture his attention. He folds that news right over. I make a mental note: *Uninterested in the convoluted.* His sense of nationalism, then, is held by the strongest of all foundations: soccer (is there any greater devotion?). I imagine both of us in the stadium, faces painted in the dual colors of our favorite team, eyes wildly tracking our favorite players. Or a more nuanced scenario: We will be getting ready to meet friends for lunch, and he will come by the room, lean against the doorway. *We have to be back before seven*, he'll say. *There's a game tonight, and traffic coming home is bound to be a disaster.* In our new İstanbul life, we will have to consider such things.

Every morning, I repeat my patrol.

Three days into my a.m. observations, just as I'm heading out the gate, my grandmother asks me to help her water the garden plants. I must start with the mint by the wall separating our garden and the diagonal neighbor's, she says, then work my way back to the tomato vines below my bedroom window. I curse under my breath and reluctantly walk over to her, holding out a hand for the hose. She tightens her grip on the nozzle.

"Why," my grandmother asks, "does it take you forever to buy bread on days we don't even need it?" She presses her thumb lightly up against the nozzle, creating a gentle spray of water at my feet.

"You spend an hour buying the bread. An hour! The other day you returned with nothing, then went straight to the Small Club to swim. That was the day we had actually run out, and your mother and I had to subsist on cucumbers and tomatoes and cheese and honey and eggs for breakfast with nothing substantial to fill our stomachs. Now, I know you are not that stupid. You are your father's daughter, after all."

The comparison to my father stuns me, but I have to focus on keeping the truth behind my morning routine under wraps. I try to remember when it was, exactly, that I came home empty-handed. The days blur together. "I use the errand as an opportunity to take a nice, long walk," I say. "I read in the back page of the newspaper that early-morning walks are the best way to activate one's metabolism."

"Ah, you mean you read about it in the newspapers that you forget to buy?" My grandmother starts to spray me up and down, and I shriek as the water splashes in my face. I hold out my hands as a surrender.

"Stop! Yes, in the newspapers. Morning is the best time to stretch out your body. Grandma, stop it!" I scramble to hide behind our garden's fat palm tree.

My grandmother slides her thumb back down and waggles the nozzle at me, the water now limp. "You come home at three every night. Then you wake up at seven to buy unnecessary bread and stretch out your nineteen-year-old body? It's I who should be getting up with the sun and exercising my stiff joints at dawn." She pauses for a minute, considering the idea. "Maybe one day I'll come with you."

At these words I run back and snatch the hose from her. Then I walk resolutely over to the mint. "Maybe," I say, terrified about the potential accompaniment.

"How about after you're done watering, we go out together?" she asks. I start humming along to the pop song playing from the Small Club.

"I said . . ."

I shudder, feeling my grandmother's breath on the back of my neck.

"A little promenade today, after you're done?"

I continue to water the mint, soaking the plant.

"Hm, what do you think? A walk, the two of us?"

"Well, you see, the thing is—"

"Ada!" The scream erupts in my ear, and I jump. "What are you doing, trying to drown the mint? Have you ever watered a plant before in your life?"

I move on to the palm tree and spray up at its fronds, tossing the hose back and forth to create a rainbow effect. My grandmother stares at me, unamused by my artwork. She shakes her head in despair.

"I cannot believe it. I just cannot believe it."

"Their leaves need water, too."

"Give me that hose. Go! Go on your mysterious excursion. Don't bring us back anything. I don't even want to read the news today—it's all terrible, anyway. Go ahead now, get out!"

"Okey-dokey." I hand her the hose and scamper off, just as my mother appears on the terrace, yawning in her nightshirt.

⚓

I am floating on my back in the sea, happy. Through the water I can hear the muted yells of children as they race down the pier and jump in. I throw my head back and flip upside down, grazing the beds of tall seaweed. The water is cold down here. I feel safer in the depths. Moving through the quiet seafloor, I can feel my body, my own presence. My movements are heavy and significant. Is it time to come up for air? Is there a raft, a person, above me? I break the surface, feeling the sun on my face. Everything is loud and bright again. I swim to the pier, climb up the ladder, and towel off.

The others are at the table, indulging in endless games of chance. That's what I call them, though my friends try to argue how deeply I underestimate the role of strategy. But I've always had more faith in my luck than in my reasoning. I am the undisputed queen of backgammon. Every few games, when all five of the home slots are blocked and my opponent's broken piece has nowhere to land and my opponent therefore no reason to roll, my shout can be heard across the café: "Sorry, buddy, school's out for the summer!" Don't worry, I console them with a smile. Remember, he who loses in the gamble wins in matters of the heart. The logic, I am quick to clarify, is not necessarily symmetric.

Now that I'm back, we can start a game of Okey. Ozan shuffles the overturned tiles, annihilating any discernible pattern. We help him stack the tiles in groups of five and set them against the backs of our wooden stands. With a spare tile in one hand and a die in the other, I roll a six and set the tile on the sixth stack in front of me. I roll again, a two this time, then pull out to reveal the second tile from the bottom of the stack. A red two. Add one and—"Red threes are wild," I inform the group, then go about distributing stacks to each player. As I turn to pass Bulut his tiles, I notice Levent on the raft. When did he get there? Was he there while I was in the water? I quickly finish what's left of the distribution. Then, in the tiniest incremental movements, my sight makes its small leaps, like a skipping stone, back to the water. My reconnaissance missions are generally limited to the morning hours. In the afternoons, with my friends, it's tough to remain inconspicuous. But today, I sneak a glance.

Levent steadies himself on the edge of the raft and dives in, barely making a splash. He had probably been there for a while then, drying off in the sun. Time to cool down. Then he pulls himself up from the tiny ladder hooked to the side, and as he's stepping up, his gaze rests on the northern end of the beach. Is my mother swimming? Why does he care about my mother? I feel a bolt of jealousy. I strain to see, but I'm sitting too low; the café's plexiglass window smears the view. I fake a yawn and stand to stretch, but my movements are too abrupt and the clatter that follows disrupts my attention before I can get a good look. Three faces turn to me in slight alarm.

"All good there, Ada?" Ozan asks, righting the stacks of tiles that I knocked over.

"Yep, I just—I thought I felt something." I make a show of checking under the table for cats. Nothing but a bunch of sandy feet. "Yes, all good. Carry on." I want to check on Levent just one more time, but I can't risk drawing any more attention to myself. I stamp my feet on the floor to regain focus and get my head back in the game.

Bulut rearranges the pieces on his stand, clacking along pleasantly, then slams a green eight on the table for Aslı, who's on his right. We're running counterclockwise. Ozan wins nearly every game, which means each of us has to buy him a can of Efes beer for the following three nights. Every summer we dream of breaking the chain, but so far it's only happened once, when Aslı took a round and we were so ecstatic that we couldn't even wait until evening. We bought beers from the Small Club and shook them up as we marched onto the dock, Aslı leading the way. Then we clicked them open and poured them over her head, right before Bulut and Ozan tossed her *altı okka* into the water. We'd sell our souls for another break in the cycle.

"Hey, Bulut." Ozan juts out his chin, motioning toward the front of the club. "That's the guy you were telling me about the other day, right?" All of us turn in our chairs to see Levent slipping out of the showers. I freeze. Bulut twitches his nose, nodding.

"What a pervert." Ozan spits out the word like the shell of a sunflower seed, and it sits dark and wet among the sleek white tiles. I fix my gaze squarely on the table, frightened about the new information I'm about to hear. Aslı nudges her brother for details.

"So? And? Yes?"

"Remember?" asks Bulut, annoyed. "He's the guy who skinny-dips in the middle of the night at Sıfır."

I visibly relax. Quirky, but not sufficiently incriminating. Another mental note: *Free spirit, young at heart.* I twist my face into my best rendition of a disgusted expression, and flash it up at Bulut.

"Mmmm, so that's him!" Aslı furrows her brows as she cranes her neck, taking him in. Now that Aslı's looking, I can freely turn toward Levent as well. He has sunken fully into the season. At our first encounter, I had considered him well tanned, simmered over. But now, with his arms darkened and his shoulders peeling, I can only remember his previous presence in a cloudy haze, a pure white winter. The contrast with today shuffles up the images of the past. These days, his shark-tooth necklace doesn't catch my eye like it used to. Its leather string has nearly melded with the color around his neck. He's truly shed off every trace of obligation and regulation and routine. Of whatever it was that tied him, on the off-seasons, to the deeper mainland.

"How do you even know he skinny-dips?" Ozan asks.

"Our parents saw him when they were taking a walk down to get *tost* from that famous stand a few *sites* over," explains Bulut. "Right before they got to the Big Club—it's not that well lit there, but they could still see, you know?—they noticed a guy walking back from the dock to his pile of clothes. Two in the morning, they said. Just swimming in the dark by himself. Isn't that sick?"

"Maybe he likes how quiet it is at that hour," I offer up. Everyone stares at me, confused as to whose side I'm on.

"Well, we always knew Ada was a weirdo." Ozan shrugs.

"Ada, he's a man in his fifties skinny-dipping at an abandoned dock in a family *site*," says Bulut, looking concerned that he has to convince me. "Not to mention," he adds, "what's a bachelor doing buying a house here in the first place? Is that not strange to anyone? No guy his age would willingly stay here without having relatives to visit. This place is nice, but man, it's got zero nightlife. It's meant for grandmas and grandpas and the people obligated to visit them. People like him summer in places like

Çeşme or Bodrum. Places where the beach clubs serve sambuca shots and there's actual stuff to do."

Aslı lifts her sunglasses to her forehead and stares hard at the man, trying to recall where she knows him from. My shoulders tense, and I say a small prayer that she doesn't remember our interaction from earlier this summer.

"There's something off about him that I can't put my finger on," Aslı says. Her head snaps toward me, and she blinks rapidly as she tries to strengthen the thread of connection. Nothing connects.

"He's kind of hot, though," she says casually. "Like, for an old guy." Of course he is. He has the aquiline nose of a sultan. Built like a fortress, the lines of his muscles pushing out under toughened skin. I remember his feline smile from that night at the Big Club, that sly spark in his eyes. His perfect dolphin dives into the water. The world seems to open up for him as he walks through it, in reverence of his stubborn beauty.

"Oh, so that's your thing now," Bulut teases his twin. "Middle-aged men?" Aslı sneers at him, then catches sight of his Okey stand. She leans over and starts to rearrange the tiles, but Bulut pushes her hand away. "Stop looking at my board! And what are you even doing? It's better in these groups, see?"

"No, you moron, I don't see. Honestly, how does your brain even work? You'll be waiting for two tiles that you already have in order to complete these guys here."

"Oh. Okay. I get it now."

"You have to think about your *chances*," says Aslı.

There's a giggling from behind. Around the table next to us stand Göksu and the younger girls who made fun of my singing, the ones who put on the dance show at the Big Club. They're huddled together speaking in hushed whispers, and every few seconds, a long-lashed pair of eyes flutters toward us. Ozan sighs loudly, then turns in his chair.

"Hey, gossip girls!" he snaps. "How about you shut your traps, what do you say?" The girls look up innocently toward him, and Göksu bows her head. But when he turns away again, I can hear them tittering, the vibrations of their suppressed laughter nearly violent.

"They've been obsessing all week about the incident on our boat trip," Ozan tells us. "Aslı told them off the other day, but they won't stop blabbering. It's ridiculous. Also," he adds, "half of what they say isn't even true, they're making things up for the sake of a good story."

Aslı notices my dejection, and starts to sing. *"In this tiny town of ours by the sea . . ."* She bobs her head to the rhythm and belts out the opening lines of a jingle we made up years ago, about the rapid-fire spread of gossip in our *site*. I understand that she's trying to tell me that it's not about me, it was never about me, it's just about the nature of information in this town. But of all the ways I could be remembered, I'm not happy that this is the one that's currently furthest in the running.

"People have nothing better to do . . ." I mutter.

"Than to talk about me!" Aslı concludes triumphantly. She clasps her hands together at her chest and looks at me, face bright.

But the song doesn't help me feel better, and I want to hear exactly what the girls are saying. I tell everyone to shut up for a few minutes so I can eavesdrop. We all pretend to quietly do something else while bending an ear toward the girls. Ozan and Bulut senselessly rearrange their tiles over and over, Aslı drops her head into her arms and feigns sleep, and I stare with a concerned look on my face at the front page of a newspaper, clicking my tongue in disbelief.

"If I were her, I'd never be able to live it down," the triangle-faced girl says, her voice lower now. "In fact, I'd just give up and summer elsewhere." Tittering, the girls curl their hair behind their ears, their fingernails cut to the quick but neatly polished in matching metallic teal. They run a thumb under, then snap back to the skin the shoulder straps of their multicolored swimsuits. The onion bulbs of their knees bend and lock as their bodies adjust to carry the weight of the gossip. They point at themselves, at something on the table, out toward the sea, but the gesticulations are a farce. They are always talking about me. Maybe they'll even continue talking about me until summer's end, and then for years to come.

I put down the newspaper and ask Bulut when we're going to swim to the island. My request is abrupt, and Bulut is startled at the break in the silence. He turns seaward to consider the distance. The past three days have been relatively serene, the waves appearing only in the late afternoon. Winds, if and when we have them, pour through the streets like warm milk and politely skim the surface of the water.

"Later this week," he says, and starts to get excited. He glances at the girls' table, then back at me. "I'll come by the villa early one morning on my way down here. I'll wake you up and we'll head in together."

We shake on it. I'm about to ask him about the curse, then quickly decide against it. If he doesn't know about it already and I'm the one to tell him, he might change his mind. And there is no way that I'm letting Bulut change his mind about this. Someone at the girls' table lets out a high-pitched giggle. I am going to do this swim even if it kills me.

With the island matter settled, I'm able to focus back on the game. I press my thumb along the sides of the rows, taking inventory of my tiles. There are too many groups in couples only, missing the requisite third. Scanning over the vague possibilities of combinations, I think about which pieces are likely claimed by the others and select a budding set to break apart. Strategizing is difficult; I decide to fall back on my luck. I recategorize my tiles, pick one at random, and pass it on over to Ozan. He stares at me for a few seconds before snatching it up.

"As per your previous announcement, Ada," says Ozan, quickly rearranging his tiles, "red threes are wild." Then he turns his board around and, with a flourish of his hand, presents a completed set.

≈ ⚓ ≈

Every morning, by the time Levent walks down to the Small Club, I am on the terrace breakfasting with the other women. He gives no indication of recognition, not even a nod as he passes by. The only consequence of his appearance is the immediate tension between my mother and grandmother, then its slow release. Each time he disappears beyond the oleanders, my grandmother relaxes her shoulders and starts to complain at length about insignificant domestic matters. The consistency of the white cheese at the Thursday farmers' market, how the cucumbers aren't as firm as they once used to be, many years ago. The devolving taste of tomatoes. Not once has Levent passed by without my grandmother commenting on the inadequacy of something on the breakfast table. How it required too much effort to procure, the abhorrent price at which the farmer had tried to sell it to her.

"How are we feeling about Levent these days?" I ask one morning as he walks past. The question dangles loosely in the air, and I take a page from Aslı, ready to analyze any and all reactions as an answer, trusting everything but the words that they might say.

My grandmother, her mouth half open in preparation for a critique of the cream and honey she was already gesturing toward, presses her lips together. My mother calmly sips her tea.

To my mother, my grandmother says, "This could have been so different, had you stayed." She moves her hand away from the cream and motions toward the entire spread of the table. "Look at this. There is enough food for everyone in my home, but I am alone, all by myself for most of the year. Never," says my grandmother, now addressing me, "never abandon your mother, Ada, do you understand? It's difficult to fathom how frightening it is to live in solitude, away from your children, unless you experience it yourself. And I do not wish that upon anyone." My grandmother touches the upturned demitasse of her coffee with an index finger for a temperature check, but keeps the cup upside down.

My mother gets up and crosses to the edge of the terrace that looks out over our rose garden and the sea beyond. She crushes her hands into fists and balances them on her hips, below which her black sarong flutters in the breeze like a trapped butterfly. Her back turned to us, she surveys the effect of the winds on the sea, nods at the shy clouds on the far end of the horizon, perhaps considering how they, too, are hesitant to approach the sun.

This is typical of her behavior these past few days. She has been more of a dreamer than usual, coming and going to the present moment. The cryptic transition is alarming. I can't figure out how she feels about having Levent appear back in her life.

"Your mother was supposed to marry him," says my grandmother. "They were little lovebirds in their youth. But she ruined her chances. You know, Ada, it's important to let your life flow like water. You shouldn't fight against your fate, like your mother has."

My mother turns around and leans against the terrace railing. "If you would just allow me to explain the matter to my daughter," she says, but is cut off yet again.

"Everything had been planned," my grandmother continues. "You know, you both know, what a skilled planner I am. I do God's work when people are too lazy to figure it out for themselves. God's work, because some people forget to live the lives that have been laid out for them!"

Like all master manipulators, my grandmother usually does a fine job of keeping her emotions in check. Always controlled, she generally contracts and releases her anger in line with the exact levels required to incite feelings of shame or weakness in the opposite party. Now, however, I can almost see a crack in the veneer. This seems to be the one plan she was unable to bring to fruition, the only one that managed to escape her realm of power. As I watch her seethe, I scoop up some cream and honey with a slice of baguette. I take a bite, then immediately spit it out.

"Something's wrong with this," I say, sticking out my tongue in disgust. I inspect the dipping bowl, wondering if something sour had spilled into the cream. "I think it's gone bad."

"That's your fault, Meltem," my grandmother says, her anger giving way to smugness. She waggles an index finger. "As I was just about to say before all this talk of Levent got in the way, you were the one who bought the cream from the town center yesterday. You should have given it a whiff, checked whether it was still fresh. Obviously, it's past its prime." She retracts her arm and once again taps her finger against the bottom of her demitasse. "You never did understand the intricacies of timing."

9

THE PAST

On the last day of July, I settle inside my mulberry bush at the usual hour, but Levent doesn't show. Since our encounter in the olive groves last week, I have avoided any direct encounters with him at the Small Club. But my morning sessions have continued. It's the only way I can learn more about him without anybody getting suspicious. I want to avoid Aslı and her judgment, my grandmother and her puppeteering, my mother and her potential fury, the talk of the townspeople.

I have never been with an older man before. Or, really, with anybody outside my usual parameters of time and space. All my boyfriends, past and present, had been attainable within the radius of my own circle—save for my middle school fling, but that relationship had been destined for interruption. Nobody else has ever offered me the opportunity to step inside another sort of life.

I try to pass the time by looking for fat mulberries, picking through the leaves of the bush. The berries are soft and ripe. This makes me smile at first, but then annoys me. If the fruits are on time, and I am on time, why is Levent late? It's impossible to begin the day without seeing him.

Just come out, I plead. *Just come out for a second so I can see you, and then I promise I will leave.*

The minutes pass, and soon the chill of the morning lifts as elegantly as the arms of a maestro. Sunlight pours in, each ray piercing its own small burn on my skin from the spaces between the leaves. The town starts to stir. First there are only the smaller noises, like the padding of feet down the stairs and the hinges of screen doors. Then those fade into the background and the people are set into relief. Mothers and fathers and children and grandparents step out onto the scene.

"Ada? Is that you?"

Neslihan sets down her shopping bags from the market and pinches out her T-shirt. Sweat has darkened the area below her breasts into half-moons. "What are you doing squatting in a mulberry bush like that? Is everything all right?" Her presence stuns me into silence, but I quickly assemble myself back together. I wasn't aware that I could be spotted so easily.

"Just . . . resting in the shade." I glance at Levent's balcony to make sure that he hasn't come out and seen us. Still empty. Good. "Do you live on this street?" I am ready to give my entire life for her to say no.

"A bit farther up, then the next street over. Have you eaten yet?" Neslihan reaches down for her bags. "I ran out to get some things for breakfast—why don't you join me? In fact, you'll keep me great company. Oh, and look," she says. "There's Levent's house. His car's not under the pergola, must've gone off again to İstanbul for work. That man," she says, shaking her head. "That man, that man, that man." She squeezes her eyes shut as if in apology for some unspoken memory, then hands over a couple of her plastic bags to me to carry. I climb out of the bush feeling foolish, and together, we walk to her villa.

Neslihan's villa looks just as it's supposed to—like everyone else's. She tells me to wait outside on the terrace while she prepares breakfast, and I forget to insist that I help and instead follow her directions exactly. Only when she comes out with multiple breakfast plates—bread, cream, honey, cheese, eggs, grapefruit, tea, olives—on two trays that she's struggling to balance do I recall that everyone here says one thing but means another, and that my unhelpfulness will ultimately be reflected on my mother. As she sets down the plates and a trivet for the tea kettle, I rearrange the items for improved surface optimization. Somehow, the table seems even more cluttered when I'm through.

"Well," says Neslihan, and flashes a big smile as she takes a seat next to me. Her wrinkles flow like rivers down her face; she hosts them proudly. There is no judgment in her voice. "Do you know, spending time with you is almost exactly like spending time with your mother?"

"You're not the first person to tell me that."

"That's because it's true. Actually, it's quite strange. When I'm with you, I feel as if we're right back at university together, reliving those memories. It's more powerful than seeing her now, even. Now, when I see her, I just remember that things have changed, that we've grown old. But you, you bring me right back." She pours me brewed tea from a small stainless steel kettle, and fills the rest of my glass with hot water from a larger one. For herself, she pours out different proportions, a darker glass. I cautiously tap my spoon against a boiled egg. It cracks easily.

"Why were you so upset about Levent?" I ask. I can tell upon touching the glass that the tea is much too hot, but I force myself to gulp down half of it anyway. I've given up on the proper etiquette for my egg, and the tablecloth is now littered with bits of shell.

"Your grandmother," says Neslihan, and I can't tell if she's heard me or if she's heading down a different path entirely. "Your grandmother is a real piece of work. I have no idea how Meltem lived with that woman for all those years."

I shrug. It's easy to vilify my grandmother, and I often slip into the habit myself. "You know," I say, "I think controlling the people around her is the only way she knows how to love." Neslihan gives me a sad smile then shakes her head, signaling that, to her, the ends have never justified the means.

"So what do you think," she asks, "about the whole thing?"

"What whole thing?" I must have missed something she said.

"Well, you know, of course, that it was completely her doing," Neslihan says, slathering Nutella on a piece of toast. She keeps flipping her knife over each time, intensely piling on the hazelnut paste. "I mean, it's got Mukadder's name written all over it." Her knife slips, tearing the bread. She looks sadly upon yet another misfortune caused by my grandmother.

"When it really started to get bad was after your grandfather passed away," Neslihan says. Now I understand that she is starting at the beginning of a story, though I am not sure which one. I put down my spoon and listen closely. "Mukadder *teyze* wouldn't let Meltem do anything. Just locked her up in a room, nothing to do but read. In high school, we'd all go to the movies in Beyoğlu. A cinema, can you think of a more innocent venue? Meltem would have to stay at home. 'Meltem doesn't like the movies,' your grandmother would say. 'Meltem doesn't like the movies,' bullshit! We'd go up to their door, maybe ten of us or so, and we'd plead with Mukadder *teyze* to let her daughter out. But she'd stand her ground. You drank that tea quickly, would you like some more?"

I shake my head no only once, and so she pours me another glass, darker this time.

"Mukadder *teyze* sewed all your mother's clothes, even though they had the money to buy outfits from the Avenue. Don't tell her I said this, but Meltem spent half her life dressed like a sack of potatoes. The most embarrassing part of it all was that she wouldn't even rebel. Whatever the authority said, your dear mother would comply. 'Just sneak out,' we'd tell her. But in her mind, a mother's word was no different from the law. It was strange to me, the way Meltem saw the world, that it was all thoughtfully prepared and that she was born into something perfectly set. The authorities would remind her of the rules should she ever step out of line. She thought of everything as a story already written, beginning to end, and all she would have to do is to play the part that was given to her. But you know"—and here Neslihan leans to give me what I assume to be a conspiratorial pat on the shoulder—"you and I both know that that's not how things work around here. You want something, you fight for it, don't you? When somebody tells you something, you question it. Your mother never really got around to understanding that."

"Their relationship couldn't have been that bad," I interject, suddenly feeling a bit defensive about my mother. "Or maybe my grandma relaxed a bit while my mom was in college? She managed to travel to Paris her senior year of university, remember? That's how she met my dad."

Neslihan laughs so hard that she accidentally sucks in a strand of hair, then gracefully spreads her fingers across her left cheek to dislodge it. Regaining her composure, she counters my point. "As if Mukadder *teyze* would have ever let Meltem take a vacation like that, alone, to Europe. She wouldn't even let her study at the conservatory there, even with a voice like hers. That's when your mother cracked. She rebelled, finally, but it wasn't just because of the relationship between her and her mom. Someone else was the catalyst for that. You know the reason she ended up taking that flight to Paris in the first place?"

"No."

Neslihan seems surprised at my response. She peers over to the edge of the terrace where the attached neighbor's own balcony begins. She gets up to look all the way around the dividing half-wall, making sure that no one's grandmother or grandfather is sitting on the other side.

"You really don't know?" she asks again. Her hands clasp together in front of her, asking a different question.

"Maybe I do, a little bit," I lie.

"Right," she says, regaining her previous enthusiasm. "Right! Of course you do, you're her daughter, and Paris is, after all, where she met your father. It's a story that's not even hers so much as it is your own, wouldn't you say?"

"Definitely."

Neslihan relaxes and takes a deep breath, drawing the scenes back into her memory. "Levent's family and your family—your mother's family, I mean, well, you know what I mean—they'd known each other for years. Neighbors on the Avenue, where folks of a certain *type* tend to live. His family was in textiles, business booming in the Middle East. Your grandfather a successful surgeon. People match these sorts of things up, don't they? It's like one of those card games. Money, geography, status, match! Meltem was never allowed to do anything, but your grandmother did let her go to see Levent whenever she wanted. He was the only exception because they knew the family so well.

"As kids, the two were inseparable. Even though nothing at all happened between them in the early years—they'd get together, play marbles, toss a ball around for İstop—it somehow became known that they'd end up together. I'm not quite sure how it started, but these spun-up truths happen all the time. Or at least they did back in those days.

"Your mother, certainly, had feelings for him. I don't know why, he was dating other girls left and right, but she was either completely oblivious or chose to ignore it. We tried to tell her, but she wouldn't listen. 'Oh, they're just friends,' she would say. Or, 'Oh, she's just a cover.' A cover for what? I think it was hard for her to realize that the only thing she had access to and the only certainty she thought she had in her life might be something worth questioning. The thing you have to realize about most men, Ada, is that they are ultimately unremarkable. The edge of them that excites, that seductive energy which you think is desire? It's not desire, and it's not about you. It's the thrill of a challenge, that rush of potentially getting away with something. That's all it is. Meltem was so obedient and malleable that there wasn't that much to excite Levent, even though she was very beautiful. The chase, the secrecy of things—these are the ways men feel youth and vivacity. The best gift you can give a man is to make him feel young again. Needless to say that there was no secrecy surrounding him and Meltem. Of course not. Their eventual partnership was the most expected outcome of all!" Neslihan looks out wistfully toward the street and gently raises a finger. "Maybe, maybe, and please, never repeat this to your mother, but if Meltem had played her cards right, if she had snuffed a bit of the attention or pretended that what all the adults had laid out for her regarding the course of her perfectly tailored future didn't interest her, that she would chart her own path, by God, then maybe there would have been a little bit of that thrill that Levent was looking for, and he would have pursued her instead of chasing his libido up and down the Bosphorus. She might have even been able to make an honest man out of him. But!" Neslihan's eyes flash. "But there is never any use in speculating what could have been.

"Now let's discuss the worst of it."

I sit up straighter.

"The worst of it was, the two of them had never even discussed any sort of commitment to each other. Even as they got older and he reached for her hand under the table, or he bought her flowers from the Romani women on the street, or they kissed on the Caddebostan promenade. Those—insignificant, really—actions provided enough seeds of romance for Meltem to see the rest of her life laid out in front of her. And what a beautiful life it would have been, had there been any truth to it.

"Anyway, it's interesting that Meltem wasn't the only one who had bought into this fantasy. Their little love affair was really all anyone could talk about. Even the ice cream shop boy down in Moda, who scooped raspberry and pistachio into rose petals when your mother came around, knew that his attempts at artwork were in vain. He'd say things like, 'Don't forget to send me an invitation to the wedding,' and Meltem would blush. Near the end of university, Levent and your mother began sleeping together. Come to think of it, he was probably the only person that she *could* have slept with, since Mukadder kept such strict surveillance over where her daughter was at all times.

"I don't know if I can emphasize to you how fascinating it was to watch this certainty develop from something that—at least it was clear to me—simply did not exist. Do you understand what I'm saying, Ada? It just didn't exist! My cousin lived on the European side and I would visit her sometimes, and twice I ran into Levent in Beyoğlu with his arms around another girl's waist. Two times, two different women. And yet the mothers of the families discussed engagement rings, wedding venues, the housing prices up in Nişantaşı, near where they assumed their kids would surely end up working. After all, both had gone to the best schools. After all, everything matched up.

"Then, of course," says Neslihan, "the inevitable happened." She looks at me when she says the word "inevitable," seeking permission to continue. Because even if I don't know this part, what she means to tell me is that

I would have pieced it together from what I already know, and therefore, what she is about to tell me is not gossip but logic. It simply follows.

"Your mother got pregnant. To be honest, she didn't seem all that upset about it. It was our senior year of college, and I guess she thought that a wedding would take place soon after graduation. When she told Levent the news, she later said to me that he seemed to take it well. Most men, I suppose, are evasive during these matters, and any time a man does not get up and run the other way after hearing something like this, it's taken as a good sign. But this time there was nothing to be evasive toward because Meltem didn't ask him any questions. She did not ask him, *Do you want me to keep it? Are you planning on marrying me?* What you need to understand is that she had already answered these questions in her mind, so there was no reason to ask them out loud. Sometimes you can get answers to questions that you never ask. But the answers to questions you *choose* not to ask—" Neslihan bites her lower lip, shaking her head. "Oh, those are never the answers that you want.

"Anyway," she continues. "Everything came to a head at the graduation party. It was so humiliating that I almost wish I hadn't been there to witness it."

I nod as I sip my tea, the type of nod one would give while recalling an event in the backwaters of a memory. Neslihan takes a long pause, considering whether she should continue. "The party," I repeat, encouraging her onward.

"Yes. The party. It was held by our university, at the ballroom of the Grand Tarabya, on the northern European shores. Meltem came wearing another horrid creation of her mother's, a yellow dress with poufy sleeves. We told her she looked great, but of course what she actually looked like was a lemon soufflé. Levent arrived late, about an hour into the event. And he wasn't alone.

"Have you ever seen someone's reality shatter, Ada? Really witnessed that process? It's like a fast death, a transition from one world to the next. You could actually see the ripple through the crowd, the way everyone's expressions shifted when they saw Levent's date. She was absurdly tall, wearing this glitter jumpsuit, somehow balancing that body of hers on stilettos. I'll never forget: She had a cigarette hanging out of her mouth, and all the men in the room would have given anything to be that cigarette. Her face was curved like a fox's, and the reflection of her outfit shimmered across the silverware. Arms all over Levent like an octopus, touching him throughout the entire dinner, absolutely no sense of shame. People began to get uncomfortable, even those who didn't know who Levent was, who he was meant to marry. It was too much. Your grandmother had to leave the table. She couldn't control her face; you would have thought she was having a stroke. Your mother just sat there quietly, her hands in her lap, slowly shrinking, disappearing into her dress. She knew that once she went home, behind closed doors, Mukadder would let her have it. That marriage would have been your grandmother's greatest achievement, but it was destroyed before it began in a way that she couldn't have ever imagined.

"What killed Meltem wasn't that Levent had come with another woman, but that the woman was someone so absolutely different from Meltem. Brazen, in the spotlight. Animalistic, in a way. Couldn't care less about decorum and all that. And even though Meltem hadn't listened to us when we had tried to tell her about Levent's playboy ways, seeing him there that day, with her, in front of everyone—she finally understood.

"She understood that her fantasies held no solid foundations, that the two of them had never actually promised each other anything. Not once had Meltem and Levent spoken about the future, their feelings for each other, or any plans to start a family. It had all just been, as she told me afterward, a feeling in the air. And anyone can read the air in any way she wants. It's like coffee grounds. Your mother saw only what she wanted to see, without once requiring an ounce of proof. She had not considered what had or hadn't been said, what had or hadn't been promised.

"Meltem sat through that entire graduation party in hot shame, even after Mukadder had left. She was stubborn about enduring the humiliation until the end, maybe somehow feeling that she deserved it. I don't know. Later that night, when she got home, Meltem took a pair of scissors and cut through that stupid lemon dress, walked down to the Marmara seaside behind the Avenue, then set the fabric on fire. The next day she called the hospital for an appointment and ended the pregnancy. Mukadder found out through an acquaintance at the hospital what had happened, and that was when she kicked her out."

I sit with this information for a few minutes. The child my mother didn't have, in my mind, is the perfect child. They would have never had to wonder whether one parent was taking something away from the other, whether the lives they had pulled each other into were desired and familiar. The baby would have been born into a setting that was perfect and uncomplicated. Had things—of course—been different.

"Mukadder didn't mean to kick her out, of course, these were just words said in a fit of rage. But what she didn't know was that Meltem had built up quite a bit of savings tutoring students in French at our old lycée, and she bought a plane ticket to Paris for the semester break. I had no idea that she was gone—I found out when she came back. Apparently, she had booked a hotel in the Marais, and the first night gone to a bar. Imagine!" Neslihan says, and a minuscule piece of cheese flies out of her mouth. She picks it up with the pad of her thumb, tosses it back inside. "Your mother, alone at a bar. She told me she had ordered a Campari! That is not the girl I knew. A man—your father—notices her, this red-lipped woman in a new silk jumpsuit, and they get to talking. He'd just graduated from an engineering school in California and was interrailing around Europe. She is so taken by him, by his complete ignorance of the world where she has grown up, of her past, that from that moment on, she never leaves his side.

"Never in Mukadder's wildest dreams would her daughter be living so far away from her, from the life that she had painstakingly designed. But something had shifted, and your mother wouldn't answer to anyone anymore. After so many years, she decided to live for herself. Did that mean that she was doing something she truly wanted? Now of that, I'm not so sure. But she had to start from somewhere, and where she decided to start from was the opposite of what her mother wanted for her. Some might call it rebellion. But rebellion, as you know, is a different sort of obedience." Neslihan sighs, looks around at the table. Consumed with conversation, we'd barely eaten anything. "Oh, Ada. The world can change to such a degree that you can no longer recognize it. The past seems to be but a story you tell yourself, with no evidence of its passing.

"Levent never ended up marrying that girl, of course not. Everybody could see that she was just a fling, nobody even knew what sort of family she was from. But it's hard to see that logic when you're so emotional over the whole darn thing. It has always been so tense for Meltem, returning here every year, especially those initial nights in İstanbul. All over again she'd have to suffer the pain of remembering the life she thought she could have had."

We sit in silence for a while. An iridescent fly hovers over the spread. Considering the honey, it slides its hands back and forth in prayer.

"If you're not going to eat anymore, then I'll start clearing the table." Neslihan moves to collect the plates, awaiting, out of the corner of her eye, my insistence for another portion, or an offer to do it myself.

But I am too preoccupied with my dizzying discovery. There was no one in my mother's past that she could return to. No one! Not Levent, who was never an actual option, just a fantasy, and not, more importantly, to herself. Her life before was the same as her life is now: a passivity that allows her to be tossed around by men and my grandmother, relegating her existence to the liminal spaces. Fist in the air, chanting at the Republic Day Ball.

I do not owe my mother anything, I realize. I hold no responsibility toward guiding her back to the life my father tore her from. From now on, the only person I have to look out for is myself. One by one, the bread and the cream and the grapefruit disappear from the table. I feel much lighter.

10

THE FORTUNE

It had been a long and confusing back-and-forth with the baker, but I finally managed to fulfill my mother's pastry order for today's tea-time. Standing outside the shop with a box of warm cinnamon rolls, mulling over the ice cream selection in the Panda freezer, I spot Levent across the way at the grocer's register once again. He's looping plastic bags through his arms as the grocer's boy leans over his massive notebook, languidly scrawling out an IOU entry. Before he can even finish his bookkeeping, I'm there on the scene, scooping up the remaining bags from the counter.

"Don't even think about it, I got this," I say, and swat at the air, at the hands and arms I had expected to intervene but do not. The groceries are heavier than they seemed from across the market. I clench my abdomen and try to walk naturally.

"Wait!" Efe calls out. He points with his pencil at one of the bags on my arm. "That one's got the watermelon. You should let Levent *Bey* carry it."

"Oh, but she's a muscular girl," Levent says, watching the scene with amusement. I can feel his gaze on me as I move out into the market and wiggle my fingers goodbye at the grocer's son.

I'm a few steps ahead of him, blinking the sunscreen out of my eyes as the thinning handles of the bags dig into my wrists. A second after I walk through the rear exit of the market, I realize my mistake. I've now given away that I know that Levent lives behind the market. To avoid any sort of embarrassing interrogation, I turn left instead of right, and continue on in the opposite direction from his villa, toward the water, toward the soccer field and all its withered grass coming up on my left. I keep walking, struggling under the weight of the bags, but Levent continues to amble slightly behind my lead, humming an upbeat melody I don't recognize. I try to ignore the pain by thinking about how very soon, Bulut and I will make our way to the islands. There they are, right on the horizon. By the time we get to the children's park, I need to set the bags down on the sidewalk. They gape open to reveal their contents. In addition to the watermelon, there are five Topkeks, a bag of Haribo gummy bears, at least a kilo of sunshine-green figs, and several bottles of water. In the park, young girls hang upside down on the monkey bars.

I pull up my tank top to wipe the sweat from my forehead and ask Levent where his villa is.

"You seemed to know where you were going," he says, watching me closely for a reaction. "Why so uncertain all of a sudden?"

This is a difficult comment to parse. His groceries are so heavy. Why would he make me walk for so long in the wrong direction?

"Oh, sorry, I assumed you live close to the water. Like us," I manage to stutter. "Why suddenly move to a town where you don't know anyone if it's not to a house near the shoreline?" My nervousness takes hold again, and I start rambling. "Toward the water, anyway, that's the direction I'm used to going in. Besides, you never stopped me. Also—"

Levent lets out a laugh, cutting me off. Behind him, a girl on the monkey bars swings her body back and forth, her arms crossed at the chest. I watch her. When I focus again on Levent, I see my reflection in his sunglasses and am taken aback. I look a lot younger than I imagined myself to be. My face shines with sunscreen.

"Ada?" He says my name differently than usual, quickly, sharpening the corners of my soft vowels.

"Yes?"

"Tell me this: Why do you think we keep running into each other?"

The girl on the monkey bars begins to lose her grip. Levent doesn't see it, but I do. I see her left leg untangle from the thin metal. I see her hang unhinged while a woman who had been sitting on a bench slicing apricots open with her fingernails shrieks and throws herself forward to save her. The girl tries to swing her leg back on, but it won't curl up properly at this position; it can't catch like it should. I can't see the woman in the space between the bench and the girl. I can't understand how she went from one place to another, because one moment she is sitting with her apricots and the next moment she is under the bars, arms outstretched. Slowly, the girl's other leg unwinds and she falls into the arms of her mother, who collapses to her knees with the weight of her child.

All this escapes Levent's attention. He is fully focused on me and waiting for an answer. There's a playful smile on his face; the question is meant as a sort of joke—no, it is a test masquerading as a joke. It's a way out for him while pulling me in deeper. I am trying not to panic, even though I am feeling smaller and smaller. But then I remember how he had asked me, among the parked cars, to follow him. How he had climbed up the ladder and sat down next me on the second story of nobody's house. There is something here; it's not all in my head.

"This place is basically a village," I say. "If I don't see someone for two days, I assume they've already wrapped up for the summer, headed back to the city."

Levent's face falls. "My house is behind the market," he says, dropping the inquiry. He turns and points back up the street. "We take a left up there, by the fig tree."

"Okay." I kneel down and heave the bags up, then backtrack toward the market. All my previous fatigue has faded. The handles continue to sear into my wrists, but there is no pain associated with the feeling. I press on. I pass the soccer field, pass the market, take a left on Levent's street, lift my arm high enough, bringing the watermelon to my hips, to unlatch his gate. Then, one by one, I carefully place all the bags on the glass table of the terrace, the same table where every morning, Levent spreads olive paste on his toast and dips the tip of his knife into three different types of jam.

"What do you do on October 29?" I ask. Levent steps back, startled by my abrupt questioning. He's unable to see all the connecting lines and paths I have drawn in my mind.

"Republic Day? There's usually a parade down in Beşiktaş. My friends and I wear our red shirts, take our flags, and walk with the crowd. One year, we went across to Anatolia, to join the walk on the Avenue."

I tell him that my grandmother lives on the Avenue in the winter.

"But you've never been in town for the twenty-ninth?" he asks.

"Never ever." I push on the side door to reveal the inside of his house. The door pushes back. It's locked.

I stare at it. Nobody locks their doors in this town. Nobody even needs actual doors. All you need, really, is the screen door to keep out the mosquitoes and the stray cats. Locked doors are for city apartments. Levent pulls out a key, fiddles with the lock for a few seconds, then kicks open the door.

For weeks, the interior of this villa had been central to my fantasies. Every morning as I watched Levent disappear into its depths after breakfast, an erect Camel balancing on his lips, his swim trunks hardened from having dried out on the balcony overnight, I imagined the environment through which he navigates. I had considered the items my mother had brought over from Turkey, her belongings a snapshot of a time that she continues to live in. Would he have that same painting of the Galata Tower? I wonder. The same small bust of Atatürk, the same silver tea trays?

The locked door, as it turns out, protects nothing.

Levent has lived in this house for only a few weeks, and the walls within it contain minimal traces of human life. A daisy-shaped flyswatter rests on a heating register. There's a mahogany desk that's too dark, too heavy for this season, that has been pulled back a bit from the wall to make use of an outlet, from which a cord snakes up to a cheap table lamp. Despite the desk's relocation, squared edges of dust maintain their

original contours. The ceiling lamps were removed by the previous owners, and primary colors of cable dangle uselessly from the living room
ceiling. In the kitchen, a few citronella candles are littered around the
stove. Past owners haven't bothered to remodel the home, and it still
has the same speckled stone tiles, pink and gray, originally installed
throughout the development—the colors of seashell insides and beach
pebbles. Levent, then, moved in immediately after purchasing the villa,
giving himself no time at all to remodel. My toes curl over my slides,
afraid to create any contact with the dust-ridden surface, and I check
for cockroaches and scorpions underfoot. I manage to make it safely to
the kitchen.

I find an open bag of pistachios and pour them into a small bowl,
which signals to Levent that I am here to stay. In response, he pulls and
shuts drawers, looking for a tablecloth he knows does not exist.

"I'm headed to İstanbul again next week," he says. "A few days, for a
work meeting."

"İstanbul's my favorite city," I say. He laughs as if it's a joke he's heard
before.

Levent's kitchen has a gas stove, so I make us some Turkish coffee—
one of the few items in his fridge—while he sets up a table inside. Re-
moving the plastic lid from the tin, I bring the coffee grounds to my nose
and breathe in deeply. I scoop a few spoonfuls into a copper *cezve*, add
some water, two cubes of sugar so that it's palatable enough for me, and
set the mixture atop a blue ring of fire. Then I stare into the muddy water
in the *cezve*, waiting. A good coffee maker needs to be able to sense the
transition between the billow and the boil, to pinpoint the exact instant
before the first air bubble pops and the coffee loses its shape. In Levent's
filthy kitchen, I know exactly when to snap off the flame. I carefully pour
out a thick foam into each demitasse, its golden lather a contrast to the
sky blue cups with cream-colored rims. Old traditions may fall by the way-
side, but they never fade completely. A woman who can brew coffee with
a perfect coating of foam must make for a good wife. A good wife, then,
is a woman who can always sense the moment *before*. The slight shifts
in the sounds and the heightened pauses, the tension before the event

occurs. That's what they mean, though they never say it exactly. Men want a woman attuned to the final omen before the point of no return.

We quietly crack open pistachios and sip the coffee together at a round kitchen table, indoors so that no one sees us. Yesterday's newspaper serves as a tablecloth. I work open the shells with my fingernails. My general strategy is to coax at first, then force them open when they won't submit. Click. Then the tongue. I am patient, knowing that not everyone can move as quickly as I do, but Levent's expression remains stagnant. Mostly, he seems detached, and when his face softens, it softens the way it would as if he were speaking to a child. But there are moments—and they have happened more than once, so I know that it is not just my imagination—when his gaze takes on a sense of wonder, a wash of fear. The combination of which, I know, is desire.

Once I finish my coffee, I remove the saucer from underneath and place it atop the demitasse, which is empty save for the muddy grounds that are impossible to drink. Though they appear slick and wet, the dregs turn to tiny specks of sand as they travel down your throat. I flip the saucer and cup over and rotate them in the air three times, make a wish, then set the pair back on the table. Levent's coffee sits finished in front of him, cooling right side up. No fortune for him? I ask. He answers that he doesn't believe in set paths in life, or in anything written. He barely, he adds, can believe the progression of his own life.

"This is going to sound weird, maybe, but sometimes I feel like I'm getting younger," he says, a proud look on his face. "As you age, you tend to find that more and more opportunities have closed themselves off to you. But for me, it's the opposite. The longer I live, the more ways I see that one *can* live. The more cities, the more women, the more potential to do good work in this world."

"I think," I say, "that there is one perfect life for everyone, and if you happen to miss it, you're stuck in eternal limbo. There is a place where you flourish, where you feel at home. Where people bring out the best in you. Every place, every person, isn't created equal."

"Isn't that limiting?" asks Levent. "Especially for someone like you."

"What do you mean, especially for someone like me?"

"Someone who feels so obviously at home and connected here, but lives elsewhere."

I stop breathing.

"I see you at the Small Club," he says. "There's a force, an agency about you. Maybe I notice this because your mother didn't have it. She seemed at ease, but if you looked closely, you could tell that she was waiting for something. A constant state of hesitation, the particular feminine strain of fear that it carries. A woman expecting company who is committed to dusting the furniture in the entryway, one eye always flickering to the door. But you, you don't wait. You walk toward things. You are the type of woman who could be ringing the bell. Maybe you don't trust yourself to every time, but you know, deep down, that you can. Do you understand?"

I nod, trying to understand.

"Have you ever thought about moving here?"

"I've thought about it." My voice is meek, and I focus on my struggle with a clamped pistachio.

"But seriously, have you seriously thought about it?"

"Not seriously, no."

"Why not?"

How could I answer that? How could I tell him that moving here was all I had ever wanted, to be among people who could pronounce my name correctly, to live in a world where my face and my name and my culture and my daily life aligned, where I could settle in softly and gently to a place where I belonged and everything made sense, and I would stop being questioned about who I was, and where I needed to be?

"I guess it never seemed like a real enough possibility, like something I could do on my own," I say. It was the first time I'd come face-to-face with the admission.

"Everything is a possibility," says Levent. He spreads his hands on the newspaper like two continents. "In this world," he says, "in this very large, large world, you can go any which way you want. You can even go backward. The future—or the past, if you wish—is yours for the taking."

I finally split open the pistachio. Levent smiles at me. But then, as I lean over to check the temperature of the coffee cup, his eyes narrow. "The

Western girl and her Eastern omens!" he groans, and sweeps up my cup and saucer. He heads to the kitchen to run them under the tap.

"It's all over your face now, I recognize that look," he says when he comes back. "It traps you." Then he moves closer to me, and I feel the rough touch of his finger as he lightly drags it across my forehead, the place where fates are written. He smells of sweat, sunscreen, and that inner crust of summer. "This is where you fall back into her. Don't do this, you're better than this! You're asking for permission from the stars, waiting for the certainty of a future from the fates before acting on it. And I can tell you, this isn't going to work out for you any more than it would work out for anybody else."

I like the woman that he has decided that I am. I like her so much.

For a while we sit there, looking at each other. He doesn't kiss me, but he flickers forward for an instant, almost as if it were a glitch. Had I blinked, I would have missed it. I don't want to give him the satisfaction of having said something that has the potential to change my life, but I know that the impact he's had is clear from my expression, from my silence. The spell breaks only when he mentions it again: He's taking a quick trip to İstanbul on Sunday. For work. A week from now, to present to the board Monday, rest Tuesday, and head back to Ayvalık on Wednesday. He counts off the days on his fingers, and their names add a rigidity to the air, shaping constraints around us. It's been a while since there has been any talk of scheduling in this town. It's clear that he cannot understand his own offer, so I repeat it back to him.

"You want me to come along," I say. It is easy not to think of Ian, who is far away in another life. Maybe my grandmother was right. Maybe I am my father's daughter, after all.

"Excuse me, young lady?" As Levent sits back down, he lands on the edge of the chair and struggles to regain his balance. "What exactly do you mean?"

I cringe at the phrase "young lady." How condescending, how could he suddenly take away all the power that he had given me just moments earlier? I feel everything slipping from my grasp, and the words tumble out desperately before I make sense of them. "I'll wait for you at eight a.m. by the olive groves between the *sites*. Pick me up from there." Levent presses the insides of his wrists up and down his thighs, smoothing them back to steady. I continue on. "And don't worry, I'll make something up, something believable. I'll tell my mom I'm going somewhere else. Çeşme, maybe. Aslı's family has a house there." A clock ticks loudly, the second hand sweeping up its rounds. There's still the teatime at my grandmother's to prepare for, the pastries I need to deliver. I get up, say goodbye, and leave Levent directionless in his confusion. He will soon understand that I am serious, and his car will slow down on the path to the next *site*, and he will scan the roads for my silhouette. I know it.

All the things Neslihan told me last week pop up in my mind like warning signs, but they're irrelevant to me. I am not my mother. I have the potential to belong to this country in a way that she was unable to manage, to grasp the attention and attraction that she couldn't hold on to. Levent's interest in me proves it.

What is a daughter, if not another chance?

By the time I arrive home with the pastries, it's well into the late afternoon, but no one's set up the table in the garden yet. I walk inside to find my mother twirling the cord on the landline, her face beaming as she speaks into the phone.

"Of course," she says in her accented English. My body blocks the sun, and her eyes flicker toward the source of the shadow. "Sorry—sorry—I have to go now. Bye." She hangs up but misses the hold, and the receiver topples to the ground. After she picks it up and places it properly, she slowly spreads out her fingers, as if faulting some undiagnosed rheumatism instead of the interruption of my presence for her clumsiness. "Did the baker have the cinnamon buns today?" she asks.

In my mind, I wind back the clock. It's seven a.m. on a Monday in California, and on Mondays my father has his briefing with the London office. He always leaves the house an hour earlier on those days, has done so as long as he's been with his company. There is no way she could have been talking to my father.

"I was talking to your father," my mother says.

I pause, giving her a chance to correct herself.

"He says hi and kisses you on the nose." She heaves her body from the chair and takes the pastry bags from me, going to the kitchen to plate them.

You're not making any sense, I say, following her. It couldn't have been him, you're lying to me. My mother's shoulders drop, and she's crestfallen at the counter for reasons unknown.

"Ada," she sighs. "These aren't cinnamon. You got tahini. Did you tell him *tarçın*? I wanted the spiral rolls that he made the other day."

Oh, whoops. I told him *tahin*.

"Okay. You do understand that they're not the same thing?"

Well, *you* somehow manage to mix up Dad with—

"Look, Ada," says my mother, and she stands in the doorway arms akimbo, staring me down. "Call your dad back if you want to, go ahead, ask him if you don't believe me. Just please, don't tell your grandmother. As if she doesn't already have enough insults to hurl at me, now she's going to shove it in my face that I've raised a daughter who doesn't trust her own mother." She bites the inside of her cheek and arches her eyebrows as she considers her failings. Then she wheels around and goes to the garden to set the table.

There is a dance-like step down the stairs. "This is so exciting, isn't it?" chirps my grandmother. She stops in her tracks as soon as she notices me. "Oh, it's you. Sorry, I thought you were Meltem. Where's Meltem?"

"What's so exciting?" I ask.

"The news," my grandmother says, stretching out the last word like a guilty toddler.

"What," I say, doing my best to keep my tone measured, "is THE NEWS?"

"Oh, it'll arrive when it arrives." My grandmother hums a little tune and bobs her head from side to side, amusing herself. She giggles at my frustration. Then, changing her mind about whatever it was that brought her halfway down the stairs, she backs up to her bedroom.

⁓ ⚓ ⁓

After teatime, my mother and I take a walk. She kneels at the edge of the road and grips the bottom of a tall, dry reed. "Moon or star?" she asks. Her pinched thumb and forefinger move up the stem, gathering its stiff flowers into the space between her fingers. She pauses at the top, holding the minuscule bouquet, and waits for an answer.

I don't understand the question.

"Ada, just choose one."

Fine. Moon, then.

She flicks her wrist, and the flowers fall into an indiscernible pattern at her feet. If they had been clustered together, she explains, it would have been a moon. Dispersed like this—"A star," she says. "As you can see, your wish will not come true."

I stare at her.

"Oh," she says, remembering. "You were supposed to make a wish."

I tell her that I have not played this game enough times to understand the expectations of proximity among the reed flowers. You could have chosen any galactic object, I say, and I would have believed it.

She tells me that all children played this game at her age, and that the moon and star are quite separate for her. "It's so clear," she says, tracing the outline of the fallen flowers with her foot.

I tell my mother that she is exhibiting egocentric behaviors. I tell her:

In Australia, there is a group of Aboriginals who orient themselves and the world with cardinal directions. When they gesticulate, they adjust their hand motions depending on the direction they face when telling the story. If they are facing the other in the direction of north to south, their gesture in a story about a man coming up to them from the east would differ should their positions change. When they navigate, they are acutely aware of their place in the world.

My father, for example, might belong to this group. He understands the world not only through cardinal directions but through hierarchy as well, and can track all trajectories, from our family to planetary movement. He fills up the car and camps alone for days at Yosemite. When he's fallen off the trail, he simply looks up at the stars and resets.

But you, not you. You close your eyes, open them, and are surprised to find that you are somewhere else.

My mother nods. "I follow the wind," she says, then leaps, light-footed, over my useless fortune.

11

THE LONG SWIM

Bulut stands knee-deep in my grandmother's tomato vines, lobbing fistfuls of sunflower seeds at my window. Never have I seen him in this light before, light like at the edge of a glass, refracting on the bridge of his nose, gilding the stray strands of his hair. In fact, never have I seen any of this garden under such a clean slant of sunbeam—the hardened fibers of the fat palm's fronds, the fragility of the pomegranate blossoms. My perception of shapes and colors has always been polluted by the *site* noise and the heat of bodies in motion. At this hour, all that is either left behind or up ahead, and we are alone in the clarity of morning.

It is far earlier than I have ever woken up for my patrols. I hold up two fingers to the window, then tiptoe down each wooden step, ensuring the other two women remain safely locked in sleep. The clock on the wall at the bottom of the stairs reads 6:10 a.m. Today, we are swimming to the island.

The Small Club is empty. There is the slightest tinge of warmth to the air, but it's slim enough to ignore, easy enough to instead imagine that we're here on the off-season, unafraid of shuffling up our timing and geography. The sun simmers in its youth. Not yet at a burn, just slowly exploring the contours of its own heat. We walk to the lawn in front of the dock, and Bulut stretches out his sinewy limbs; they are like woven seaweed. His chest is deeply cavernous. We slip into the water from the left edge of the T-shaped dock, and shiver, electrified with the cold. I dive deep, deep down to the icier pastures so that when I emerge back where the sunlight hits, I am toasted and feel welcomed.

"Let's start slow, warm up a bit," says Bulut. I'm worried that he'll tire easily. Maybe I'll have to carry him on my back, leaping through the waves to keep his head above water. But that shouldn't be a big deal. I'm a strong swimmer. We'll make it.

My first university swim meet was at my home campus against a school from Southern California, a couple weeks after Ian and I met. As someone who held no regard for courting customs designed to generate mystery and allure, Ian arrived with a bouquet of tulips and took a seat at the top of the bleachers. From there, he watched me place first in the 200-yard freestyle and third in the 500-yard freestyle, even though there was an hour between the two events.

"The 200 is actually much harder," I told him, toweling off by the edge of the pool before disappearing into my oversized parka. "It doesn't seem like it, but it is. The 50 is just a sprint, you race your heart out from the moment your feet leave the diving board. For the 100, the four laps are pace, faster, as fast as you can, then kill yourself. That's really what Coach says: 'Kill yourself.' Every last thing you've got, you gotta leave it out there, in the pool. Try to race yourself out of this body; they've got a new one waiting for you at the finish line. They're going to have to pull your dead body out of the water, that's how hard you have to take the last twenty-five yards. For the 500, it's all about the pacing and staying strong, then the final push. But the 200? It's absolute torture. What the hell are you supposed to do with the 200?"

"Pace for half, then kill yourself?" Ian suggested. He had skipped down the bleacher steps after my finish and cornered me poolside as I was heading to the locker rooms for a shower.

"No one knows what you're supposed to do," I said. I kept talking, I couldn't stop, nobody had ever done anything like this for me before. Who was this boy from my physics class? What did he see in me to pursue me so intently? "You can try pushing the whole time, but that's impossible. If you go below your max for even a lap, the distance is short enough that you'll never forgive yourself for taking your time. It's a mental battle between what you should do and what you think you can do. You're constantly reassessing." I frowned, annoyed that I had the energy to speak for so long after my 500. I had even been able to pull myself up out of the pool without any help, only seconds after I had lifted my goggles to scan the scoreboard.

"Sounds like you're drawn to the more impossible things in life." Ian awkwardly tossed the bouquet from one hand to the other, unsure how to offer it to me. I collapsed my arms inside my parka and focused on taking off the straps of my race suit, which were digging into my shoulders. "For placing first in the mental battle," he said abruptly. He jutted out the flowers toward me, even though there were no hands at the ends of my sleeves to accept them. Instead, I stuck my nose in the petals, taking in their scent.

"I don't think tulips have a scent," corrected Ian.

"Ahhhh," I sighed, having released my shoulder straps. "Everything has a scent, but I can't detect it right now." With two practices a day, my sensual experience of dry land was always trapped in a chloric fog. The chemical scent would never scrub off my body. I'd tried and tried, even using a *kese* my mother had bought from Turkey to exfoliate her skin. "I'm like that joke about the fish, you know," I said. "So used to the world they live in, they have to ask, 'What's water?'"

Bulut and I start off with an easy breaststroke. As I'm concentrating on my pulls, bits of my conversation with the grocer's son drip back into my mind. I hesitate on whether to bring up the curse with Bulut. On the one hand, if Bulut hasn't actually heard about the curse yet, he might latch onto it as an excuse to return to shore. The fear of the journey is already apparent in his tight-lipped expression, and he is, I notice with alarm, a fairly slow swimmer. I'm already several notches below my usual warm-up speed in order to accommodate his pace. On the other hand, what if he does know and it's something that I don't want to hear? Whether it's true or not, the curse is shame-inducing enough that neither Bulut nor the grocer's son has been able to say it out loud. At least not to me. And yet it's not awful enough to prevent Bulut from wanting to swim to Barren Island in the first place, or to convince me to do so with him.

In the battle between painful curiosity and blissful ignorance, the scales tip heavy.

"Hey," I say casually. "So . . . do you know anything about this curse?"

"The curse about the island?" Bulut's even more nonchalant than I am pretending to be. "I mean, I know," he says, dismissing the severity of my shock with a wave of his hand, "that it's cursed. The island we're swimming to. There's that legend."

Palm splayed, I skim my wrist across the surface of the water, splashing him in the face. "You knew that we were swimming to a cursed island and you didn't even bother to tell me?"

"Technically, you knew it was cursed and didn't tell me until we were . . ." He looks out toward the horizon. It's difficult to gauge the distance when everything around you is the same, and nothing is in relation to anything else, which is how things are usually described. Time is also affected by this. We had been swimming for half an hour, maybe. Maybe two hours. Bulut finally manages to complete his sentence. "Until we were well on our way," he says.

The wind has picked up. Far ahead of us, still far enough not to matter, whitecaps start to form. "And were you planning on telling me about this curse?" I ask.

"I knew you weren't aware of the legend itself," he said. "If you had been, you wouldn't have agreed to the swim. Not that I was trying to trick you," he adds quickly. "It's just that I don't believe in any of these things, and you're always off with that circle of cards or looking for signs everywhere and all of that, I thought it might affect you if you knew. Besides, I—"

"Of course I still would have come!" I cut him off. There are worlds of difference between my own fortunes and the legends that are spun up by people who are not me. The insides of a coffee cup are nothing but trails of mud until I gaze upon them, until a slumbering knowledge arises within me that shapes them into the future. The clock fortune is only fifty-two frayed cards, manufactured in a plant somewhere outside the city lines, until I cut the deck and make the wish. The stories about myself, about my future, I write on my own. The more I want something, the more times I lay out that clock, the more likely it is to happen. The signs of the universe are always in movement, adjusting to what you do next. It is a dance; you are in step. What would I do with a legend? What *could* I do with a legend? A legend is an intangible tale that is neither here nor there when it comes to the unraveling of my own lifeline. No one else's story could dissolve my desire to swim to this island. Vacationers, breakfasting on their terraces, coming and going on the rosemary path, huddled around a table at the Small Club, will whisper about this achievement for years. *Ada and Bulut*, they'll say. *Ada (and Bulut). They swam to Barren Island, just because they could.* No one will mention my dance on the boat or remember where I spent my winters.

But I still want to know about the curse.

"I was just thinking," Bulut continued, "that when we get to the island, how about I tell you the legend then? That way, we'll have the right backdrop for the story. And it won't seem so weird. And maybe you can tell me something in exchange, like . . ."

"Like what?"

"Hmm. Like, maybe a secret."

A secret. My secret is that I am going to İstanbul with a man that my mother may still be in love with. My secret is that I am trying to make my mother happy, but it is not working, all the doors are closed, but there is a way that I can make myself happy. My secret is that I watch Levent over breakfast, his Adam's apple grazing up and down the thick skin of his throat as he sips coffee from his London mug, as he takes a fruit knife and cuts himself a slice of white cheese from its tub, piercing the block at the top. My secret is that each night now, the cinema of my desire begins as I drown in the Aegean because I do not know how to swim, and Levent dives into the sea to save me.

"What kind of secret?" I ask Bulut.

Bulut treads water for a bit, thinking. "Maybe . . . one you haven't told anyone before. And I promise that it won't leave the island. It'll mark the occasion somehow, add a little something to our adventure, to have this sort of story between us. We'll reclaim the island. It will henceforth be known as the Island of Secrets."

"As opposed to Barren Island?"

Bulut flinches. "Yes," he answers.

I wonder if I'll let him watch me as I tell him, or if I'll make him turn around, close his eyes. As everyone knows, a large part of a secret is expressed through the body and the face. To really understand some- one's secret, you have to watch them tell it. You have to pay attention to the movements of the eyes, the arch of the brows, the twist of the lips. The hesitation immediately prior to the reveal, the hot terror in the gap between the end of the story and the reaction of the listener. Aslı taught me this.

"Yeah, that's fine," I say cautiously. "I trust you."

"Because you know I'll take it to the grave, right?"

"No," I say, and laugh. "Because even if you let it slip, no one would believe you."

"You said you checked the weather today?" I ask, pulling in longer and longer strokes to steady my arms. The wind is strong enough to lift sev- eral strands of my wet hair, and howls into my ears like the calls in the labyrinths of seashells. The thick white flush of the whitecaps moves in closer to us, though it doesn't seem like we've been moving any closer to the island.

"Ada . . ." Bulut's face has grown pale, and his previously determined expression starts to wane. "It's not looking so good out there. I actually don't think we're going to be able to make it."

"Did you check the weather or not?"

"I don't need to check the weather. The weather is in front of your face. The waves in the distance, they're a lot bigger than you think, and the wind is picking up over here already. We have to turn back."

"Oh, no way. Bulut, there's no way you're leaving me to do this alone." I estimate the distance. Forty-five more minutes, fifteen more years. "Listen, how about this—let's just book it. For five minutes or so, straight ahead, okay? Keep going until you get tired, and we'll get much farther than you thought we could've, and you'll feel better about our pace. I promise." He turns to me, but his focus is beyond me, on the safety of the site's shoreline. "We've been moving so slowly because we've been dawdling, chitchatting the whole way. It's time for a serious effort now, and it'll go by much faster than you think."

Bulut turns from the mainland to the islands, then back again.

"You made a commitment," I remind him. "You made a promise. We're writing our own story today, remember? What the town will talk about when they talk about us."

He gives in. We submerge our faces back into the waves and plow through as fast as we can, our feet disappearing in their own whitewater. My fingers press together on the strokes so tightly that I can almost feel the bones touch.

Soon, I sense the currents shift. Either because it's late morning now or because we're farther out at sea, or both, the waves come in, growing choppier. Every few strokes, as I turn my head for a breath, the water dips into my nostrils and floods into my open mouth. I have to stop, cough it out. Around the fourth time this happens, a thin panic sets in, and I stop to wait for Bulut. I kick frantically as I tread water to keep my chin above the undulations. He's nowhere near. I can't see him. I can't see anything. Where is the dock, the mainland? Everything is too far away to be distinct, and none of the islands have gotten closer at all. I stick a hand in front of my face. It's dissolved into a sickly lilac. "Bulut?" I call out. "Bulut!" The wind whips my voice and carries it elsewhere. Waves slam into my body and I splash back at them with attempts at playfulness, trying to ease the shivers running up and down my arms. I think of Aslı's warning: *When it's man against nature, nature always wins. Every. Single. Time.* I prepare for another wave coming toward me, puffing out my chest to crash against it, but it swells with so much power that it knocks me over. Water seeps into my eyes and blurs my surroundings. All I can see are whorls of blue, of sea and sky. My panic swells.

"Ada!" Bulut's voice echoes from far away, and as I blink out the seawater, I see his bobbing head in the distance, turning back toward the pier. I watch his crab dance as he raises his arms as high as they will go and then makes a motion with one hand crossing his neck. *I'm done.* Coward! He motions for me to come along. I shake my head no. *Ada (and only Ada) swam to Barren Island.* Bulut calls to me again, then dives back in and swims toward me. I wait. As he resurfaces, he gasps for air.

"I am not letting you swim there alone," he says, then splashes around for my hand. I immediately pull it away. How could he do this to me? We had planned and decided and waited and dove in, and all that's left to do is to keep going. But when I look at Bulut, I realize that even if I am brave and strong enough to continue, I am not heartless enough to let him head back alone. His skinny limbs thrash and blur under the water, struggling to keep his head afloat.

He grabs my hand again and pulls me toward him, hard. "You're coming back with me."

"All right," I say, and turn my back on the islands.

12

THE DICE

During the most crowded hours of the Small Club, as the trash bins overflow with sand-crusted Fruko bottles and the children scream as they shove each other off the raft, my mother naps in an air-conditioned bedroom on the other side of the street, trying to pass the time. My mother swims her longest swims at night.

This evening, she moves in and out of the still water, the only human as far as the eye can see. I'm supposed to call her to dinner, and I wait for her to notice me. Beyond my mother are the islands, my islands, none of which I have been to. I sit down at the edge of the dock, on the damp wood half covered in plastic carpeting, and watch the sun set into the silhouette of the mainland, the reaching arm across the gulf.

I often wonder whether I became a swimmer to be more like my mother, or if it was a desire born solely from my own preferences. When I watched her in the sea throughout my early childhood in Datça, it seemed important that a person should be able to navigate both land and water, as if not knowing how to swim were as damaging of a limitation as not knowing how to walk. That was the greatest lesson my mother taught me, one that she seems to have now forgotten: Wherever you are—and you will be in many places—you must learn to move fluidly.

It was my first summer in Turkey. I was four years old and playing on the shore, as my mother recalls, watching her swim, when I threw my shovel aside and began to walk into the water. My grandmother was next to me and snapped to attention, but my mother shook her head and told her not to meddle. "It was so bright that day," my mother said. "There were diamonds glittering all across the sea." I winced as pebbles and shells cut into my feet but only whimpered softly to myself. When the water had started to lap at my chest, I turned toward my grandmother and waved. She stood up and motioned for me to return. "Ada," she called out, "that's too deep for you out there." I turned back around, raised my hands high, and threw myself into the sea. I desperately held my head above water, floating and kicking until my mother scooped me up in her arms.

That is how I learned to swim.

On the pier in front of the Small Club, I wave to my mother, then repeatedly lift an imaginary fork to my mouth. She says something that I can't quite hear, a half sentence that hangs in the air. But I know what she must mean: a joke about my grandmother, eyes on the clock. In the summer, there is only one designated time for things, and that is when they happen to happen. But because my grandmother enjoys her illusion of control, mealtimes are our concession. Our small sacrifice to the matriarch.

I stand up and wipe the wet grit off the back of my shorts, then head to the showers to wait for her. Nearby, a spindly teenager with a goatee works his mop around the legs of the café tables, and a woman and a man on opposite sides of a single sun bed play a game of backgammon.

The man counts his moves at a snail's pace, holding his round wooden piece vertically and clacking it on the board to track each step. One-two-three-four-five-six-seven-eight. "Not eight—five-three!" his partner corrects. She explains that the number on each die must be counted separately—you cannot simply add up the numbers to get their sum. One die can do what another cannot. She tosses for her turn. Six-three. Her piece sluices through the air with the memory of a thousand games, landing on its

destination triangle. The silent kills made along the way are now an-
nounced. She holds up one of the man's dead. "That was the six," she says.
She holds up another. "And this was the three. Do you understand now,"
she says, balancing the two pieces on the heightened center of the board,
"how the numbers are more powerful when they are distinct? How I
could have made two kills with six and three, but only one with three and
six, and only one with the nine?"

The man sucks in his cheeks and nods with a glow of admiration.

Footsteps that could be mine. I turn away from the game and see
my mother walking toward the outdoor showers. She's wearing one of
my bikinis. Black and white stripes, with a gold sailboat charm hanging
where the triangles meet. Her fingers keep moving up to her chest and
touching the charm.

"I hope you don't mind," she says.

Dinner's ready, I tell her. Grandma made *mantı* and she'll murder us
if it gets cold. She spent all afternoon while you were napping rolling
dough, slicing it into squares. Sorry. Otherwise I wouldn't have cut your
swim short. That was a nice sunset.

"Wasn't it?" My mother twists a red flower knob on the long pipe, its
paint peeling. The water pours over her face, blurring her features, but her
smile is uncontainable. I can count all her crooked teeth. She's speaking,
but the water swallows her words.

"I know something you don't know," she repeats.

What is it? I ask. I am terrified that my mother knows about the
İstanbul trip.

She winks.

You think you're so mysterious, I tease, easing up, but you're going to
slip. You'll slip over breakfast tomorrow, as early as that. You'll give a hint
unexpectedly as you're lost in thought pouring tea or salting cucumbers,
and I'll put together the final clue.

My mother laughs and winds the knob back up. She grabs a lone towel
hanging on the drying rack, throws it around her shoulders like a cape.
We walk together through the Small Club, both of us barefoot, her grin
still wide.

Tell me what it's about, then, I say, careful not to sound as if I'm begging. Then I add: At least.

My mother stops in the middle of the oleander walkway. My grandmother sees us from the terrace and gets up from her chair. Though visibly upset by our lateness, decorum prevents her from yelling across the street. She gestures violently, a flurry of fingers.

"I thought that was obvious," my mother says. She leans over to stroke my dry hair. Salt water drips from her fingers, down my forehead. "It's about you."

13

THE NIGHT SWIM

In the middle of the night, Ian races through Schumann as I twirl in the common room, but I wake at the crescendo and understand that there are no right-hand trills, only a mosquito. I slap at my ear and turn on the lights, then stand naked by the doorway, listening, watching. The battle doesn't take long, as killing without waking the others is an art I've perfected throughout my many summers. My slaps are swift, light, and effective, as evidenced by the rust-colored speckles on all four walls. I don't like the fact that what I leave behind in this country is only destruction, never a creation, but at least, I think, it's something. By the time I've silenced the buzz, I'm so full of energy that there's no chance of sleep. I pull on some clothes and leave my room. The clock at the bottom of the stairs reads 2:43. My friends are probably still out, but I have been returning home earlier these days, tired from my morning patrols.

I close the gate behind me and head north. Across the street, the Small Club continues playing its night set, and pop star Demet Akalın croons over a man's voice in a remix that cuts her words into staccato segments. I understand now why the girls with the Chupa Chups were laughing. I had incorrectly paired endings and beginnings, my syllables swapping partners in an absurd dance. I walk through the park, the market, and the basketball courts, but can't find my friends. They're not at the Big Club, either, where only a few of the tables at the restaurant are occupied but the staff stays on, plunking ice cubes into tall *rakı* glasses. The faces of the guests are slung with a semblance of fatigue, but conversations scatter effortlessly.

Behind the Big Club lies Sıfır, where I stomp through the withered grass until I find myself in a field of dried seaweed. It crunches under my feet. The lights of the Big Club weaken by the time of their arrival here, and it's difficult to make out the thin wooden dock at the far end of the beach. A pathetic, rickety passageway for those who flinch at the sensation of seaweed, or prefer not to punish their feet on the sharp shore pebbles. There is no reason to have built a dock like that, something that is neither magnificent nor useful. As the beach is situated between *sites*, coming here is no one's preference. Those of our town will always go to the Small Club beach, where the dock is sturdy and the waiters attentive. Those of the neighboring *site* have their own cafés and beaches farther down, near their own center. It's either here or there. Sıfır's only purpose, it seems, is to warn someone that they are in the wrong place. *You are here*, it says. *But you shouldn't be.*

When I reach the dock, I move cautiously, testing my weight with each step. Even though it can't be more than five meters long, it takes forever to reach the end. Water laps in an errant rhythm against its sunken legs. I get on my knees and pass my hands along the wooden boards to make sure that none of the planks have fallen off, that there are no spaces between the boards large enough for my foot to plunge through. But as I'm feeling around for gaps, my hands come across a different sort of texture. One, two, three sets of fabric. Clothing. I run my fingers along its edges, hold it up, stretch it out, squint as my vision adjusts to the darkness. Someone's polo, maybe. Boxers with an elastic waistband, a pair of jeans. Who left this here? I look around for an answer, but there are no ripples of movement, no sign of life beyond the dock. Only a blank reflection of white opal reveals itself in the small, shallow breaths of the sea. Then the water breaks open and a face appears like the moon.

"The jellyfish are out," says Levent, swimming over to the dock. "But if you don't mind a bit of an electric shock, it's absolutely stunning. Silence. Like floating in nothingness."

His voice calls all the elements forward, and the strong scent of brine rises to meet me. All of a sudden I can see the contours of the dock, each speckle of sand, the browned, crisped edges of the seaweed along the shore. The gleam of flat orange skipping stones among the pebbles. Levent places his hands along the edge of the dock and raises himself up so that he's resting his head on his crossed arms on the wood. Moonlight glints off his shark-tooth necklace in small sparks.

"What do you think?" he asks.

"What do I think about what?"

"Joining me for a night swim."

I settle onto the edge of the dock and dangle my feet into the water. "Maybe."

"Ada," Levent laughs, and I wonder what's so funny. He takes a deep breath and cocks his head. "You know . . . you know that I see you every morning, watching me eat breakfast in that mulberry bush?"

For a minute, I lose all my confidence. I see myself the way that he must see me. Crouched among the leaves, seemingly shrewd, cloaked in false security. He could see all the ways in which I was pretending. The sense of being seen terrifies me. Then I realize that I don't have much left to lose.

I kick water in his face. "I'm going with you next week, are you ready?"

"To the city? That's a joke."

"It's not a joke."

I run my fingers along the hem of my shirt for a moment, then another moment, and maybe a few more seconds, and that's probably enough. I take it off. I strip down until everything that had been on me is folded into a neat pile to my right. I'm in only my underwear, which, I realize, is just one of my swimsuit bottoms. Cotton underwear or lace lingerie— these are for the other seasons. Levent's eyes flicker madly under thick eyelids, and I sit there for a while, enjoying his reaction. If I don't move at all, do I still remind him of someone? Gripping the edge of the dock, I lower my body over it and slide into the water, wincing as splinters in the wood scratch against my back.

"I'll swim," I say, "but you're not allowed to touch me." I tread water for a few seconds, then dive in fully. It's warmer than I expected, and as I swim underwater, I extend my arms out from my sides, lengthening my strokes. I am unafraid of the schools of fish that swarm at this hour, the jellyfish that glide in their translucence, eager to sting.

As I break the surface for a breath, I hear him call my name.

It's easy to lose sight of me. I move softly, nearly imperceptibly in the sea. My wet hair hangs down my back, parceled into long, dark ropes. After a while of traveling out toward the invisible horizon, I turn around and swim back in his direction, toward a place to moor.

14

THE MOVIE STAR

My mother places a bowl of hazelnuts on the glass table in front of me. "You swim too much," she says, "and eat too little. Have some snacks."

I pop a couple into my mouth without looking up from today's crossword puzzle, with whose boxes I've done little but traced over and over again in blue ink. The clues are simplistic, all about knowing and not-knowing. Nothing like the *New York Times* crossword, where wit and mental acuity play into your chances of success. What does this mean? I keep asking my mother, tapping a pen at the clues. I do a mental count of the letters as she lists off synonyms. What does that mean? I chew on the plastic pen cap, aggravated. The reference to a celebrity gazing expressively from the middle of the page tugs at me, but I can't figure it out. At a certain point, my grandmother returns to the terrace, having rinsed our plates. She yanks the newspaper from my hands, plucks out my pen, and takes both with her over to the porch swing. She puts on her reading glasses and kicks herself off the ground. The swing returns a long, yawning creak.

"Don't waste too much brain power over this," my grandmother says, scribbling in answers one after the other. "You either know it or you don't. No fun if you get the answers from someone else. You think too much, all the time, and that makes your face frightening. The creases, the glares, the hardness. You must learn to stop thinking and relax your face. Look at your mother. She's perfected that stoic, empty expression for a more approachable demeanor. Meltem, show me that look, let me see what I've taught you."

My mother looks at my grandmother as if she is about to kill her.

"Is that true, do you agree with her?" My mother collapses back into her usual, soft countenance. "Do I walk around with a stupid look on my face?"

It's not that it's *stupid*, I try to explain. It's more like—

"Dense. Airheaded. Moronic," my grandmother snorts. "Any of those work?" She fills in a few more boxes. Then she moves her glasses slightly down the bridge of her nose and holds out the paper at arm's length with both hands, snapping out the fold.

"This is Kemal Sunal, you uncultured fool," she says to me. "One of the most famous film stars to ever grace the screens of Turkish cinema."

Shit. I can't believe I couldn't recognize him.

My grandmother stares at me from above her reading glasses. "Don't tell me you couldn't recognize Kemal Sunal," she says slowly, fearing my response.

"Ada was born and raised in the States," says my mother. "How do you expect her to keep up with Turkish cinema?"

"Quite correct, Meltem. And whose fault is that?" The swing screeches following a heavy push. I cringe with the noise. My mother reaches across the table and grabs a handful of hazelnuts, her fingernails gently scraping the bottom of the bowl. Then she leans back and a shadow briefly passes over her face.

In an attempt to rescue my mother from the debris of my grandmother's insults, I try again to search for the words. *It's more like . . .*

⚓

"She has a certain naïveté," said Levent in the dark. I was floating on my back, looking for shapes in the stars. Big frying pan, little frying pan. "But I don't know how much you know about all this."

"I know everything," I said, recalling my breakfast with Neslihan. I could feel the water displace and caught sight of Levent's head. He was swimming around me, circling my star shape.

"How old are you, anyway? You're not yet at the age when you can understand any of this."

"It's not that complicated," I said. "My mother had made up a fantasy about a life with you that just wasn't true. Sometimes, the wreckage of something that didn't exist in the first place is even worse than the unraveling of something real."

"Right you are, young lady. But there's another element to this, which is that your mother is—or was, I can't claim to know her anymore—not what I would call an autonomous woman." In the expansion of his breast-stroke, Levent's arm caught onto my hair. He broke our no-touching rule, but I let it go. Somewhere in the Big Club, a light turned off, then another. In the next few minutes, the sound from the tables slowly drifted away until all that remained was the silence between the *sites* and the gentle nighttime glow of the building. "She's incapable of taking any action of her own. Don't believe me? The first time she tried it, it completely knocked her off course and swept her away. She went and married some man she ran into at a bar in Paris. Come on, now. Paris? And don't think for a second that I believe it was because she'd fallen in love with him. She got carried away, that high that comes with being in charge of making your own decisions for the first time. I've come across these types of women several times in my life, Ada. The kind who can't make a decision on their own and have to look for people to latch onto in order to continue on anywhere. They either stay stagnant or go where they are taken."

"Maybe she had fallen in love with him," I said. "Maybe that was a direction she wanted to go in, not one she was taken in."

"I doubt it. Every step that woman has taken has been due to a push or a pull."

I didn't like hearing it like this. It was one thing for me to feel the weight-lessness of my mother, and another for someone like Levent to claim it as fact.

"She decided to get rid of the baby," I said, and when I saw the look on his face, I knew that I had told him something new. He stopped encircling me and stood up in the sand.

"What are you talking about?"

I opened my mouth to explain, but then I stopped. I could have told him, *There was almost another one of you.* I could have told him that there were things, great things, on a par with acts of God, that my mother was able to do and decide on her own. But there was some-thing in his eyes that grasped at what was happening, and was begging me not to say it out loud and make it true. He did not want the confir-mation.

It was time to move away from my mother and back to me. "And with me?" I asked, carefully navigating the path back. I wanted to hear again how he saw me differently, the things he had told me in his villa.

"What about you?" There was gratitude in his voice for leaving the past behind. "You are a different person altogether. You don't have those sorts of problems, not as far as I can tell."

"That's not what I'm asking," I said, even though I supposed it was. "What I'm asking is, how do you feel about me?"

"I don't feel anything about you. You're just the daughter of someone I used to know."

My floating body folded up in anger, but I was too short to stand and face him. I swam up to him, as close as I could without touching him.

"It's very uninteresting," I said, "how you can only think of things in relation to each other."

"I've known your mother since I was a child," he countered. "It's not really possible for me to think of you in any other way except in relation to her."

"Try again," I said. My tone made it clear that this was a demand. I slowed down the movement of my arms and legs, treading water as silently as I possibly could. The sea was so quiet and the night was so dark, all the sensations fading away one by one, that I felt that if he could not see me as someone very separate tonight, then he would never be able to. My face was very close to his. Ever so slightly, Levent tilted his head. Then someone called my name. Our background flooded in again in full force, and I shielded my eyes from the brightness of the moon.

The voice belonged to Aslı. "Helllllooo?" The pebbles crunched under her feet as she made her way onto the beach, the sound amplifying with each step. Next to me, Levent inhaled sharply. An electricity crawled up my skin. Something had bitten me.

The small shock of a sting spread its bolts over my legs, up my back, from my hands to my arms, and when it reached my chest, I lurched forward, and planted my arms on Levent's shoulders. I pushed him into the water. "Under," I hissed. He looked up at me in surprise, but he allowed me to sink him into a bed of seaweed.

I scaled the dock ladder as quietly as I could and threw my clothes back on before racing down the wooden planks. "Aslı, hi!" But as soon as I called her name, my foot was bathed in a strange warmth and there was a searing pain around my thigh. My leg had fallen into a gap in the pier. I must have screamed, because Aslı screamed, and then I heard the start-stop of her footsteps, trying to navigate their way to me in the dark. I attempted to push myself out with my arms and free leg, but at the angle, the jagged edges of the wood cut into my skin.

"I don't even know where to begin with this," Aslı said in bewilderment, surveying the scene. She had been on her way back to the park after using the restroom at the Big Club. I reached out to her, and she took my hand and squatted down, trying to get a sense of the amount of space she had to work with. Then she took off the denim jacket she was wearing and shoved it into the gaps.

"If I try to yank you out, it will be worse," she said. "You're going to have to push yourself up with your hands, okay?"

I steadied myself on my palms and strained to hear whether Levent was making any noise. Not a sound from the sea. Then I pushed, and my leg kicked up against the denim and broke through the plank behind me. Once I finally wrestled myself free, I collapsed onto the dock and quickly zipped up my shorts. Aslı lay on her stomach, scooping up salt water to pour on my leg. The wounds burned. For a moment, the pain stopped, and I noticed that Aslı was occupied with something else. She was looking out over the dock with her face scrunched up.

"What was that?" she asked.

"What was what?" I scanned the darkness for any signs of Levent. Nothing at all. He seemed to have disappeared.

"I heard something."

"It's night, so the larger fish are out."

"No, it wasn't . . ." She gathered herself up and sat on the dock with me, mindlessly stroking her wet hands up and down my leg as she kept her gaze on the sea. "I don't think it was a fish. I don't know, I can't figure it out. It's eerie here at night." She shuddered. "Are you trying to kill yourself out here, swimming alone at this hour? If you have some freaky nighttime-swimming fantasy, we can all go together off the dock at the Small Club. It's safer there. Someone would actually hear us if we yelled for help. First it was the island swim, now . . . you're not invincible, you know. Oh, sorry, honey," she said as I whimpered. "I know it hurts." She patted my leg to signal the end of the caretaking, then got up and held out her hand. I clung to her as I balanced on my good leg and looped an arm around her shoulders for support. Limping back out to the beach, I breathed in her comforting scent of pomegranate shampoo and cheap beer, happy to have a friend.

"*You* heard me, though," I said. I was trying to win the argument, but immediately regretted it.

"Oh, that's right," she remembered, then stopped in her tracks. "*Try again.* Wait, who were you even talking to?"

"Myself. Well, a jellyfish, really. I'm pretty sure I got stung." As we approached the street, I held out my leg out under the light of a streetlamp. "It's all messed up from the fall. I can't tell what happened. Do you think if it's a sting I'll have to do something about it tonight—hey, Aslı? What's going on? What are you looking at?"

Aslı had turned back toward the water, considering something. "Sometimes," she said, "when you can't see, you can figure out what you're looking at from the outline. Do you know what I mean? For example, for a few seconds, I saw the lighting of the Big Club black out, foot by foot, as if there was someone or something walking across the dock. Were you alone out there?"

"In this tiny town of ours by the sea . . ." I began to belt out.

"Ada, I'm serious. Do you remember what Bulut was saying about that man? Was he around?"

"People have nothing better to do than to talk about me!" I completed the line on my own, doing my best to maintain the melody, but it was obvious that my voice was shaking. I had just started on the next verse when Aslı crouched down and motioned to her back.

"Get up, you dummy," she said. "I'll carry you home."

"Okay, but I'm wet." I held on to her shoulders and jumped up as she threaded her arms around my knees. "Thanks for not interrogating me," I whispered into her ear as we passed the park. She replied with a sly, soft chuckle. As if I were her only shot at an answer, as if this town weren't crawling with informants.

⚓

It's more like you have a certain naïveté, I tell my mother. She sighs and goes back inside, taking the bowl of hazelnuts with her. Over her shoulder, she says that maybe once she's out of the way, my grandmother and I can debate the point further and come up with an exact definition of her allegedly idiotic expression. Soon a folded crossword puzzle zips across the table and lands in front of me. The pen rolls along after it.

"All done," says my grandmother, taking off her reading glasses. "I may be old, but I'm still all right in the head, aren't I? Not going anywhere soon, I can tell you that much." She taps at her temple and whistles the jingle from the Channel D commercial break, which I recognize from movie night at Aslı's. I put my feet up on the terrace railing and inspect the scars on my legs, still unsure which of the marks belong to the sea creature that attacked me in the night and which can be attributed to my fall. There are so many of them. I uncap the pen and chart my own constellations.

15

THE BIG CLUB

Tonight Ozan, the twins, and I are playing cooncan at the Big Club while passing around ketchup-flavored potato chips. It's windy, and the cards keep flapping off our table. We scuttle after them silently, everyone too afraid to comment on the change of weather. Only two weeks until September.

"Bulut, did you already finish the chips? Isn't there another bag?" Ozan lunges over Aslı and snatches the chips from Bulut's lap. "How Western of you, taking it all for yourself. Ada's supposed to be the selfish American here." He grins at me and reaches underneath the table, pulling out a plastic bag filled with beers and snacks we had bought from the grocer for the night. He shifts to take a key chain out of his pocket and pops open three bottles of Tuborg, leaving Bulut empty-handed. "Sit there sober for a while," Ozan says. "Let's even this out. After all, we might not have many more opportunities." Then his tone takes a turn for the serious, and he strokes his beard. "After all, my dear friends, this might just be our last summer together."

"Enough with that," Bulut murmurs, and I can tell from his voice that he's worried. I'm sensitive about it, too. We're all on edge. Soon our lives will transition to adulthood. It has already taken me too many unpleasant conversations to justify my trip here, the first summer of my college years. Another summer by the sea while everyone else interns and saves up their dollars and shuttles up and down the peninsula to their various office parks. Ian, of course, responsible Ian, is getting ahead with his summer at the hospital. It wasn't even a question for him whether he should vacation or work. We are in college now; summer no longer means what it once did. The thing is, I can't think of any direction I want to move in other than closer to Turkey. How can I move closer to who I'm meant to be if I stay in California?

But adult life, I know, has a way of masking true desires with the dreams of others. Once responsibilities begin to creep into our schedules, once we experience withdrawal symptoms even at the mere thought of being away from our phones, our computer screens, once we see the money in our bank accounts and the closing window of time to spend it—will we choose to come back to one another, here? When our partners become serious candidates for our lives with sights set on five-star resorts and drinks in beheaded pineapples, will we return to seaweed-strewn beaches to laugh with old friends, fingers and tongues orange from Doritos, in a place where everyone knows everyone else, where the possibility of gossip electrifies every deviant action?

Will we even want to?

"Yeah!" I shake a finger at Ozan. "This topic is off-limits."

To each other, my three friends are family, and never too far away. In fact, all the residents of this town disperse only within a restricted radius. From time to time, I hear stories of *site* acquaintances running into each other. It's tough to recognize someone out of their swimwear, but not impossible. What would it be like, I wonder, to walk into a Starbucks in the business district, see Aslı in a wool peacoat, snowflakes melting on her shoulders? Would I even recognize her as she sips cinnamon-dusted *salep* with her city friends? Everyone else in this *site* would. They would understand that that is, indeed, how most of her life passes.

"You know what would have been rad," Ozan says, changing the topic. "If you guys had actually made it to that island."

We all remind him that he was originally against the idea, that Bulut and I had ventured out despite his warnings.

"I mean, of course I didn't want anything to happen to you," Ozan says. "It's dangerous no matter how you look at it. It was a stupid idea. But if you were going to do it anyway, despite whatever people said, then it would have been pretty cool if you'd actually, well . . . done it." He pauses, trying to get the words right. "I agree with you, Aslı. The *lahmacun* maker's son probably didn't swim there. I actually don't know anyone who has, just a few folks who've gone with their boats. Maybe one washed-up windsurfer a few years ago. But swimming there? And someone our age, like, not a professional? Man, that would have been legendary."

All of us fall silent as we construct our own fantasies around the alternate reality. I'm the first to speak up. "I would have kept going if Bulut hadn't practically begged me to turn back." Bulut looks up at me, surprised. The waves were harsh that day, and I know that my own fear had been obvious. I swallow my guilt down, hard. *Let me have this*, I think.

"I guess it was my fault," Bulut admits, being kind. He reaches for the snacks and takes out the pretzels I had bought for myself. Then he tears open the bag and tosses a few pieces in his mouth. "Maybe I chose the wrong day, or maybe I didn't train hard enough. I mean, I didn't even train, not really. Whatever it was, the point is, we never made it. And that's the end of the story."

Ozan wins the hand at play and leans back, neatly setting the cards into their deck. He takes a look around the club. "Hey," he says, alert. "That dude's here again." At the northern edge of the club, out in the direction of the abandoned beach of Sıfır, sits Levent, lighting a cigarette and nodding at a waiter who's just served him a glass of red. Aslı shakes her head.

"I noticed him staring at us a few minutes ago," she says. "That guy really does give me the creeps. What do you say we get out of here? Let's grab some more beer at the market and drink over at the park instead."

The boys nod and begin to shuffle out, and Ozan tells the waiter that they can add tonight's IOU to his family's name. I stay in my chair until Bulut asks me what's wrong. I have one second to think of an excuse.

"Ada, beers, park? You deaf or what?"

"I, um. I'm going to head home. I think I got sunstroke from today. My head's all loopy."

"You want to head home already?" Aslı tilts her head to check the moon. "It's not even midnight yet." Then she understands, and shoots me a disappointed look.

I simply nod, as though words require too much effort for my fatigued state.

A chorus of voices bids me good night, and the three of them walk across the street to the park. Even though we are four, they are all one. In the winters, they will be close together, the separate cities of the cousins only a train ride away. They will remember each other and forget about me.

The summer's inevitable end mocks me. Once I'm back in California, I'll reset to my old self. What will it matter that I spend the hot months here?

I stay in place for a minute longer, doing my best not to make eye contact with Levent. One more minute, I think. If he doesn't come over in one minute, I will go to him. But less than ten seconds later, I hear my chair screech back, feel my legs working across the terrace, and I am deeply inhaling the sharp scent of tobacco.

"Hey," I say, pulling out a chair for myself.

Levent slides his packet of Camels toward me as an acknowledgment of my arrival. I slowly pull one out. Not because I want to smoke it, but because I want him to light it for me. I lean toward him with the cigarette in my mouth, but the flicker of the flame is quick and the moment is over before I can even enjoy it. With small inhales, I struggle to figure out whether I can feel the smoke tumble down into my lungs or not. When I open my mouth to release what I've taken in, nothing comes out. Levent can probably guess that it's my first time with a cigarette, but I can't tell if the smile on his face is at my expense, or if it's a reaction to how close we are. I will just hold the cigarette, I decide. Like a pencil, and let it burn on its own. I wonder if he has finally decided to believe that I'll be coming to İstanbul with him.

A waiter passes by our table and I expect Levent to signal to him to bring me something, but he doesn't. So I reach over for his glass of wine and take a long drink, then set it back down. I pause for a reaction.

"Maybe you should get your own," he says.

"Maybe you should have ordered one for me."

He leans in and lowers his voice. "So what you told me that day when we were at my villa, in the sea . . ."

"I meant what I said. I'll be there, waiting for you." My mother might not be a woman of action, but I am not my mother. "I'm working on my plan. No one will suspect anything, don't worry. So tell me," I say, "where in the city will you take me?"

"And how is school going?" he asks, his tone suddenly paternal.

"What?" I study his expression, which seems concerned, genuine. "What are you talking about?"

"Ada?" Behind me, my grandmother's voice. I slowly turn to see both her and my mother, dressed in far more stylish outfits than their evening muumuus. Did they know that Levent would be here? I immediately drop the cigarette and smother it with my shoe.

My grandmother is wearing gray slacks and a rose pink button-down, maintaining her innocence in all matters, and my mother is wearing a burgundy jersey dress that I realize is mine. "Ada, what a surprise, to see you here!" As they approach the table, my mother darts a confused look at me. I do my best to seem bored, as if Levent were just another family friend who had flagged me over to his table for small talk. Nothing out of the ordinary for our *site*.

"Let's order a round of drinks, shall we?" suggests my grandmother. "I see you've already started on the wine. Yes, that sounds perfect. Waiter!" she calls, her voice shrill. "House reds for us all."

Levent slowly inches his glass closer to his side of the table, so that there can be no mistake about who's been drinking it. My mother clears her throat. "We were just talking, on our way here," she says, "about how we spend such little time in İstanbul. I think that maybe Ada and I will leave Ayvalık earlier this year and spend a few extra days in the city, instead of taking the bus up just the day before our flight."

Oh no no no, no talk about İstanbul. We can't discuss this, not now.

It's too close to the reality of our upcoming trip, and one of us will crack, and my mother will know that something is up if both Levent and I start acting strange. I fix my gaze on his face, making sure he knows that I know that he cannot mess this up.

"I don't know why you never stay there, Meltem," says Levent. His voice is breezy, as if he's practiced hiding his emotions for years. I'm impressed with this act, just tossing away the fact of me so completely.

"The memories, I suppose." My mother looks at him shyly, and I nearly cringe. She has completely fallen under my grandmother's spell, it's clear, and she is ready to fully welcome this potential romance. She just has no idea that it's no longer available to her. Underneath the makeup that she so inexpertly has applied to her face this evening, she is also blushing. I look away and focus on a waiter who is operating the *tost* grill near the ice cream freezer. "But I'm thinking that it might be time to make new memories."

"Yes!" says my grandmother. The waiter arrives with three glasses of red, and I ask him for a sour cherry vodka, which is the only cocktail I can think of that will go down fast. "I was just thinking," my grandmother continues. "Levent, remember how we would always have tea at the Hilton with your parents? And then you two would run off, go to the movies in Beyoğlu for those films we thought were so immoral." She laughs, ridiculing the misjudgments of her past, making light of her oppressive regime. Her heavily ringed fingers coil around the stem of her wineglass.

"Yes, the movies!" cries my mother, matching my grandmother's enthusiasm. I stiffen in my chair. Her volume cannot bring those memories back, I know this, but her vivacity stuns me. I want to draw it out. I stay silent. "That theater," she continues, "with the cozy patisserie next door, profiteroles dripping in chocolate sauce." My mother cups her hands to make tiny cream puffs and shows her empty fists to Levent. "We should go, you and I, when I return to İstanbul." I turn sharply to my mother, noticing that she did not include me in her return.

When we return, I correct.

"When we return," she says automatically, eyes still on Levent. She doesn't even understand the importance of the omission.

"Of course I remember." Levent smiles, but the corners of his eyes don't lift at all. "But we'll need to find someplace new. They tore down both of those places years ago, don't you know? They're nothing but fixtures of the past. And of course, Beyoğlu itself isn't what it used to be, anyway. Nowadays we all spend our weekends on the northern European coast, that's where the good nightlife is. A lot has changed since you've last spent any time in the city, Meltem. It would be unrecognizable to you."

"It's really no longer there . . . ?" my mother asks, her voice trailing. "The profiteroles?" She coughs and lifts a wineglass to her mouth. "Oh, I can't drink red wine," she says quietly, and looks sideways at my grandmother. I motion to the waiter to bring her some mineral water.

"But if you were to move back," my grandmother says, riled up now, "I'm sure Levent could help you discover the city again. It would be just like old times . . ."

"Well, now I don't know anymore," says my mother. She slides a straw into the green bottle the waiter has brought over and twirls it around the tiny opening. "Maybe the past should just stay in the past."

"To hell with the past!" My grandmother waves her hands, dismissing all notions. "I am talking about the future! İstanbul is always here, whenever you're ready. Now, tomorrow morning after we've had our breakfast, we can look at the calendar and decide when you're going to head back to the city. And I can even come with you and stay for a while in the apartment, get everything all set up for the winter."

"We have a calendar in the house?" I ask, looking up from my drink. My mouth is still on the straw, but it's pulling on air. Draining my vodka took a matter of seconds. My grandmother rolls her eyes at my obscene manners.

"Then that really is a waste about the villa," says Levent. He starts to tap out another cigarette, but suddenly his eyes grow wide. My grandmother gives him a stone-cold stare.

"What do you mean, a waste about the villa?" my mother asks.

"Nothing," says Levent, averting his gaze.

"Nothing," says my grandmother.

"Where is the calendar? Grandma, is it in your room?" I am now working through my mother's abandoned wine and second-guessing my familiarity with the villa. How can there be something I don't know about in that villa? What are all its other secrets?

"There seems to be something you are not telling me," my mother says. She stops twirling her straw. "Tell me now."

My grandmother pretends not to hear her. Her attention flits around at the other guests and she clucks something about how it's too busy at this time of night; if people knew what was good for them, they would be home, sleeping. The elderly are not meant for such liveliness, she concludes. It's clear that she does not include herself in this category.

Levent sighs. "Your mother bought the villa I live in. She convinced me to spend the second half of my summer here, instead of in Bodrum, so that we could spend more time together," he says.

My mother whips around to face my grandmother.

"Of course I did!" cries my grandmother. A few gray-haired heads turn toward our commotion, then huddle back into their own tables. The murmurs of their gossip ripple out to the other diners, and soon the entire Big Club bubbles with anticipatory energy. "You think a bachelor would ever decide on his own to spend a summer in a town like this?"

I knew it, I knew it, I knew it. "I knew it!" I yell, then realize I've let on that this is something I've been thinking about. I slouch in my chair and make myself as small as possible. Thankfully, there is too much going on for anyone to pay any attention to me.

My mother turns to Levent as if she is seeing him for the first time. She visibly recoils. "My mother convinced you to come to our *site*? This wasn't just a coincidence?"

"Oh, he would have come on his own, eventually," says my grandmother, silencing Levent with a movement of her hand. "It's just easier this way, a quicker way for you two to reconnect."

"Only a fool would refuse a house by the sea." Levent shrugs, as if he'd been offered a holiday present he was too polite to return. "My house in Bodrum," he says quietly, "is up on a hill."

"Oh," says my mother. "Oh, oh." She takes the wineglass back from me and winds her fingers around the stem, not snakelike like my grand-mother, but with a force that turns her knuckles white. I hear her deep breaths. Then her arm snaps straight, and she empties the glass onto the floor. The wine splatters all over the white tiles.

A collective gasp rises from the diners, but my mother is focused solely on my grandmother.

"Meltem!" My grandmother is in shock. The gossip boils over; no one attempts to hide it anymore. I can hear people talking about us, saying our names. My grandmother motions to a waiter, then points down at the wine-stained floor. "Please, we had an accident," she says.

"Not an accident," my mother says brightly.

"Meltem, how's your husband?" asks Levent. I laugh wildly, amused at how easily he thinks he can untangle himself from all of this. But perhaps he is used to that, I think, remembering his past. The alcohol has gone to my head already. I am flickering.

"Terrible," wails my grandmother. "The man has been having an affair, and Meltem thinks she can salvage it. I think it's time for her to cut her losses and move on, wouldn't you say so?"

"Well, ahem," says Levent. "I can't comment there, that's really up to Meltem."

My mother is shocked by the transition of the topic, and we are look-ing at each other, trapped in the distant conversation. My grandmother and Levent carry on; they are elsewhere and have forgotten about us. The dilemma my mother is now faced with is old news for them. Everyone ignores the waiter mopping around our feet.

"Let me ask you something, Levent," my grandmother says, pursing her lips. "Where are your parents? They're in İstanbul, no? And don't you find that comforting, that they'll know they'll always have you to take care of them in their old age? I've been lonely ever since the day my hus-band passed—oh, thank you, well, we've made our peace with it—and you know what the American style of caring for parents is, don't you? They imprison them in nursing homes. Tell me, what's the use of having children if you're going to spend your old age withering alone in someone else's poorly decorated idea of a home?"

"Ada," says my mother. She stands up. "Let's go." I am obedient and follow her. My grandmother calls after us—"Be courteous, Meltem, we've only just sat down!"—but Levent does not, and I am too afraid to look back at him with an expression that will confirm that yes, despite everything that happened tonight, I am still coming. What does it matter that my mother couldn't keep him in her grasp, that my grandmother had to resort to manipulation and trickery to get him back into their lives? I am not them; there is something special about me, and Levent has seen it. There is something about me that draws and connects me to this country, and he is the one who can lock me in place.

Once we're on the main street, my mother turns to look at me for a long time. I am anxious but feeling safe because there is no reason she should be mad at me. She should be mad at my grandmother because my grandmother was the one who made the plan.

"Ada, that man Levent. He is a bad man, okay? I don't want you spending any time with him. Why were you even at his table?"

I can't remember. I tell her that he called me over, which seems reasonable until a few seconds later when I remember that it's a lie. She considers this and looks pained. I mention that I thought he was a good family friend.

"No!" My mother throws her hands in the air, exasperated. She spins around in her sandals, unsure what to do, where to go. My dress flutters around her. She looks down at the street along the water that leads toward our villa, then turns back to me. "Do not talk to him, do not go near him, if you see him at the beach, stay away. I thought he was a good man, too, but if I had used my brain, instead of following along with everything your dear old grandmother says, trusting her instead of trusting myself, I would have discovered it sooner. Don't make the same mistakes I made. Soon you will find that the summers aren't as temporary as you think, that your summer life and your real life have intertwined and are inseparable from one another, and that all your actions have consequences, no matter the season." She takes a deep breath. "I'm sorry. I promised myself when I had you that I would never tell my daughter what to do, that she should be her own person. And here I am, no different from Madame

Mukadder. But please. Learn from my mistakes." She pauses, relieved by the look on my face. I am listening. "Are your friends still out? Are you going to meet them now?"

I want to go home, I tell her. I do not tell her that it's because I still need to pack. Because in three days, I am going to the city with the bad man, and nobody can stop me.

16

THE LIES

The next day, my mother and I head to the town center so that she can get a new bottle of her extra-high-SPF sunscreen from the pharmacy. When we arrive at the main square with the Atatürk statue, I make a beeline for the ice cream vendor and ask for mastic flavor in between two pieces of helva, while my mother gets one scoop raspberry and one scoop chestnut in a waffle cone. The boats are slowly pulling away from the marina, heading out on their day cruises. I let my mother walk ahead of me, then switch over to her left side, out of direct sight of the *Eftalya II* crew.

My mother speaks with the pharmacist as I read through the brand names lining the shelves, silently mouthing them out. They are mostly in French. The pharmacist runs her fingers along my mother's arm and comments on her skin. "A little too late for these sorts of preventative measures, aren't we?" she asks as she rings up the sunscreen. I swerve around to glare at the woman, and check my mother for her reaction. If she is upset, then I will destroy the pharmacist. But my mother remains calm.

"It's true," she says, "that the sun ages you. But when I look in the mirror now, what I see are all my summers along the Marmara when I was younger, the days when I was close to my family and living in my country. I live elsewhere now, but do you see"—and here she runs a finger along the inside of her wrist, up to her elbow, pulling the sagging skin along with its light touch—"how I can carry everything with me in this way? None of it is gone."

"I apologize for the misunderstanding," the pharmacist stammers, her porcelain face flushing. "Your skin is truly beautiful. The color of a—"

"I know it's beautiful," says my mother. "I don't need you to tell me that."

Her hand hovers over the clasp of her wallet while the pharmacist waits. My mother frowns, then silences her face and deftly works her fingers into the pocket of her purse, pulling out a few bills and coins at random. She places them in her palm and offers up the variety. The woman raises her eyebrows, taken aback by the responsibility of counting out the change.

"Thanks for the sunscreen, have a nice day," I say. I grab my mother's arm and drag her out the door.

Once back on the street, my mother shakes her head. "They changed the currency a few years ago," she says. "I still can't tell them apart."

It's because you've been gone, I respond.

"What was that?"

Never mind, I say.

We walk along the skein of the town's backstreets, stopping to admire the jewelry stands. Turquoise stones, elaborate silver bracelets, sea-creature charms. At one of the displays I see a shark-tooth necklace and remember that I am leaving for İstanbul soon and still haven't lied to my mother about it.

Aslı has a summer villa in Çeşme, I tell her, making sure that each word I choose is absolutely necessary. The worst liars are caught in their home-spun webs because of extraneous information. She's invited me there—she and her family are going down on Sunday. Does that sound okay? I'll only stay a couple days.

"Sunday?" My mother evaluates her reflection in a mirror as she holds up a silver earring to the side of her face. "Sunday," she repeats. "When is Sunday?"

I tell her that it's two days from now. My mother asks about the price of the earrings to a woman in a paisley skirt standing near the door of the jewelry atelier. When the woman gives a number, it's clear from my mother's face that she cannot determine whether the price is too high, or too low.

"In dollars, it's quite cheap," she whispers to me. Then, at her normal volume, "Yes, that's fine. Çeşme's gorgeous, you'll love it. Just make sure they feed you there, okay? Oh, and come back by Wednesday." One by one, she flexes her fingers. "Yes, Sunday, Monday, Tuesday, Wednesday. You know what they say about guests. They're like fish. Three days max, or you start to stink. Excuse me? I'll take these, thank you."

I ask her if she thinks that Grandma will agree with the plan. Maybe my mother can help convince her when we return home that night? My grandmother is quick to make a scene whenever I take additional time away from her.

"Oh, there's no need," my mother replies. "That woman's reign is long over. You know," she adds, fastening her new earrings, "I am very happy that I found out they tore down the old movie theater in Beyoğlu. Very, very happy." Then she links her arm in mine, and we continue with our shopping.

⁓ ⚓ ⁓

Later that afternoon, in a series of best out of five, I hesitate during the first two backgammon games. On the third, I rap loudly on the board.

"Hey, Aslı." She looks up at me, annoyed that I broke her concentration. "I need you to do me a big, gigantic favor."

Aslı has been staring at the two six-doors I set up after the toss of an early *dü şeş*, double sixes, speechless at my consistent luck with the game. There's a sensation that overtakes me as soon as I grip the tiny dice. My vision sharpens, and I am electrified by the adrenaline as my mind races through strategies to break an opponent's piece. I know that for every toss, the numbers that eventually end right side up will work to my advantage. The feeling is strong enough for the other player to sense it, thereby completely destroying their morale.

"Remind me, did we bet on anything?" she asks. Then she picks up the dice and rolls them lazily on the board, taking on the airs of someone for whom defeat is inevitable.

"We didn't, and come on, don't be like that. It takes the fun out of the whole thing, and we've only just started," I say. "Remember: There's always a chance."

"What do you need?"

"You have to promise not to tell anyone."

Aslı smiles at this. "I won't," she says, "but I can't promise you that they won't find out."

"Just do your best."

"Tell me what it is already." Her focus is back on the game, plotting out her next move.

I lean across the table, clasping my hands at my chest until I manage to direct her attention back to me. "On Sunday I need to head out of town for a few days, and I told my mom that I'd be going down to Çeşme with you. But I'm actually going to İstanbul."

"What?" Aslı pauses her player midway, the round wooden piece hovering above the slim triangles. "How am I supposed to go along with that story? We all practically live on top of each other. She'll spot me at the beach and figure it out. I'm giving you ten seconds to think of a new plan."

"I know, I know, I know," I say, counting ahead to where she's about to place her piece. Wrong move, definitely the wrong move. "But my mom almost never sets foot in the Small Club itself except to talk to me—she won't see you. And she only swims in the late afternoons and evenings, anyway, otherwise she sits at the drop-off at the north end of the beach in her tent. The only thing I need from you is to not walk past our house when you head over here."

"But there's no other entrance to the Small Club except through the oleander path."

"There's no other official entrance, you're right, but there is another way to get here. In the mornings when you come, hop the fence near the end of the beach, across from the children's park." I scoop up the dice for my turn and roll. One of the numbers lands me right on an unprotected piece of Aslı's. I break it and set the dead player in the middle of the board.

"Why don't you just tell her that you're going to İstanbul and not get me wrapped up in this whole thing?" Delicately, Aslı picks up the dice from the board and massages them in her hands.

"It won't make any sense to her, why I would do something like that alone. She'll want to come with me, she'll ask about logistics. She'll wonder why I want to go to the city by myself in the middle of a sticky urban summer when we could just book our bus tickets to return earlier and spend an extra few days in the city together. My mother picks up on nonsensical inconsistencies like that. There's no way she'll fall for it."

"Oh," she says, and presses her hands closer together, nearly crushing the dice. "I see where we're going with this. You're not going to İstanbul alone, are you?" When she asks, her eyes work their way over my entire body. I pause for only half a second, but can see that she already has her answer.

"The less you know, the better," I say. "I don't want to make you complicit in anything. Now roll already."

Aslı leans into her chair without lowering her gaze. She's looking for the tell, but after our encounter at Sıfır, everything should already be quite clear to her. I keep my cool anyway, staying as nonchalant as possible about the whole thing. Out of nowhere, as if she's just remembered something, Aslı starts to laugh.

"All good there?" I ask.

She looks at me, a bit more serious now, but I cut her off before she can reprimand me. "I know you think he's creepy," I say, "but I don't really want to hear it right now."

"All right, all right," Aslı agrees. Then she shakes the dice with a renewed vigor, releasing them onto the board with a flourish. I immediately
map out all possible moves. Each die could land one of her pieces on my
only two singles on the board. She hits one; then she hits the other.

"I'd be careful about this trip, though," she says, placing both my pieces
into purgatory with a big smile. "Looks like your luck's taking a turn for
the worse."

17

THE ROAD TRIP

On the border between two *sites*, I stare at my lavender-painted toes in the quiet chill of morning until Levent's SUV pulls up. His knuckles crack white on the wheel, but there is a forced serenity to the rest of him. Like the way he tilts his head back into the headrest, the dusty road reflected in his sunglasses, concealing any panic that might linger in his gaze. Even his forehead is masked in a wide-brimmed baseball cap. I wait by the side of the road, unacknowledged. My hand travels to graze the knots of my mother's white eyelet dress tied at my shoulders. I'm frightened that they might undo of their own accord, suddenly aware that they are holding on to the wrong body.

Finally, Levent shuffles around to check that the doors are indeed unlocked, then lifts a hand in an exasperated gesture. *What are you waiting for?* I walk up to the car, get in. It was difficult, I suppose, to erase away the possibility of his saying, *She flagged me down, she opened the door and hopped in,* but that is a possibility I don't want him to have. The way the story has to go is that it was something that we both wanted, and all the actions and reactions need to be played accordingly. I know what one-way desire can do to a person. It can exile her to unknown countries.

The leather slides cool and hard under my legs. Our only glance at each other is when I turn to toss my duffel bag in the back seat, but all I see in his sunglasses is a reflection of myself in motion. A canary-yellow-and-navy medallion jerks around from under the rearview mirror as the car hobbles out of our *site*. I'm surprised that soccer fanaticism had won out over the usual evil eye protection. I almost comment on the lack of talismans, but then click my tongue *no* in conversation with myself. Instead, I turn up the music, and am satisfied to hear that it's Fikret Kızılok in the CD player. Things are moving along as planned, and there is no need for talismans, anyway.

Through the window, the olive groves that shielded our rendezvous in half-built homes flash past us, and we head toward the single lane road that runs by the water. I recognize the next song and sing. I remember my mother singing it, just a few years ago. We had been walking out of a restaurant on the Avenue with tired eyes and bags of takeaway, and as the song faded behind us, my mother picked up the thread and continued with the lyrics.

"Those aren't the words," Levent says, interrupting my memory.

"What?"

"He's saying 'My wineglass fills with you,'" Levent explains, holding up a calloused finger. "Not 'You become my fate.' It's *'kadehime,'* not *'kaderime.'*" I reach up to wrap my own fingers around his and pull down. I press the finger against my thigh, roll it around with my palm. He lets me.

"Don't talk to me like that," I say quietly.

"Like what?" Levent keeps his attention steady on the road.

"Like a parent." I turn down the music so I won't have to listen to anything that I can't fully understand. "As if everything I learn, I can only learn through you."

We drive in silence for a while, him stopping at gas stations for snacks and restroom breaks unprompted by my needs. At a Petrol Ofisi, I fill a styrofoam cup with coffee and am mixing in cream with a stir stick when

Levent comes up to me holding three cylindrical packages of cookies. Chocolate with vanilla filling, vanilla with chocolate filling, and chocolate with chocolate filling. "Which one do you want?" he asks. His question is serious.

"They're all variations on the same theme," I answer in English.

"What?"

"I don't eat cookies," I tell him. I don't want him to get the wrong impression of me. "I'm an athlete. Isn't there any trail mix or something? Or fruit?"

"You're a kid," Levent says, offering up the cookies again, as if I hadn't gotten a good enough look the first time. The green-and-white branding glares in the fluorescent lighting. "Kids love cookies."

I mock his eager facial expression. "Levent, I'm nineteen years old." Then he breaks out into a full grin, the first light on his face I've seen all day. It feels like an accomplishment, being able to make him smile.

"I'll go find the trail mix," he says. He tosses the cookies on the closest shelf, where they don't belong, next to a package of onion rings and raisins, and methodically works his way through the aisles.

Back in the car, I set my packets of hazelnuts and dried apricots—Turkish trail mix, we'd joked—on the dashboard, not ready to start snacking until we are back on the highway. Maneuvering out of the station, Levent takes off his sunglasses to lift and lower the brim of his dampening hat. Rivulets of sweat run down his eyebrows, drop from his lashes onto his cheeks. He runs a hand all over his face. "What's wrong with this air conditioner?" he mutters, fiddling with the dials. The car is new, and there is nothing wrong with the air conditioner. I roll down my window and change conditions for the worse.

"Don't, Meltem, the hell are you doing, it's boiling out there." His words hit him just as he's tapped the button on his side to bring my window back up. He pauses long enough to sense the air, to see whether I've noticed what he's said. Then he's brave enough to look at me, but his expression has been hardened through years of practice and shows no sign of remorse. "I mix things up sometimes," he says, his lips twitching into a half smile. "Try not to take it personally or anything."

We pull into the on-ramp of the highway, spiraling out. "It's all right," I say. "You did say we resembled each other."

"The way she used to look," he corrects, and tilts his body back to apply pressure on the gas. "Before all that time passed." There is a soft lurch as we transition from one speed to the next, and then we are acclimated, even the surface of my coffee steadying, as we continue at our faster pace.

⚓

Our next stop is not until an hour later, in the town of Susurluk. We park beside the intercity buses, and immediately to our left is the blue-and-white coach that I take every summer. Its logo, a female centaur, holds her bow and arrow with a steady aim. I swell with pride at the fact that I am no longer bound by the bus schedule, the last remaining rigidity of my summers. Isn't that what it means to live somewhere? It means there are options, other lives than those prescribed.

"Susurluk is famous for its *ayran*," says Levent.

"I know." I slam the car door behind me, and shudder as I adjust to the aridity. We're deep inland now, and with each breath, dust settles into my nostrils. Parts of the earth work their way inside me.

The rest stop resembles a lower-tier mall with an expansive food court. I head over to a small shop for some shampoo and conditioner, and end up buying a brand whose commercials I had seen in İstanbul. A woman with flowing hair turns around at the end of the shot as a man outside the frame narrates, "Head-turning, voluminous hair." I figure that Levent probably doesn't have any shampoo for women who don't already have voluminous hair. I also pick up a box of candied chestnuts for my mother, as a thank-you for her unwitting permission.

At the food court, I order lentil soup, meatballs, and eggplant stuffed with minced meat. Levent orders a cheeseburger and a Diet Coke, then tells the cashier, "And an *ayran* for my daughter." As the young boy at the register reaches into the fridge for the frothy yogurt drink, I run my hand up along the side of Levent's body, then back down his arm, feeling the goose bumps rise. He flinches but says nothing. The cashier pretends not to notice and passes Levent my drink, who hands it to me with a slight tremor. The entire interaction goes unmentioned. When we sit down at the table and begin to eat, Levent looks over at the shop where I bought my volumizing shampoo and asks me if I'd like to hear a story. I say yes, always.

≈ ⚓ ≈

At his job (Levent tells me), he's a top-level executive at a grocery store chain. It's headquartered in Paris with global branches, though from his İstanbul office he's specifically responsible for the Middle East and North Africa markets. Years ago, as part of his onboarding, he and another fresh-faced colleague were tasked with visiting various stores in the region with the goal of getting to know the workers and enhancing their operational understanding. The stores they visited ranged in size and geography: small mini-marts on the outskirts of İstanbul, gargantuan hypermarkets between towns, and discount stores along urban avenues with heavy foot traffic. Born and raised in İstanbul, Levent was familiar with the urban shopping experience, and often bought his own groceries (to the extent that he did purchase them, instead of going out to prix fixe dinners with colleagues and friends) from the same, well-known brand to whose corporate office he headed each morning in his tailored suit and silk tie.

The onboarding kicked off with visits to a few İstanbul branches. However, Levent and the new colleague soon extended their radii outside their usual spheres to stores in neighborhoods they wouldn't have been able to locate on a map. At one particular market, as he met with staff and inspected the shelves and committed to memory the location's top-selling products, Levent happened to notice an unattended shopping cart near the main exit. The cart had been filled to the brim with bottles of detergent, packets of sponges, boxes of biscuits, several packages of minced meat, rolls of paper towels, a bundle of mandarin-scented candles, and a host of other random items in flashy, colorful packaging. Levent challenged himself to pull together a customer profile as he observed the brand names and products. A family? A bachelor? Two young female roommates? As he held more and more customer segments up for trial, he realized that the exercise was futile. There was no—could not be any—rhyme or reason to the unmade purchases. He didn't make much of it, mentioned it to no one, and filed it away as an interesting anecdote as the two colleagues continued with their training.

As they traveled to more and more stores, the number of abandoned-cart sightings by the door began to increase. Carts that had been lovingly filled with all sorts of home items and kitchenware, then left by the exit. Levent contemplated each cart of this sort that he came across, racking his brain to understand the inherent pattern that must surely be among them. But, similar to the first cart, they were all a hodgepodge of unrelated items, from boxes of paper plates to bottles of lemon-scented *kolonya* to Eti Cicibebe cookies, and the only thing they had in common was that they were all full, each one packed with as many items and brands as possible. Cheap and high-end, brand-name and generic. He wondered out loud what they could mean, but his fellow executive merely shrugged, indicating that as a born-and-bred İstanbulite, he had never been able to make sense of the outer-city mindset, either. Finally, at the sixth store where abandoned carts abounded, Levent brought up the matter with the store manager.

The manager smiled as Levent explained the bewildering sights he'd seen. Instead of giving a direct response, she asked him to follow her to the control room, where a series of monitors displayed scenes from each corner of the store. The store manager tapped on a screen to bring Levent's attention to a young couple in gray scale and clearly in love, fingers entwined while pushing a shopping cart together. Slowly and deliberately, the couple worked their way down each aisle, browsing and selecting products with brows furrowed in concentration. The girl wore a long dress patterned with fat roses, her hair clipped back in bird-shaped barrettes. The boy sported a button-down that hung off his lanky body, then was tucked into a pair of pants held up by a thin belt. His hair had been slicked in pomade.

As the couple meandered down the aisles, the store manager continued to tap on the relevant monitors so that Levent and the other executive could follow the journey. The girl gazed adoringly into the boy's eyes; the boy put an arm around the girl's shoulders. Into their cart they tossed organic chicken breast, soy-marinated tofu, generic pasta sauce, high-end bleach for white cottons, fabric softener on sale. Into their cart went dog food, then cat food. Levent watched with his mouth half open until the very last monitor, the one connected to the camera by the main doors, showed the couple heading toward the exit, each smiling an impish little smile as they parted ways with their cart just before the cash registers.

The store manager turned to the two trainees and crossed her arms.

"Well?" she asked. "What do you think just happened?"

Levent and the executive were dumbfounded.

"Date night," the store manager explained. Behind her, the monitors resumed their coverage of everyday, predictable shoppers. They checked prices, placed items back. "It's the packaging, the color, something outside of their dreary lives. Play-pretend, you see. All the products they can never afford, for the home they'll never have. Multiple pets. Windows to clean, personal bathrooms to disinfect, carpets whose wine stains need to be removed. Four-course dinners to prepare. For the hours that they're among the aisles, these shoppers are living out a fantasy."

⚓

Levent pauses at the end of his story for my reaction. He doesn't seem satisfied with my shrug.

"But don't you think it's bizarre?" He pierces the air again and again with a french fry, trying to make me understand. "Isn't that absolutely insane?"

I think of our day together in the olive groves, the eggs I had imagined Levent sizzling for me on the stove while I woke up on the floor and washed my face. I understood the shoppers perfectly. I could have spent even more time in the bathroom, preening in the mirror that wasn't there, brushing my hair with my fingers hooked like claws.

"Totally," I agree. "Absolutely insane." I break off pieces of bread and sop up what's left of my lentil soup.

⚓

I can't tell exactly when it is that we reach the city limits of İstanbul. There should be a road sign in blue, following a previous blue sign with a red slash through it, but I miss both. Without spotting the signs, it's impossible to tell. It's not at all like the plane landing, where for a long while you are not, and then, suddenly, as the wheels make contact with the runway, you are. There's heavy traffic on some streets but not on others, and after several stop-and-starts, we find ourselves on the crest of a hill in Arnavutköy, parked in front of a five-story apartment building overlooking the Bosphorus.

18

THE CITY

We are farther up the European coastline than I have ever ventured before. My grandmother's condo near the Marmara Sea remains empty somewhere southward, below, behind. I slide onto a black leather couch, still heated from the late-afternoon sun. It catches at my skin and squelches, complaining that it needs more time to conform to my body. The house is minimalist. I see no resemblance to any items my mother carried with her across the ocean. The only things of any note are a few comic books horizontally stacked on a bookshelf and a framed photograph of Levent in a cap and gown, for his university graduation. I turn and wait for him to tell me what we're going to do.

Levent occupies himself with everything that is not me. He puts things in their places, cleans the edges of the apartment. A soft light under a big-screen television drifts to sleep, awakens, drifts off again. Levent runs a rag all across the screen and its frame. He does the same with the beveled mirror above the king-size bed in the living room, which reflects a scene out the window: two boys in their underwear splashing in the

Bosphorus. Their jumps upset a fishing boat with tangled netting, which now rocks in the current they've created. As Levent works the rag over the glass, the scene sharpens, and water ripples cleanly through the walls.

"It bothers me to come back to a place looking like this. Usually I call the housekeeper, but this time . . ." His voice trails off, but what he means to say is that my presence would have made it awkward.

"Really?" I ask. "Your Ayvalık villa is a disaster. I could never have guessed you were so careful about cleaning."

"Well, I don't really live there," he says. "How's the dust? Are you able to breathe?" Levent cranks a lever and pulls open a floor-to-ceiling window, behind which is a short, glass balcony railing. The boys sharpen another turn inside the mirror.

I nod, signaling that my airflow is perfect.

"Excellent." Levent sits on the edge of the bed and sighs, tossing the dust rag back and forth in his hands. When he finally looks up at me, I feel my weight double. In İstanbul, both of us take up more space, grow substantial. Now I don't have to make up everything anymore. In fact, there, right there down the hall, is the kitchen where Levent really will make me eggs in the morning. My desire has been frothing at the edges like coffee in preparation, foaming dark and thick on the sides, crawling up along the copperware. I twitch and smother the fire. Not yet not yet not yet.

Levent says something about the schedule for the next few days, how his meeting will be in the morning but we can get together in the afternoon and explore the city, take another day to relax, and head back to Ayvalık the following day. On Wednesday, he clarifies.

"I'll order in for us tonight," he says. "Kebabs okay?"

"We're eating in?" I prop myself on my elbows on the backrest of the couch. "My first real trip to İstanbul, and we're eating in? What's Arnavutköy famous for? Let's have whatever that is."

Levent shakes his head. "It's famous for its seafood restaurants along the shoreline, but we can't do that. Too many people know me here." He notices the disappointment on my face and resets. "It'll have to be dine-in tonight, Ada. I'm sorry. How about tomorrow I take you out, and tonight, we order from the kebab place around the corner?"

"Yeah, fine," I say, falling back into the cushions. "Kebabs are fine." *Kebabs are for tourists*, I think.

From the open window, the stifling city heat pours in as the boys wrestle in the water, each trying to push the other down far enough so that they can step on shoulders with their feet and sink the other slowly to the seafloor. Behind them a tanker trudges along, bearing its rust-orange cargo. People do not know how far away the things they want are, the mountains and oceans they have to traverse to get to them. "How spicy is it?" Levent asks from the back room, ordering through the telephone. "Could you make it less spicy?" It's important to make things look easy.

Summer air surrounds one differently in the city. It's speckled with dirt, and there's a haze to it. It's not that clean-cut sun with its Aegean breeze. It weighs on the body and cakes like clay, doesn't slick down with sweat, isn't licked off by salt water. I shuffle around to crane my head back on the couch, my throat arched to the sky, as if waiting for a drop of rain. I swallow in the solid air.

Arnavutköy, I will tell my mother, *is famous for its seafood restaurants. But you don't have to worry about remembering anymore. I'm here now.*

Though Levent's apartment has several other rooms, nearly all the furniture has been collected in the living space. The leather couch, the television, the bed, the wooden dining table that's pushed out toward the edge of the balcony railing. He's set the table already with plates and water glasses, as well as a single unlit tealight candle. While Levent unknots the plastic bags and lifts out the styrofoam packages, I take the candle and light it with a flame from the gas stove. There's a tiny IKEA sticker underneath. "There we go," I say, setting the candle back on the table. "That'll give us a bit more ambiance." Levent looks up at my comment but says nothing. With two spoons, he distributes the food from the boxes to our plates. Yachts skim the water, their greens and purples glowing aliens among the softer lights. The second bridge turns on its infant bulbs, which intensify as the sky darkens. As I unfold a napkin across my lap and take in the view, I have to admit that maybe this is better than having gone out on the town. I bite into a piece of lamb kebab and am disappointed to find that it has already cooled from its journey over.

"Mmm." I hold up my fork in a gesture of admiration. "Good choice."

Levent fiddles with the stereo near the television. I wince at each cacophonic eruption until he turns up the volume on Satie, *Gymnopédie* no. 1. The music pours in with the thinnest thread of static. "I have a talent," Levent says, "for choosing the ideal music to match the current moment."

"Is that so?" I tease him. "And what is it about our current environment that led you to this selection?"

He mulls over my question, as if it weren't a perfectly natural inquiry after such a comment. "I suppose . . ." His eyes flash toward the bed. "I suppose it reminds me of something peaceful." I make a sound that suggests I'm unsatisfied with the explanation, but will make an exception and tolerate a simple adjective. "Have you heard this piece before?" he asks. I nod. "Oh, really?" He seems surprised. "Well, what does it make you think of?"

I think of the day Ian and I were driving back from Potrero Hill, after having seen the house where I didn't want to live. "It makes me think of places that aren't mine," I answer. Before he can ask me what I mean, the water outside shatters itself. It begins to rain, a hard, abrupt summer storm. Levent quickly gets up to close the main window, and we look out at the world through the glass. How unexpected, we murmur, mesmerized by the shift in the weather. How untimely.

⚓

After dinner, Levent takes out his laptop to review some spreadsheets, and I pick up the phone, walk down the hall, and close the bathroom door behind me. Perched uncomfortably on the edge of the Jacuzzi, I try to think like a rational person might. "I'm here, he wants me here, he brought me here," I repeat under my breath. Out of the corner of my eye, my reflection sneaks a look back at me. I look frightened. I imagine

Levent, hear the thumping footfalls on the dock like a heavy metronome, watch the sleek contortions of his body as he folds down, extends out, and slips below the surface of the water. Then there is the man who ordered in kebabs, ran a rag over his television set. But then there is the man who, every night, I fantasize about rescuing me from the Aegean.

There is only one person who might be able to talk me out of this. Before I can change my mind, I dial Ian's number.

An automated recording informs me that the party I'm trying to reach is currently unavailable. There must be some mistake. I redial. Again, the lady robot. I stare at the phone in my hand and calculate the hour. It's Sunday morning in San Francisco, early enough that Ian shouldn't have left the house yet. There is no reason that he wouldn't pick up. Unless . . .

Unless he's realized that something's wrong. That it's not normal for someone you're dating to forget about you for an entire summer, calling to check in only when convenient. *It's just that I'm not indoors or near a phone that often*, I would say to him, trying to explain the infrequency of my calls. It's unnatural for someone you're dating to not even entertain the thought of spending the summer together, especially after you take her to an orange-and-green house on a hill with two beautiful palm trees, because you know that she will love it. Ian's not an idiot, but I have been treating him like one.

How did I ever think that I could get away with this?

I dial the number for our summer villa, but it's my grandmother who picks up.

"Hello?"

"Is Mom there?"

"Oh, Ada. It's you." My grandmother sounds strangely disappointed, but her voice quickly readjusts. "No, your mother's out for her sunset swim. Everything all right in . . ." She pauses before she gives the name, and my heart skips a beat as I try to remember all the lies I told, who I told them to, the order in which I told them. ". . . in Çeşme? That's where you are, right?"

"Yeah, everything's fine, I just wanted to talk to Mom for a bit. I'll call back another time. Bye." I press the End Call button before she has a chance to say goodbye, then throw the phone to the opposite wall. It cracks, and the batteries tumble, along with the receiver, into a bidet.

"You all right over there?" Levent calls from the living room.

"Yeah, I'm fine," I say. "I think I'm going to take a bath."

"What?"

"I THINK I'M GOING TO TAKE A BATH."

Crunched into the Jacuzzi, I slowly peel off my mother's dress and toss it over the edge onto the bath mat. Then I turn the jets to their hottest setting and let the water rise up to meet me. Maybe it's a good thing that nobody will be able to stop me, I think. Maybe I really can get away with living the life I've always wanted.

I soak in the bath for an hour, taking in large mouthfuls of air whenever I feel a rush of sadness about my mother. So close to home, yet locked in a villa in the middle of nowhere with my grandmother. Held hostage at the edge of the world by a man who entertains American women at Greek restaurants. Eventually, I climb out and brush my teeth with toothpaste for sensitive gums, wash my face with coconut-scented hand soap, gently pull my pajamas over my pruned body, and step into the living room. Levent doesn't even look up. I slow down my movements, open the comforter with an exaggerated gesture, yawn loudly as I crawl under the sheets. But Levent continues to type from the couch, his fingers contorting themselves for the shortcuts. After a few minutes, he heads to one of the other rooms and comes back with a blanket and pillow, which he tosses on the couch for himself. "Good night, Ada," he says. "I'll see you in the afternoon, after my meeting." He tells me that he'll likely be up before me, but that he'll leave a note about where we can meet after everything's wrapped up at the office. I pretend that I am already asleep and give no answer.

In my dream, my mother has aged into an infant who cannot remember anything from her life as a young woman, and so I head into the forest to forage for her memories. *Here you are with your raspberry-pistachio cone in Moda, here you are feeling the breeze skim over the Bosphorus, wondering how it can be possible to live and love in any other city. Here you are at the*

Grand Tarabya, watching another woman take the starring role of your life. I feed the scenes back to her with a tiny spoon in between her cries.

The sun from the window wakes me up early, and the first thing I see is the second bridge, its long lines of vehicles humming back and forth. There are signs on the bridges once you reach the other side, saying, *Welcome to Europe*, or, *Welcome to Asia*. It's a short distance, but they still celebrate the crossing.

Levent's left a note on the table, detailing logistics, keys, and where to meet him in Beyoğlu in the late afternoon. It's got a sketch showing how to get there and bills set aside for estimated taxi fare. And then some, I realize, counting it out.

I shower with my volumizing shampoo and wander around the apartment trying to pass the time until my hair dries. As I poke around the drawers on the television console, I spot a packet of playing cards.

Hello, old friend.

I sit cross-legged on the parquet and shuffle the cards into a bridge. The fluttering calms me, and I can almost hear the cries of the kids among the tables with their tangerine floaties, the whoops of boys in a stampede as they race to jump off the dock. I make my wish, cut the deck, and lay out my clock fortune. When the deck begins to shift from the monotony of its back design to the scramble of colors and numbers and royalty, I check the middle of my circle and notice that a king has yet to arrive. In fact, not only are there no kings, but there are no jacks, either. None of the men are here. Slipping out of my trance, I take each new card out of the pile with extreme concentration, turning it over deliberately. All the cards that have been flipped over are in their correct spots. I'm sure of it.

The jacks finally appear, interspersed with their kings. I try to determine the chances, but arrive nowhere. The penultimate card is a queen, and from underneath her appears my very last card, my final king. I set him squarely in the middle, hands shaking. I stand up, eyeing the cards from above. Everything is correct. Every card on its hour, every number in its place, all the royalty in their thrones. I leave the set as it is on the floor so that I can see it when I return in the evening, in order to confirm that this happened and understand what it means that it happened today, in this house, in this city. I stand up, collapse as the blood drains from my head, and try again. The message is clear: I am going to get away with it.

⚓

I am alone and have not yet been touched, but the city is beautiful and that makes it okay. Joggers hustle down the promenade in bright neons, their foreheads shimmering with sunscreen. The water is an electric blue, unburdened from its night of trading tankers between the seas. Fishermen unfold camping chairs along the shoreline and sit with their large yogurt buckets filled with water and feed. A cabdriver honks as he slows down for my decision, then speeds up after my dismissal. There's time; I'll take the next one.

When the taxi I do flag down drops me off at my requested destination, I realize I've made a big mistake. İstiklal Avenue is the one place in İstanbul I know on this side of the Bosphorus, but it's also the most crowded and tourist-drenched area of the city. Everyone who has been to İstanbul, even for the briefest of stopovers, has walked along this pedestrian thoroughfare, taken photos of the vintage red-and-white tram that runs its length. There is nothing special about this place, I reprimand myself. But I am here now. I buy an ear of steamed, salted corn from a vendor and begin the long walk from Taksim Square toward Galata Tower, remembering to look up at the cafés and erotica shops and hidden venues on the second floors, third floors, fourth floors. If I'm going to walk down a well-worn path, I may as well notice the sorts of things that might escape the fleeting attentions of others. Let others take their photographs of the Republic Monument in the square, frame the incongruity of fast-food establishments in neoclassical buildings, or capture the mangle of bodies that can congregate on a single avenue in the only city that connects the world. My sights, on the contrary, will always be set slightly higher.

I give myself over to the flow, but can't quite catch the rhythm of it.

My feet scrape the ankles of the men in front of me; I slam into low-set strollers beneath my line of vision. I appear in several photographs I can't think quickly enough to sidestep, and accidentally drop my half-eaten cob to the floor after running into a pomegranate juice stand while trying to avoid the oncoming tram. After a series of near-accidents, I take to the side streets. *I've been coming here for years*, I tell myself, trying to feel more comfortable. (*You've been coming* here *for years*, says Aslı, gesturing to the Small Club. *Notice the perimeter of what you're used to.*)

But in the side streets, I trip over the blank spaces where bricks shaped like farfalle have been removed. The tired gazes of old men sipping tea atop wicker stools trail me on my backtracks as I turn from yet another dead-end alley. I gaze enviously at the shopkeepers and restaurateurs who stand in front of their buildings and smoke, their arms resting across their chests in the crook of an elbow, watching the parade of the day go by. *Don't you already know this place by heart?* I ask them silently. *Haven't you already seen it all, living here, in every season, at every hour of every day?* Nobody knows that I am not actually alone, that I am here in this city with someone. In fact, I am going to meet him shortly. In fact, despite it still being early, I am going to start heading there right now. I may not look it, but I have somewhere to be.

I return to the main avenue with a renewed sense of purpose and scan the sky for the famous Genoese tower and its directional guidance. The sun, of course, is of no help in the noontime. Clumsily dodging ditches, tourists' ankles, and skewed brickwork, I walk toward our rendezvous point. But just as I'm about to reach my destination, an imposing set of gates flashes on my left. These are not new to me; I have seen them before. I stop to inspect the gates and quickly recognize them from my mother's photo albums. These gilded gates are the entrance to her high school. So this is where she studied. I crane my neck to get a better look at the impressive insignias placed over the wrought iron. The gates, flanked by stone columns, are several times my height. I peer through them for a glimpse of the academic buildings, but the thin spaces between the railings reveal only segments of a grander facade, mostly hidden by the courtyard trees.

For the next hour or so, I trace all possible paths to the gate within a

quarter-mile radius. I walk down each direction from the avenue, inch-
ing along the inclines and huffing back up the zigzags of the alleyways.
Each time, I return to the lycée through a different route, having lived
through a slightly different experience, the colors and scents and sounds
and slopes shifting. If I work through all possibilities, then I will have
taken at least one walk to school in exactly the way my mother had. In
a very small way, I will know what it's like to live her life. My hair starts
to meld to the back of my neck, and my blouse, sleeveless and airy, has
soaked through to the skin. I clutch the iron rails with both hands, knowing that they will never open for me.

≈ ⚓ ≈

"What the hell happened to you?"

In a café named after and owned by one of İstanbul's famed photog-
raphers, monochrome prints hang on the walls, chronicling the city's history. At a table in the corner, in the refracted afternoon sunlight cutting
in through the stained glass windows, sits Levent with knitted brows.

"I took a very, very long walk," I say, flipping open a menu.

"You walked around here? Ada, it's a hellhole out here. I only asked
to meet here because my last meeting was at the hotel down the street.
You could have at least explored the Cihangir neighborhood, maybe sat
in a café instead of spending time around this plague of people."

"I like this area," I say. I almost start to tell him about the restaurants,
the alleyways, the little boutiques once you go off the main road. About
how fascinating it is, actually, to watch the tourists and the trams and the
corn on the cob vendors find their spaces around each other in a chaotic
yet choreographed dance. But instead, I excuse myself for the restroom.
There, in a tiny capsule with walls papered in advertisements for women
from past decades, all in shades of pink and magenta, I wash my face. I
stick my hands up my blouse to pat down the sweat with paper towels.
I look in the mirror and turn my head from side to side, touch the heat
emanating off my flushed cheeks. *Why didn't I go to Cihangir?* I ask myself.
Where is Cihangir?

We order salads for our mains and profiteroles in heavy chocolate sauce to share for dessert. As Levent chews, the lines around his mouth deepen and release, and the skin between his chin and neck softens. His youth is concentrated in his eyes, which bounce wildly around the room in a valiant effort to never meet mine. They jump from a photo of the Galata Bridge fishermen to the open doorway, resplendent with sunlight, to the raw, peeled skin of my left shoulder, to the countertop with the cash register and splayed brochures detailing this month's cultural events, sponsored mostly by banks. I keep trying to catch his gaze, chasing his eyes left and right and up and down with my own, but am always one direction behind.

Finally, his focus settles on me. "It's kind of funny," he says as I swirl shapes in the chocolate sauce with the tines of my fork, "that I'm the only person you know in this entire city."

"How does that make you feel?" The truth of the situation hits me only after I ask him. I am just a guest. A visitor, limited to the whims of my host.

"Responsible," he replies. He dips a finger into the sauce, running a thumbprint through my creation. "Powerful."

As the afternoon falls, we walk to Galata Tower, then down to the mouth of the Golden Horn, where we cross the bridge to the historic peninsula. "We can come here," he says, "because here, there are only tourists. Nobody I know will be on this peninsula." I understand, I say. Levent buys us two tickets for Topkapı Palace, paying extra for the harem. He does not remember much of the palace history, but instead relies on the brochures at the reception. He offers me one. "It's in English," he says when I look at him in surprise. I had planned on him being my guide. We walk through hallways of İznik tiles and waiting rooms of the past, with him always hanging back by several steps, and I pose lavishly in front of Bosphorus views by the golden pavilion where fasting sultans once awaited sunset. I am so happy to be in İstanbul. I jump into star shapes and blow kisses at the camera I've handed him. Levent puts his hands together and pleads that I take it down a notch.

"I don't care," I yell across the tourists streaming into our untaken photograph. Museumgoers turn to look at me, chuckling at my enthusiasm as they flap their brochures like fans. "This is your city. I've got no skin in the game." These people from Canberra and Bristol and Montreux and Kuala Lumpur and Djibouti—would they even notice the incongruity of our ages when they themselves are wandering so deeply inside other centuries? Later on, I hum loudly while strolling along the walkways of the Basilica Cistern to hear my melodies bounce along the damp stone walls. I gaze up at the circular medallions in Hagia Sophia and converse with a cat sunning itself where the light comes in near the *minber*. In the Blue Mosque, I smile widely at everyone standing with me in line as we wait to take off our shoes, layer cotton scarves over our hair. At the moments when Levent is not annoyed, I catch him watching me with an intrigued look. It is as close as he allows himself to get to me—a curious gaze from his end, a wink from mine, then an embarrassed expression from him—even though we are far from any nosy neighbors, listening behind dividing walls.

Along the Golden Horn, the crowded lines of the fishermen drape over the Galata Bridge still and steady, breaking up the panorama like cracks in an old film.

I begin to fade into a fever of nostalgia for city transformations I had never lived to see, those even beyond my mother's lifetime. They flash one by one in my mind's eye: Forests diminishing, cranes littering the horizon as skyscrapers paint the landscape with their pinstripes. Ottoman caïques (entire centuries, I had missed!) morphing into taller and fuller steel passenger boats; the swelling of İstanbul's population, the crowds gathering at the wharves darkening a larger portion of each snapshot through time. And then, and yet, there is the Bosphorus. Through all the years, she's stayed exactly the same. Who saw her then could recognize her now, time travelers seeking solace in the familiar. The queen of it all, wholly uninterested in her admirers, their absences. Preoccupied instead with her own beauty, the heavy draw of her silken train.

≈ ⚓ ≈

At night, when we return to the apartment, we're too tired to go out, and anyway, I'm sticky from the sweat of the day. Levent orders pizza for us. Once the boxes are empty, he sets them outside the door for the building custodian to dispose of, and brings out his pillow and blanket for the couch. Before he turns off the lights, I steal a glance at the kings on the floor.

"Hey," I whisper in the dark, lifting one arm out from under the bed-sheet. "Come here."

There's a silence, then a rustling, then the soft padding of his steps as he walks along the parquet toward our bed. Levent unbuttons his shirt, slides off his belt, his pants. Something I have wanted forever begins as he slips under the covers, and at our feet and above our heads, the water flows on, its currents switched in the reflection. He moves a hand across the bed toward my hip. I wait, then inch closer, then closer again. We start with two points of contact, then five; then there is nothing left.

As we kiss, my mother's voice in my head: *I know something you don't know.*

I keep my eyes shut until I am positioned so that when I open them I can look upon the water. Until I can see something that was exactly the same as when she had seen it.

As he turns me over, my own voice in my head: *Please oh please oh please continue mistaking me for someone else forever.*

19

THE SPA

The morning light comes in through the big window, and the edges of the furniture twinkle, a thousand stars in the room. Levent isn't in bed. I feel alone and uprooted, and try to recall the sensations from last night. The sex had been cold and transactional, meaning I had to imagine my way back into desire. The rhythms of his breathing became waves at sea, his hand running up my leg the heavy sunlight at noon. How is it that when I am exactly where I need to be, I am not present at all? This can't be it, this frustrating feeling. I'll need to try harder.

Levent is in the kitchen salting small plates of cut tomatoes and cucumbers. I lean against the doorway for a bit, watching his back. "Good morning," he says, but he doesn't turn toward me. There's a breadbasket on the counter, and I take it and carry it to the table, which has already been set while I was sleeping. Then I lock myself in the bathroom to get ready for the day. As I put on my mascara, I give myself a little smile in the mirror. So this is what it would be like—my other possible life. *Stay with this, Ada,* I think. *Stay with it.*

≈⚓≈

Over breakfast, I plead with Levent to give me the local's tour, but his only concession is to take me to a single art museum in Karaköy. "And then we're right back across the bridge to Sultanahmet," he says. In the galleries of the museum, we admire oil on canvas at opposite ends of a constantly rotating circle, as if we're tied together with string. He considers the view from a window where a tableau might have been, the seagulls screeching across the sky as the rain thunders down, with the walls and minarets of the historic peninsula in the background. I walk with my neck craned, mesmerized by a ticker above a doorway that flips to display all the names that the city has tried on, shed, been summoned by but never answered to. There are many that I do not know. I concentrate in an attempt to ink them into the more indelible files of my memory.

At the museum café, I stick a long-stemmed spoon into my ice cream sundae while Levent looks on, alert and on edge. With shaking hands, he lifts a tea glass to his lips, and the saucer clatters on the descension. "Don't worry," I say, and place a hand on his shoulder. "It's the middle of the workday. And besides, even for those who aren't working, they're all down in their own summer villas this time of year, aren't they?" He nods, and underneath my palm, I can feel him unclench. Very quickly, so fast that I almost miss it, he turns his head to the side and kisses my hand. I finish my dessert and ask for a slice of mosaic cake, drawing out the summer afternoon for as long as I possibly can.

Due to the weather, we take a cab instead of walking, and Levent tells the driver where we're going. I give him a confused look. "Isn't that a hotel?" I ask.

"That's right," says Levent.

"So this entire morning when I was complaining about how you only took me to the tourist sites, none of what I said made it into your brain? It's not enough that we have to spend all our time in Sultanahmet, but now you're taking me to a hotel?"

"Trust me, Ada, this hotel has the best massages in the city."

The driver glances at us through the rearview mirror.

"For foreigners, anyway," adds Levent, grinning.

"You're not funny at all."

When the taxi pulls over to a modern building with glass double doors, I push past Levent and sprint into the lobby, forging ahead until I locate the spa reception. While I wait for him to catch up, I scan the menu of services for the most expensive treatment, and book two of them.

We receive our massages in separate rooms by Balinese women who run electricity up my legs by pressing their elbows deep into my flesh, and inquire about my preferred pressure in broken English. No amount of kneading can untangle my muscles. I am frustrated and upset. Yesterday was fine, but I don't want to be stuck here on this peninsula when there is so much left to discover. I could be deboning fish on the shores of Arnavutköy or brunching at Rumelihisarı. But instead, I'm in a dark room with an Indonesian woman living a moment that I could be living anywhere. It's dark enough to be California. The masseuse slathers my body in globs of eucalyptus oil, and the scent mixes with the sound of raindrops that drizzle out from a small speaker nestled among the candles. When someone is no longer touching my body, I open my eyes and am pleased to find that I have slept through the experience.

I change quickly into my clothes and take a seat at reception to wait for Levent, who should be done with his massage around the same time. The only other people here are an older man immersed in a yachting magazine, sipping on a glass of water with floating plum slices, and a blond receptionist with a plastic rose in her hair speaking on the phone with a customer. The treatment has worked its magic, and I'm surprised at how relaxed my body feels. I am hopeful. Maybe Levent will take me out to dinner for our last night. If he does, I'll forgive him for today's tourism. That's fair, isn't it? He'll have to agree. I start to imagine what our evening might look like. A white-tablecloth dinner on the water, cloudy glasses of *rakı* and an array of colorful *mezes*, the surrounding tables filled with urbanite diners in silk blouses and button-downs who have just left the office and are easing into the evening with glasses of chilled white wine.

Then, at night, on the bed again. The black of the Bosphorus flashing in the mirror.

"Ready to head home?" Levent appears in the doorway, freshly showered, face flushed. The scent of the floral gel he's used in the shower reaches me from across the room, and my senses immediately heighten. Yes, I can definitely forgive him. "Hold tight while I pay, all right?"

Just as Levent turns toward the receptionist for the transaction, the door to the waiting room swings open. A conversation between two women wafts in, then booms at full force. The cadence of their voices catches me like a hook through the cheek—that smooth, honeyed American English. When the women step inside, the reel tightens, and my face lifts helplessly toward them.

Deniz presses her hand to her heart, upon the tiny buttons of her lilac-print dress that's soaked through with summer rain. "Ada?" Her voice is full of wonder, disbelieving. "Ada!" Next to her is Eliza, whose cheeks run black with a mascara that did not hold. "I didn't know you'd be in İstanbul!" Deniz throws herself on me for a hug. She twirls me around, and I catch a glimpse of Levent's shoulders jerking before I am set back to where I was. I kiss Eliza hello, and as we embrace, Levent slips behind the two women and quietly exits the spa.

My mind ravages itself in an attempt to recall any of the usual niceties. "How are you?" I stammer, and swing my arms to shake out the tremor.

"How are you, canım?" Eliza reaches over with hands veined like mountain ranges and strokes my hair, reaching all the way to the frayed ends that she pinches with her fingertips, as if to confirm that I'm really here. "Is your mother still at her treatment?"

"I came here alone," I say without thinking. I have no purse on me, no money, no jacket. Though I don't know her mother well, I do know that Deniz is too self-absorbed to be so observant about others. I pray that her mother is similar.

"Oh, this is so great, so great, I didn't think we were going to overlap in

Turkey at all." Deniz paces around the lobby, makes as if tossing confetti here and there. She speaks too loudly for this spa reception, too loudly for this country. "You said at the Republic Day party that you spent the entire summer months in Ayvalık. We just got here yesterday, we're staying at this hotel, actually! Then heading down to Fethiye for our Blue Voyage tour this weekend. Are you two still here a few days? Maybe we could all get dinner tonight in Eminönü? You're on the Anatolian side, right? At your grandmother's?" She glances at her mother, who's nodding along with each piece of information, trying to make sense of the timeline of events.

"Well, I'm not staying—"

"Yes, yes!" Eliza cries. She finally grasps the coincidence and its accompanying scheduling possibilities. "Dinner, of course!" The man with the plum water looks up and, in a thick Russian accent, politely asks us to keep our voices down. Eliza continues on gleefully.

Deniz's words are still echoing through my mind. *Are you two still . . .* Had she noticed us before, when we first got out of the cab? Me rushing into the hotel, him yelling after me? Perhaps they had been to the museum earlier, seen us there. Perhaps this was not our first encounter today. "Us two?" I ask, in the most innocent tone I can muster. I hold my breath.

"You and your mother," clarifies Eliza, completely oblivious to my impending breakdown. "There's a great *meyhane* in one of these little side streets, they do the small plates, you know. Does Meltem enjoy *rakı*? We could have a girls' night in the city. Deniz doesn't really know anyone, and you know I'm tired of meeting with my husband's old classmates all the time—"

"Excuse me." The receptionist with the rose in her hair interrupts us, her face beaming from above the counter. All of us turn, but she directs her gaze at me. "The gentleman who just paid for your treatments forgot to take his card. May I leave it with you, Miss . . ." She crouches to double-check her screen. "Miss Ada?"

Deniz and Eliza gape at me, and the receptionist misreads my terror as confusion. She clears her throat and holds the credit card in front of her face, reading the name out loud. "Levent Toprak. You two arrived together, for the Balinese massage. I'm sure of it . . ." Her voice fades out in the end, as she slowly comes to the realization that in a hotel of this sort, there are relations that are better kept secret. She must be new here.

"Perhaps I've made a mistake," she says, and flashes an apologetic smile.

"Perhaps you have," I respond. I turn back to the unexpected visitors and watch the features of Eliza's face hover ever so slightly above their originally allocated spots, hang loosely in the air, then return to their resting positions. She quickly extinguishes any expression of her alarm. Eliza and Deniz speak at once, pause to let the other finish, then begin again in unison.

"You go," says Eliza.

"You go," says Deniz.

"I have to go," I say, but instead of working my way around them, I push their bodies apart with my hands and squeeze through. Then I yelp, backtrack, and nearly throw myself over the counter to snatch Levent's credit card from the receptionist's desk. On my second and final attempt to exit, I have enough sense to navigate around the twosome, who have magically come together again. They both gape at me, dumbstruck.

I race down the hall to the elevator and jab at the call button several times. Just as the light dings on, a young couple appears from around the corner and remarks at their stroke of luck as the doors open in front of them. Nobody else can see me here. I think fast, push through the entrance to a stairwell nearby, and take the steps two at a time.

In the hotel lobby, a man in a three-piece suit plays chromatic scales on a grand piano, and spotted orchids stand tall and slender in their vases as each corner of the hard-edged furniture gleams, reflecting the light of the many mirrors and glass tables across the room. Catching my breath, I scan the lobby for Levent, but I can't separate window from mirror from wall, and the room shrinks and expands with each shift of perspective. Couples and groups float as if in a ballet—poised, serene, light-footed. People trained in the art of living in public spaces, accustomed to integrating into temporary residences. They are all younger, or have paid to look younger, and nowhere do I see the weathered face and graying hair of the man I'm searching for. After a few minutes, I understand that he has left without me.

The flinch of his shoulders as Deniz had cried out my name. As if he had not realized, until that very moment, what it meant for us to be here together. Wasn't he the one who picked me up in his car on the border between the towns? Wasn't he the one who drove up with me in the passenger's seat the seven hours it took to get to İstanbul? Levent had had plenty of time to reflect in those hours, plenty of opportunities to drop me off in a coastal village known for its barley stew or its leavened bread or its almond trees and say, *Please get out and find your own way home, I don't think that this is a good idea.* But he had not done that. Instead, he had driven on. He had unlocked his front door, gestured with a sweep of his hand, and said, *Welcome to İstanbul.*

With my head hanging low and my arms crossed at my chest, I travel through the crowd like a tear in the painting. I walk past the valet service onto the street, where, in the pouring rain, it takes me forty-five minutes to find a cab.

⚓

Levent buzzes me in and leaves the front door to the apartment ajar, so there is no welcoming or flourish this time. Upon hearing my footsteps, he rises from the leather couch. There is a pained look on his face, which sags with the years now clearly evident. Before he can interrogate me about the women—who are they, do they know my mother, did they understand that I was there with him, what are we going to do about all this—I reach into my back pocket and hand him his credit card.

"You left this there." He makes no move to take it and doesn't thank me. "The receptionist called your name. Eliza and Deniz know my mother from California, and they figured out that you were there with me." My voice is nonchalant, and he tilts his head to look at me. I had the whole taxi ride to face reality, and he is only just understanding now.

During my hour in traffic, the rain pelted my window like shards of glass. I watched the city through its minuscule refractions until each one disfigured itself and ran away. The vast gray metropolis felt more inaccessible than ever, pierced only by the minarets ascending from their hilltops. The water had been there from the very beginning, the city built around it. I was a transient face in a yellow cab, always on the move, desperately looking for someone who would ask me to stay.

Levent would never ask me to stay. No matter how well I tangled him up in his own confusion, how much I reminded him of his youth. Now, in front of me, he looks lost himself. I do a double take. A man like him, I had thought, should have all his surroundings under his command.

"Ada. You are aware that we have a problem?" Levent asks. I toss the credit card on the coffee table and slump onto the couch. Now that I am wet with city rain, I slide right in.

"I'm aware," I say. "I'm aware that I completely miscalculated everything, and that the only reason you agreed to bring me here is because you know that I'm leaving in two weeks and you'll never have to see me again." Though the heat in the city gives no sign of fall, September is creeping closer—and, with it, the onset of my real life.

"I thought it would be fun." His voice drops like a stone. I can't help myself. I laugh at the comical juxtaposition of his flimsy explanation, the gravitas of his tone. Then he moves closer to me, eyes wide, very serious. He smells like jasmine flowers in the night, but a sour sweat punctures through. "You thought this could really be something? Ada, come on. We're just having fun."

I watch his face as he remembers that convincing me of what we are isn't the main problem. That there is a much larger problem, the original problem, of consequence. "Nineteen years old," he says. "Like you said at the gas station. Athlete, doesn't eat cookies. An adult. But you know who's going to get the blame for this, don't you? Not you at all. It's going to be me." His face is worn and old, and his gaze wanders aimlessly, unable to separate left from right, here from there. "There is no way I can go back there, if your mother knows," he says. "You have to go back alone. You know, this is all your fault." He moves to the couch, then falls over next to me, lying supine with his arm over his forehead, muttering in prayer.

He looks so miserable, so pathetic. Talking to himself on his couch, nearly in tears, the new heat rising from his body, wilting out the flowers, he doesn't look like someone who could help me build a new life in this country. There is nothing powerful, or significant, or striking about him. Even in the forgiving light of this İstanbul evening, he looks utterly unremarkable.

20

THE CURSE

I wake up with the call to prayer and pack my bag while Levent's still asleep on the couch with his mouth half open. Beyond him lies my card fortune, splayed out and untouched. I stare at the cards for a while, then scoop them up and crank open one of the giant windows, the one that looks out onto the Bosphorus. I fling the entire deck out onto the street. I want the cards to reach the water and sink into the seaweed beds, but they flutter and meander and sway before finally settling atop the cars that are winding their way along the shoreline.

I walk out the door and flag down a cab. "Intercity bus terminal," I tell the driver. "Preferably one with that blue-and-white bus. You know the company?"

The next direct bus to Ayvalık leaves at 8:30 a.m., which gives me a couple hours to sit at an outdoor café and try to stomach a cheese-and-tomato *tost* with some tea. The steady rhythm of arrivals and departures at the station restores my sense of calm. I take a book out of my duffel bag, the

Turkish one that I never had a chance to start reading, and relax into my
wooden chair. When I'm nearly halfway through, a sweaty man in a white
button-down shirt calls for passengers to destinations along the Aegean.
People hurriedly embrace their families and set their suitcases down near
the side of the bus for the luggage handler in exchange for tags. I gather
my things and head to a kiosk for an ice cream, not worried that the bus
will leave without me. I've traveled on this bus for many summers. I know
that I'll make it exactly on time.

My seatmate is a frizzy-haired woman in her mid-thirties, traveling alone
and peeling fat figs with her hands, licking her fingers clean after each bite.
She sits seaside, on the right-side window, the same as my mother's designated seat on the drives down. We exchange smiles as I shove my duffel
bag into the overhead compartment.

About fifteen minutes after the bus pulls out of the terminal, a young
driver's assistant comes by with a clipboard to confirm everybody's final
destination.

"Bodrum," says the woman next to me, twisting around as she pulls
out a ticket from the pocket of her cutoffs. "Via İzmir."

"Ayvalık," I say. The boy confirms both destinations on his clipboard
and continues down the aisle.

"Looks like we're both starting the season a bit late in the year," the
woman says. Her shoulders are broad, like mine. "Ayvalık is such a lovely
place. It was one of my favorite places to summer, growing up."

"Oh?" I say. I turn toward her, intrigued.

"We had a house on Cunda Island. Now I summer in Bodrum." She
lets out a long sigh. "When I can get off work, anyway."

Her voice is soothing. As she talks through her memories, I wonder
how prepared I am for my summers to shift. I want to come back to
Ayvalık; I want to keep returning forever. I will have to, anyway, to see
my grandmother. But this is the last summer that my friends and I can
spend the full three months in this town. Soon our vacations will shrink,

and overlaps will be impossible. It won't make sense to come back because what is our *site* without its community? Untamed soccer fields, bleachers layered with sunflower seed shells. We will come back, but it will not be the same. So we will slowly move our summers to locations less populated by our elders, and where we can appear and disappear in the span of a week. We will go alone, and go as ourselves, and not as daughter-of, or granddaughter-of, or fathered-by. Places where people might know us by name—by first name—only.

"I'm Sedef," says the woman.

Sedef's a swimmer as well, I learn, participating in events around the world, including the annual race across the Bosphorus. As the bus squeezes its way out of the city, we compare our practice schedules, our warm-ups, the number of days we dedicate to dry-land training each week, our favorite events (mine the 200-yard freestyle, and hers the 100-meter backstroke). We discuss how we both prefer the Aegean to the Mediterranean, because its cooler waters appeal only to those serious about the swim. It's not for the lazy beachgoers who prefer lukewarm dips between hours of baking under the sun.

"That's what a lot of people say when I tell them I summer in Ayvalık," I say excitedly. "They ask me, why do you go there? Even among all the other spots along the Aegean, the water there is so cold and salty."

"You know, I was just thinking . . ." Sedef taps an orange fingernail on her folded-up tray table, trying to catch at a memory. "One of my favorite legends is from Ayvalık."

The bus lurches. "Are you talking about the curse?" I ask.

"Curse . . . I suppose it depends on how you look at it." She winks and offers me a fig. I take it and thank her, and she seems bemused by my eagerness. "It's old lore, really, and it's been twisted so many times and never written down anywhere, so you're sure to come across several different versions. But this version is my favorite. It's called the curse of Barren Island."

After all that's happened with Levent, investigating the backstory of the island had completely slipped my mind. "Barren Island, the one with nothing on it, no plants or anything, that one?" I ask. It strikes me as

bizarre that someone I have never met knows so intimately the islands I
see every day from my grandmother's balcony. They aren't just for me, for
us. The exclusivity of our *site* is not at all how I have always imagined it
to be, restricted to the summers and the years that I've been there. People
can come and go as they please; people have come and gone. The market
stays open in the winters for those who carry wallets in their coat pockets.

I reach up to the climate-control knob on the ceiling and twist off the
air-conditioning.

"I think so." The woman furrows her brow, unsure. "It's been a while
since I've been there. 'Barren' probably isn't the actual name of the island.
I don't even think anybody knows the real names of the islands. That's
one of my favorite things about these seaside villages. Everybody has
their own names for everything, depending on what they see when they
look at it, what they believe about it, the tales they've heard . . .

"Anyway," she says. "Do you want to hear the story?"

"Absolutely." I drop the fig into my mouth. As I chew, it softens like
honey.

There is a long silence as Sedef mentally collects all the details. Then
she begins.

Once there was and once there wasn't, very, very long ago, before
Ayvalık belonged to Turkey, before it belonged to the Greeks, before it
belonged to anybody, Barren Island stood unexplored out in the Aegean,
cold and unwelcoming in exactly the way we know it to be now. On the
mainland nearby was a swimmer who was preparing for his very first
race, swimming just a few meters farther every day. Eventually, one day, he
found himself coming upon the shores of the island. Tired from his longest swim yet, he decided to rest and stepped onto the land. But as soon
as his body made contact with the island, the ground turned green, and
trees and plants sprang from the newly rich soil. The swimmer watched
in astonishment as the island transformed from a wasteland to a resplendent oasis, brimming with lush greenery and sprouting pomegranate
trees and apricot trees and tomato vines and vine leaves and all the fruits
and vegetables that one could dream of on this side of the Aegean. Upon
this dizzying discovery, the mainlander swam back faster than he had

ever swum before and ran up and down the streets of his town crying out about the great feast that awaited them out west, out toward
the horizon. After hearing the swimmer's tale, men and women began
heading off in their rowboats, a veritable regatta on the sea. As much as
they picked and plucked from the island, nature would doubly replenish
its stock the following day. At each season's harvest, the townspeople
would again gather their oars and take to the sea. Life became easy with
abundance.

But as the years passed, something curious happened.

The first thing the townspeople noticed was that the schools had
grown sparse, and the streets had settled into a disquieting silence. The
sound of play had disappeared. Their women were unable, it seemed, to
bear children. Most would be unable to conceive entirely, and for those
lucky few who did, the babies they birthed had no heartbeat. Ashamed of
their fertility challenges, the families did not speak of their private struggles, and the severity of the matter remained unknown in the public
sphere. Later, the town council launched an inquiry to solve the mystery,
constructing timelines of activity and weather, drawing up astronomical
and biological charts.

When they worked backward, the council found that the decreasing,
then disappearing birth rates aligned with the discovery of the island and
its flora. But was the poison in the fruit, or was it in the soil? Was it in the
pebbles where the land met the sea? They began a series of experiments.
A dozen virgin women were dropped off by boat to swim around the island. Others were tasked with touching the soil with the bottoms of their
bare feet, biting into the fruit of the trees, or remaining in their white-
washed kitchens and rolling up the grape leaves delivered from the island
by the men. Researchers diligently took notes. Could the curse travel
through the trees? The charts continued, the tests multiplied, the data
accumulated. It wasn't long before an unexpected conclusion emerged.

Anything from the land, it was revealed, would strip away from women
the possibility of motherhood. Whether it was the dirt between their toes
or the ingestion of the vegetables that appeared at their front door, any
connection at all with the island meant that there would be no sons and

no daughters. The only safe method was to approach the island by sea, and take in the views of its gardens from the water. But who would do that, what end would it serve, if one could not be among its trees and benefit from their bounty? A declaration was drawn up and spread to all corners of the town: The island, and all that was upon it, was cursed. And once the visits stopped, the trees fell, the grass withered, and the land turned back to stone.

I understand now why Bulut and the grocer's son had been so hesitant to tell me the story. It's a little funny, actually. "Now that's what I'd call a curse," I say.

Sedef leans back into her seat. She looks out the window, but there is still a while until the coastline. "Sure, for some," she says. "For others—I mean, I'll just say it, for some women like me—it's actually sort of a dream. A curse, are you crazy?" She laughs. "I'd hire a boat just to take me there."

21

THE SURPRISE

From the Ayvalık bus terminal, I take a cab. I direct the driver toward our *site*, but yell "HERE IS GOOD!" well before we reach the Small Club. The driver slams on the brakes near the entrance to the *site* at the top of the hill, and I tumble out to walk the rest of the way home. It's quiet up here, where no one goes, and my body expands to fill the space offered up by the silence. It's difficult to believe that I was just in İstanbul, amid its spiderweb streets and cracked apartment buzzers and swarms of people rustling among each other like migrating storks. At the same time, it is just as impossible to believe all the other places my body has been. In tough-cushioned airline seats over black oceans, sleepless. Leaning, vodka-flushed, against the doorways of Palo Alto dorm rooms. In the middle of the sea. I glance at my toenails, the lavender polish chipped, their edges darkened with city soot. My feet seem too small and insignificant to have carried me all those places. The world, I think, must have turned to accommodate my transitions.

But I know that's not true. Everything that's happened to me has been my own doing, for better or worse. The consequences are more generous, though. Lives will change once everyone knows. I need to figure out how much time I have, how long my secret can last. The number of people who know what I've done has now made its way to five, which is three people past the breaking point of all secrets. It will not be able to hold. It will flow down the hills of the *site* like coffee dregs in an upturned demitasse. What I have done will flip inside out for everyone to see. The neighbors will wade through the mud of my fortune, shaking their heads with pity, then slapping their thighs in laughter. But my mother and my grandmother will not be able to traverse to the clean side. Mired in my ugly fortune, they'll be left with no choice but to continue their lives in the mess that I have made for them. Reputations make no distinctions among generations.

Terror of the future pins me to the top of the hill. There is nothing I can do that will lessen the blow or prevent the course of the unfolding. I can only be very careful up until then, and preserve the past for as long as possible. *Think of logic*, I say to myself. *Think of only the very next step.*

My very next step is to construct a narrative of my vacation with Aslı's family, to prepare for the eventual interrogation. My grandmother, especially, will want to know what it was that pulled me away from her for these last few days. How good of a time must I have had in Çeşme for it to have been worth the separation? A couple quotidian scenes assemble themselves in my mind's eye: Aslı and I laughing over cooncan on her terrace, pushing up orange-flavored ice pops from their conical packaging. Dinners of grilled sea bass and wine-drenched cockles with her family while the sun sinks into the Aegean, plum-picking in the neighbor's garden for a late-night snack. My stomach rumbles. I should stop for a snack.

On the market floor, the *lahmacun* maker's son plays with a miniature race car, the tiny wheels turning as he creates his own sound effects. Behind him in the window, large red stickers read *PİDE LAHMACUN*. I say hello, but he only smiles shyly in return, so I walk over to the space between the baker and the grocer, between the freezer of Panda ice cream and the freezer of Algida ice cream. When I was around the boy's age, my allegiance to the stores would shift depending on the brand of that year's most sought-after flavors. I slide open the glass of the Panda icebox, and bend over to take out a chocolate-and-vanilla push-pop.

The baker, with his white hair and white shirt and white apron, walks around in sandals with flour speckled across his toes. As I show him the ice cream so that he can note down the IOU, the baker's eyes flutter closed and he tilts his chin. *No payment necessary. My treat today.*

"Oh, hey, thanks," I say. "That's really kind of you."

My mother would not have accepted this generosity so easily. She never forgets the rule of three. *Aaaa,* she would have said, arranging her face into an expression of shock. *Completely unacceptable,* she would have said, in response to which the man would have lifted his chin higher and clicked his tongue. *I simply won't stand for it,* she would have said, and the baker would have waved his hands in front of him, implying that there was nothing to be done. Only after that final push would she have allowed herself to surrender and settle into the plastic chair next to the tray of fresh spinach rolls, toss one leg over the other, and click her sandal in and out from her heel, ready to enjoy her treat. *Well then. Only because you insist.*

I sit down right away. The push-pop comes with a red plastic hat for a lid, which I place on my head. I straighten up to keep it balanced.

"You coming or going?" The baker gestures with his spatula to my duffel bag from behind the counter, where he is placing crescents filled with hazelnut paste on a tray. I tell him that I'm returning from a short trip to Çeşme with Aslı. He nudges one crescent pastry to make room for another, then floats his hands above his creations, delaying his next movement.

"That's strange," he says. "Because Aslı was just here yesterday. She came in with Ozan and they asked for two glasses of Tang lemonade and drank them just right here on the terrace, at the tables overlooking the soccer field." He looks out behind him at the half-open door where the late-afternoon sunlight streams in. Confirming that that was indeed where he saw the girl who was supposed to be out of town, he turns to me expectantly, curious to hear my side of the story.

The hat topples off my head. "The other Aslı," I say. I bend down for it and face the floor for as long as I can. There is already flour on my toes. How did this happen? I am marked wherever I go. Very slowly, I unfold myself.

"There's another Aslı?" I've confused him now. "You mean Semra's daughter?"

Semra's daughter is ten years younger than I am. "Yes," I say, then remember the speed of the gossip through the town. "No, probably not. I don't know. I don't know her mom's name."

"Don't know her mom's name . . ." This is, of course, impossible. No one can be known here distinct from their families. "Not Aslı, then," says the baker with a wink. He's playing on her name, which means "the original."

"Is Semra in our *site?* Then no, it's not her, you don't know her," I say, still trying to dig myself out of this hole. "This Aslı's house is in the next *site* over. She doesn't come to this market. I shouldn't have even mentioned her to you. Just a friend. There is another market in the next town she goes to, she never comes here." The air feels heavy, sticking to me, stacking up in the back of my throat like the dusty bricks of those half-built homes.

"Here," the baker says, wrapping up one of the crescents in a napkin. "Take this to your mother, I know she likes them." I accept it and raise my push-pop as a thank-you, then leave as quickly as I can without arousing any further suspicion. My face burns from the interrogation, and I say a small prayer on the way that he won't mention any part of this conversation to my mother. I'll have to be sure that it's I who goes to the baker every day for the rest of the summer instead of her. I cannot give her this pastry; she will come in to thank him. I need to get rid of it.

The *lahmacun* maker's son is still there, moving his race car back and forth. "You realize that your little car's not going anywhere?" I say, cracking a fault line in his child's imagination. He looks up at me and tells me that his car has already been across the Caucasus, carved around the Black Sea to the shores of Ukraine. It has withstood the heat of the hottest Arabian deserts and is currently making its way back to a car wash in Ayvalık before Formula 1 racing in Monaco, a country he has heard has the best croissants in the world. In response, I offer him the pastry. "These aren't bad, either," I say. He shakes his head without making eye contact. I extend it closer to him, as a second offer, but he clicks his tongue *no*, then continues with the various sound effects of a car wash.

I shrug and bite into the pastry. Only then does he look up at me with a hurt expression, having expected the third offer, the official offer, that never came.

≈ ⚓ ≈

My grandmother is watering pomegranate trees in the front garden. As I approach the gate, her thumb moves to partly cover the nozzle of the hose, and she begins to spray me through the diamond-shaped gaps of the wire fence. I hold out a hand in front of my face as a visor and unhook the latch, droplets raining on me. I race up the terrace steps with limited vision. "What sort of welcome is this?" I yell.

"Serves you right for leaving us," replies my grandmother, adjusting the hose to match my distance. "It's the same Aegean, don't you know? You're here, you're there, it's all the same thing, nothing changes except for the direction of the wind. Now he's going to see you like a wet little alley cat, ha-ha!"

"Who's going to see what?" But as the words tumble out of my mouth, I hear a familiar laugh that I have not heard in a long time. Slowly, I remove my hand from over my eyes.

On the terrace, through the rainbow of water droplets still arching and falling on me, is my mother with her hands on the railing, her face lit up in anticipation. Standing next to her, grinning with all his American teeth, is Ian.

"Surprise!" my mother cries. She throws her hands into the air.

22

THE FANTASY

Overlaps are verboten. Ian is not a man of August. Ian is a man of September, and that is where he belongs. Not now and not here on my grandmother's terrace. My mother beams as if she has done something wonderful. My curated life is not hers to dismember and rearrange. There are geographies where he is forbidden. I want to scream: YOU ARE CARRYING GIFTS.

23

THE PHONE CALL

O leanders lining the Small Club entrance sway in the wind, which plucks, then scatters their fragile petals to the ground. Ian loosely holds my hand as we walk into the café with towels slung over our shoulders, and I point out all the places that we cannot yet see. Farther along is the Big Club, I say, but before that is the park, and behind the park is the market with the grocer and the baker, and then there are the basketball courts . . . but when the concrete under our feet turns to tile and the Small Club splays out in front of us, I stop short. An eerie silence permeates the café. Only a smattering of people occupy a few of the tables, and then there are my friends.

"Hello!" The three of them jump to greet him at once, as if all the energy that should have been buzzing around the café has now condensed into one table.

"How was your flight?"

"Have you learned any Turkish yet? Swear words? We can get you started . . ."

"I'm Aslı, this is my brother Bulut, this is Ozan . . ."

"Are you a swimmer, like Ada?"

They swarm around us as if they'd been waiting their entire lives to meet him. All the detritus on our table, from the empty cans of Nestea to the ketchup-smeared wrappers of *tosts* past, were only ways to kill time until his arrival. I watch the scene in a fog of confusion, wondering how it is possible that everyone knows exactly who Ian is and why no one has shown any signs of surprise, only delight.

"Wait a second, wait a second." I spread the crowd apart with my arms, silencing the group. "Did you all know that Ian was coming?"

"Of course we did," says Ozan. "Your mom told us a couple of weeks ago that he'd come in last night, but asked us to keep it a secret."

"Obviously," adds Bulut. "Because it was supposed to be a surprise. Was it a good surprise?" He turns to Ian. "Did she freak out?"

Ian shrugs, then smiles in a way that means *kind of*. It would have been hard to describe what my face looked like, but Ian tries anyway. "She looked like she was about to throw up," he says.

"That's just what she looks like when she's happy," Aslı laughs, trying to salvage the situation. "It's a very Turkish expression."

"A couple of weeks ago . . ." I turn to Aslı, who flashes me a lopsided grin that doubles as an apology. How had she kept something like this from me? As she carried me home on her back, as she broke my backgammon pieces during our final game and promised to hide from my mother, she knew all the while that this would be a bigger surprise for me than anyone had anticipated.

"We will talk about this later," I say to the chair that I'm gripping, my knuckles white. But it's not her fault, I know. It's mine.

"So anyway," Bulut says, and I can tell from his tone that he has some bad news. He swings his skinny arms back and forth, delaying the message. Someone pulls out a chair for Ian and he sits down, but no one does the same for me. I drag one over from the neighboring table and try to scrunch into a table of five meant for four. Bulut looks at me to make sure that I'm prepared for what he's about to say. "The sea is full of shit."

Oh, no.

Ian turns to me for an explanation.

The sewage leaks happen from time to time, and as word travels fast, there is no need for any announcement from the market's PA system, no need to pin any notices on any doors. The earliest swimmers to arrive at the Small Club hear the news from the staff themselves and spread it through town, the highest density of exchanges occurring at the market, or on the minibus into the town center. From balcony to balcony, families swap the details, so that even before the clock strikes noon, everyone is well aware of the situation, and avoids swimming for the next day or two. There are, of course, those who truly understand the breadth and depth of the sea, and how that renders any filth from the land negligible. Currently, two swimmers wade resolutely near the dock, signaling their beliefs to those who are simply sitting at the café and trying to enjoy the view without thinking about it too much.

"Takes about two days to clear out, though Ada usually goes in anyway," Bulut tells Ian. "The rest of us can't really stomach it."

If Ian can't go swimming today, there is absolutely no other activity left for us. What am I supposed to do with him? Should I take him around to meet the grocer's son and the baker, show him the dried-out soccer field and the netless basketball courts? Seeing those places without having built memories around the town means nothing. Everything here would seem bleak and spartan from his perspective. He wouldn't see the drunken evenings by the fountain in the children's park, but he would notice the peeling paint of the slide.

"If Ada doesn't mind, then I don't mind," says Ian. He puts a hand on my shoulder and gives me a small squeeze. I cringe as the peeled skin burns. Ian takes off his sunglasses, folding them neatly on the table, and pulls off his shirt. I gape at his chest. It's pink and tender, as if it has never once seen the sun. "You ready to head in?" he asks me.

I shake my head. I can't do it, not with him here. When I look back at the sea, it's taken on a dull gray color, and suddenly there is nothing appealing about it at all. A thoughtless child at the end of the dock wraps his toes around the edge and lets himself fall into the water. No, we will have to avoid the sea today and tomorrow. I suggest instead a game of backgammon, remember that Ian doesn't know how to play, and am relieved at the thought that teaching him will help us kill time. I order

everyone a round of coffee on my tab and ask for a board. Bulut volun-
teers to teach Ian while I switch spots with him and sit next to Aslı.

"You didn't see my mother at all, right?" I whisper.

"You're safe," she answers. "The first day I didn't even go down to the
Small Club. Bulut and I were with family and we played cards in the
morning, then went to the town center at night. The second day I took
the entrance by the fence and didn't run into her at all, then yesterday
anyway was the sewage leak, so there was barely anyone here."

"Okay," I say. For some reason I still don't feel at ease. Something tugs
at me, reminding me that I'm not yet in the clear. Ian slowly counts the
movement of his wooden pieces, but Bulut's expression remains patient.
He doesn't even reach for the dice in preparation for his next roll.

"How was İstanbul?" Ozan asks in English.

"Great," I say.

"Great," says Ian, and we stare at each other.

"You were in İstanbul?" Ian asks. The brightness in his face suddenly
dims. An electricity failure across continents; cities shutting down. "I
thought you were someplace else . . . with a strange name . . ."

"I was asking Ian," says Ozan, looking very confused. "Aslı said that
you were in Çeşme seeing a family friend." He points to me, opens his
mouth, then closes it again. He narrows his eyes at Aslı, who I now realize
is crushing his foot with her heel.

I flap my hand in the air in dismissive nonchalance. "Çeşme was great,
I thought that was what you were asking. Sorry, sorry. Saw some family
friends from California for a couple days, then came straight back because
I missed you all too much."

Of course. Of course Ian was in İstanbul. How had I not realized that
we had overlapped? It was the only reasonable way to make it to this town
internationally, to stop over in the big city and take the bus down. Likely,
he had spent a few days there, exploring the cultural capital. Roaming
around the historic peninsula, hopping on and off the ferries, rambling
down the streets of—

"Oh, damn. Excuse me." Bulut leans in his chair, searching for something on the ground. "Could you look here please!" he calls out to a waiter.

My throat constricts. Up until now, I had seen my lives clearly delineated. Living in one necessarily meant shutting off access to the other. The reality of Ian next to me sets in relief the fantasy—yes, because that's what it was, a fantasy—of living here. I feel the full and sudden impact of my betrayal. I can't move.

A boy in a polo arrives, carrying a tray. "Do you have another set of dice?" Bulut asks him. The waiter looks down as Bulut points to where the wall meets the tiles, toward a die that has lodged its way into a tiny crack.

"We have an extra game set at my house," I say, and stand up so fast that my chair flips over behind me. I run across the street to the villa, yank down the clasp of the garden gate, leap up the steps to the terrace, and slide in through the side door. I bend down to grab the backgammon board from the lower shelf of the coffee table, now taking my time. Every minute I spend here means one less minute of having to entertain Ian. The rotary rings, its tone shrill, and I yell to the house that I'll get it.

"Hello?"

"Darling, is that you, Ada? It's Eliza."

Eliza. With all the stress surrounding Ian's arrival, I had completely forgotten about Eliza. I look around the house, but no one has come indoors or downstairs—I don't know where the two of them are—for the telephone. They know that whenever the telephone rings, it's rarely for me. All my friends are always across the street.

"Hi," I say, taking care not to repeat her name.

"Is your mother home?" Her tone is somewhat careful and a tad condescending. As though, if I don't answer her question truthfully, she has ways of working around me, methods she has learned in the years that separate her from me.

"No, she's not," I say. "She's in Çeşme."

"Is she? Hm, I don't know anyone who summers there. Do you happen to have the number for the place she's staying?"

"No, I don't, sorry, bye!" I slam the phone back in its cradle, and stare at it for a long time. I walk back to the coffee table to take the backgammon board. Then, staying as quiet as possible, I head out the side door but break into a run as soon as I cross the threshold. I race out the gate, not bothering to close it after me, and down the oleander path, where the flowers seem to bend toward me in mockery. *It's only a matter of time,* they whisper among their leaves. *After all, in this small town, nothing stays a secret for long.* The board slips out of my hands, breaking at the hinge. I scoop it up and leave the scattered pieces on the ground. I'll get to them later.

When I reach the din of the café, it no longer sounds like the soothing melodies of summer. It feels like entering a party to which I'm not invited. I head toward our table and see Ian there, listening intently as Ozan explains the poem behind his tattoo. I remember everything all over again. How stupid I was, that day gazing at my painted toenails waiting for Levent's SUV, the way he kissed me quickly in the museum, aware that I kept giving and giving and receiving nothing in return. How happy he was in the gas station when I refused the cookies for kids and the veil of guilt lifted from him completely. The blood drains from my face. I look away so my pallor doesn't frighten my friends, or lead to any questioning.

Bulut takes the board from me, turning it over. "Ada, you dummy," he says. "All we needed was the dice." He holds it open in front of me like a damaged book, empty and askew. "There are no dice in this board."

24

THE WISH

My boyfriend is here for two weeks and will take the return flight with us at the beginning of September. I start to count the days.

Ian sets an alarm every morning and rises with the first note. He heads down to breakfast with my mother and grandmother while I bury my face into my pillow and ache to return to splintered dreams. He has a habit of snoozing the alarm instead of turning it off—"just to be safe," he claims—which means that minutes after he leaves, it bleats again. I wake up a second time and smash all its buttons.

I switched rooms with my mother so that she sleeps among my dead mosquitoes and Ian and I take the larger room with two twin beds, which we push together. The first night, we touch each other softly, but the thin walls between bedrooms prevent any further progression. Returning to my own body is a struggle; it's as if I had slipped on borrowed skin that can neither recognize nor respond to the warmth and patterns of his fingertips. In controlled whispers, I yelp and groan. I clench and unclench as violently as I used to so that there is no doubt in his mind that I have missed him and been lonely all the while. Though we try to fall asleep intertwined, the crevice between the beds can't be avoided no matter how much we force them against each other, and one or both of our limbs keeps sinking into the abyss. Ian finally admits discomfort, and we turn our backs to each other, but I stay awake, listening to the neighbors, the rise and fall of the breath beside me. I risked my relationship with my mother to indulge in an attraction that never gave me the roots I assumed I had been promised. I casually tossed aside everything I had with Ian, seeing him in the same way I did my father—as someone who would take me away from where I needed to be. There is too much to sift through. I divide up all my sadnesses and cry just a little bit, very quietly, every night.

One morning, I head down to the terrace for breakfast and hear Ian explaining the particular characteristics of Russian Hill to my mother, who is translating for my grandmother, and delving into a detailed compare-and-contrast with the qualities of other San Francisco neighborhoods. The ratios of tech workers to the homeless, of flat land to inclines, and proximity to BART stations, which he then ranks by stench of urine. I murmur in agreement as I take my place next to him, and notice that my grandmother looks horrified, and my mother, disengaged.

"I was never too fond of San Francisco," says my mother, forking over sliced *sucuk* onto Ian's plate. She takes care to arrange the sausages in stacks, like poker chips. "There are too many drug addicts, it's always cold, and I find it dangerous. That's why Ada is still so unfamiliar with the city, since we never go there as a family."

I am worried about what my mother is going to do when she finds out. The past few days I have been entirely on edge. Everywhere I go, I feel uncomfortable in my body. I am too cold in the water, claustrophobic in the house, melting on the streets as Ian and I walk hand in hand, sweat dripping where we touch. There is not a second when I can relax, and the anxiety of how everything is going to fall apart eats away at me.

"Ada and I have actually gone to San Francisco several times together," Ian says. "I'd venture to say she knows it pretty well." I become increasingly absorbed with the ends of my hair, slicing along the splits with my finger-nail. I struggle to remember what I can about the city. The peaks of San Francisco merge together in my mind, the houses all variations on a post-card image. I cannot recall the name of a single street. Oh, yes. Arkansas.

"I don't think *several visits* is enough to get to know a city." My moth-er's gaze jumps over to me in a series of nearly imperceptible staccatos. Then her stare rests steady. "Do you, Ada?"

Does she know? She can't know. Eliza hasn't called again, and Levent is nowhere to be seen. Yesterday I thought I was clever and unplugged the phone cord, but my grandmother had to make a call to the gardener a few hours later and plugged it right back in. My mother seems like a scorpion lying in wait inside a slipper, but maybe I am just seeing every-thing through the lens of what I have done. My arm spasms, and I knock over an empty water glass and a saltshaker. My mother rights them with her usual grace.

"For example, İstanbul," continues my mother, now with a terrifying coldness. "İstanbul is an extremely convoluted metropolis. In order to truly call that city home"—she draws out the word "home" until it encircles a restricted area that few would dare to enter—"one has to create memo-ries spanning time. What do you call it when you just skim across, 'fair-weather'?"

Ian nods, pleased to be helpful. The sun is angled precisely at my forehead, and I start to sweat.

"They are just fair-weather visitors." She lightly touches the recently stabilized saltshaker with her index finger. I unsteadily pour myself some sour cherry juice, but when I pick up the glass, my hand trembles vio-lently. Everybody notices, but nobody says anything. Ian stuffs his mouth full of *sucuk*, easing his way out of the conversation. My grandmother serves him a second helping. My mother salts the eggs on her plate.

From beyond our backyard, from a neighboring villa, a strange sound wafts through the summer air and settles over our table. It envelops us in its long wails, entrances us so deeply that, like a long, slim finger, it lifts all four of our chins toward it. We look past the mint leaves, over the metal railing, down the lawn of neatly trimmed rose bushes, to our diagonal neighbor's porch. The voice belongs to the woman from the capital city, a senior manager at a national bank. Divorced, with a sailor son in his early twenties, who comes and goes from our sleepy *site*.

The language of her words is familiar yet undetectable. My grandmother lowers her gaze and shakes her head, and my mother follows suit. Ian and I continue to stare in her direction, mesmerized by the beauty of her voice.

"What's she singing?" I ask my mother.

"Singing?" My mother looks at me. "Did you say 'singing'?"

"Can you not hear her, the bank manager? There, on the diagonal. What's she singing? It's beautiful."

"Really beautiful," adds Ian, stabbing a cucumber.

"Did she say 'singing'?" my grandmother asks my mother.

"Ada, she's praying," says my mother, releasing a deep, depressive sigh. "Her son passed away in a sailing accident."

"Oh."

"How awful," says Ian. Later, I catch him looking at me with a mix of disappointment and bemusement, as if everything I had told him about who I am was a lie.

⚓

The hours at the Small Club shed their languor and tense up, taking shape. Our days at the beach are no longer the same. They are square-edged calendar days, delineated precisely. As designated dragoman, I have trouble translating the humor, keeping up with the wit and tossing it back over to Ian. What's worse, my fluidity in English throws my stunted Turkish into sharp relief, and this is apparent to everyone within earshot of the rises and falls of my voice. In English, that easy California coastal highway. Turkish, in a relative turn, becomes choppy waters under a thundering sky.

When the boys, all of them, line up on the dock, I am unable to watch the series of jumps that used to serve as my midday entertainment. Ian lines up last, towering above the group with his height. He leaps at the edge of the dock into an imperfect, unpracticed dive, an awkward bend to his back that displaces buckets of water when he instead should have slipped in quietly, like a fish.

When waiters pass by our table, they shield their eyes from the blinding whiteness of the newcomer's skin. I pretend not to notice their nudges and winks.

One day, Ian tells me that he wants to go to Cunda Island. "I don't know it that well," I say. "But okay." He wants to see the restaurants on Cunda Island that are farther inland. He wants to see the windmills, the old Greek houses whose stone facades and colorful doors he's read about in a guidebook. On his lap, he spreads out a map during the ferry ride to Cunda, holding it flat with his palms. I lean over, and for the first time in my life, I take in the topography and dimensions of my summer. My radius encapsulates little besides our villa, the rosemary path, the market, extending up toward the town center with its marina, ice cream shops, and Atatürk statue—my radius is as insignificant as a grain of sand tucked between the toes of a satisfied vacationer returning home.

On Cunda Island, we walk past dead fish with their upper lips raised in terror, gazing dumbly from the mirror of the iceboxes. The air fills with the sweet scent of waffle cones hardening in griddles. The restaurateurs along the seaside all present their menus with toothy smiles and hacked English, and even Ian, who nodded in acknowledgment at the first few, starts to ignore their calls. The restaurants of the island soon peter out and make way for a jewelry market. We browse the trinkets laid out along the stands, and Ian surprises me with a silver anklet. I put my leg up on one of the quayside bollards and pull up my long cotton skirt, and he ties it onto me. He fiddles with it a bit, taking longer than he should because the clasp is complicated. I am comforted by the warmth and dexterity of his hands.

A sharp heat cuts down on us around noon, so we stop at a café and I order us two coffees and a deck of cards, out of habit. Before I realize that I don't believe in these things anymore, the waiter has already jotted down my desires and left.

"I ordered your coffee with sugar," I tell Ian. "First-timers usually can't enjoy Turkish coffee without it."

"You know I take my coffee plain," he says. He's watching a balloon vendor move with a parade of floating Mylar along the promenade. The garish colors flash in the sun as they turn with each step. "But if that's what you say, then I trust you."

The coffee is too sweet for him. I order him another one, plain, then I ask him to cut the deck and make a wish.

"All right," he says, his mood brightening. He pats down the sweat behind his neck with a napkin, then rests his hand on top of the cards. "I wish for—"

"Don't say it out loud!" I cry. Ian laughs, surprised at how many heads have turned toward us. "Oh, what am I saying. It's not like any of them come true anyway," I add. But just in case, I nudge the cards again toward Ian. He cuts them, and I lay out the deck.

"Why did you say they don't come true?" Ian's never considered the alignment of the stars, never flipped to the back of a magazine to read his horoscope. He's probably just going to drink the coffee until there's nothing left but muddy grounds, and not even pause to wonder whether there is an additional activity to the ritual. "What do you usually wish for?"

"My wish is always the same," I say, the words in English slipping out like water. My silence is no longer responsible for what may or may not come true. "It's always a prayer that I don't end up like my mother, living some sort of half-lived life. She's so unhappy, seems so lost everywhere she is. Haven't you noticed? Every year, we spend three months in this town. This country was once familiar to her, but isn't anymore. She's left it alone for too long. Too much has changed during her absences for her to feel at home here, and she has never managed to integrate in California. Lose-lose. Nowhere-nowhere."

"She's never seemed unhappy to me," says Ian. He looks genuinely confused.

"Of course she's unhappy!" My voice rises again, and a waiter shoots me a glance, then chuckles with his colleagues. "How can you not have noticed this? At this point, she's spent over half her life in the States and she still isn't comfortable there, even my father noticed and found someone else. How could anyone like that be happy?"

Ian shrugs. "It just didn't seem like it to me." He takes a sip of his new coffee and makes a face. "You know, I think maybe I should just get an Americano. It has nothing to do with the sugar, it's just . . . just the taste is a bit off for me, in general."

"Right, but you need an anchor," I continue adamantly. "Like, my father was her anchor in California, now their whole relationship is unstable and she has to start all over again. She had this ex-boyfriend here that she was going to live her Turkish life with, and that didn't work out. You can't just float around and land wherever you want," I add. "People need to help you get there."

"Are you sure we're talking about the same person?" Ian asks, signaling to the waiter for his third coffee.

I look up from my cards, squeezed into an oblong shape on the table. "What do you mean?" I ask. "Who else would I be talking about?"

25

THE SECRET

One morning I wake up and am surprised to find that Ian hasn't gone down for breakfast yet. He's sitting on the floor with his back to the bed, dancing his fingers on a silent keyboard he brought with him from San Francisco. I place my chin on his shoulder, and he strokes my cheek with his left hand as his right carries on with the melody. Turning my face in toward his, I let myself softly fall to the floor, then kiss him, long and hard. His hands lift from the keyboard, and he holds me around my waist, balancing my body in its crooked diagonal. I find a space for my head under the V's of his bent legs and watch his face through the gap as he plays. The sun has worked itself deeper into his skin; there's a spray of freckles across his nose, and his cheeks have shed their previous pallor of thinned porcelain. They've been roughened up now, like a sailor's. It's unexpected how cleanly his body has adapted. I had underestimated his ability to transition, overestimated the resistance of the borders. I am suddenly terrified that I will lose him.

I jingle the small bells of my anklet. I want to be a part of the music, too.

"You can't hear it," says Ian, "but this is *Moonlight Sonata*."

And then he starts the piece again from the beginning, humming out the notes as he goes.

≈ ⚓ ≈

That night, Ian decides that we should go on a walk along the water and take two glasses and a bottle of wine for the road. There is no wine in the house. Ian suggests we get some from the market.

"The market," I repeat. I have been avoiding the market, and my grandmother has begrudgingly readopted her daily routine of buying the newspaper and bread. Seeing Levent again won't solve anything; all it would do is remind me of my ridiculous fantasy and how much I believed in something that never could have happened. I don't want to remember. I want to completely forget everything that I have done and settle neatly back into my old life.

"Okay," I say to Ian. "The market it is."

On the rosemary path, I realize that I am clenching Ian's hand. I relax my grip, and he gives my hand three squeezes and smiles as we continue along. His teeth are so big, so white. Buoys in the dark sea of his mouth. At the grocer's, I grab the first bottle of wine I see and say, "All right, let's go, let's get out of here," but Ian is crouching and craning and observing all the labels on all the bottles, taking this opportunity to tread curiously into the world of Turkish enology. *Now is not the time.* I am aggravated, being so close to where I must not go, and try to concentrate on a display of Chupa Chups, whose colorful packaging makes me dizzy. I sit down in a corner near the toilet paper rolls and wait.

Finally, Ian decides on something local, and I turn the label toward the cashier as we walk out without paying. But this time, it's the grocer himself at the register instead of his son, and his arm reaches out to stop me. "I'll make a note of it, Ada," he says. "But summer's almost over, some folks are already heading back to their cities. Just so you know, I've started to collect the IOUs this week." He opens up the large notebook and runs a finger down the page for my name. "You've racked up quite a debt," he says, pursing his lips. "Remember to settle your account."

"I will," I promise. I tighten my grip on the neck of the bottle. Maybe we can take a quick peek at Levent's house. Just walk by, and I'll glance over. No big deal. If only to remind myself that he is an average man living in an average house that's exactly the same as all the other villas. There is nothing at all that is special about him. Nothing at all that he can give me that I can't reach on my own. Just a small reminder. "Very soon, I will pay."

As we leave the grocer's, I take a deep breath. "Actually," I start to ask Ian, "do you mind if instead of going straight to the shore we take a—"

Ian tilts his head in the direction of my gaze. "You want to head out this way?"

"Yeah," I say, a bit too casually. "Let's take the side streets for a bit."

"Sure."

Night instead of the first breath of morning, in mixed company as opposed to solitude. We make a left on a side street and pass a few villas until I stop in my tracks. He's there on the balcony, arms ringed with the stretching handles of several plastic bags. "Come here," I hiss, and tug on Ian's hand. Levent has turned away from us now; he's walking toward the car parked under the pergola. I scramble inside the mulberry bush and pull my boyfriend down with me.

"What are we doing?" Ian whispers, and when I turn to him, I notice that he's got a half smile; he's thrilled to do something exciting together, happy to see that there is some life left in me after all. Levent opens the trunk of his car, places the bags on top of a suitcase. I put a finger to my lips.

"You see this family here," I say, pointing to the other side of Levent's balcony, beyond the dividing wall. His neighbors are sipping *rakı*, laughing together in the dark. "Let's spy on them for a bit."

"All right," says Ian, and settles down next to me to uncork and pour the wine. I flinch with each small sound, and empty my glass as soon as he hands it to me. We stare straight ahead, watching in silence.

Levent locks the door, then goes to the side windows and closes all the shutters, placing the little hooks into their metal circles. As if he had never lived here, as if none of this had ever happened. As if Ian's visit had been a wonderful, pleasant surprise.

One of the neighbors hears the sounds of shutters closing and sticks her head around the dividing wall. "You leaving already?" she asks, and Levent nods a very formal nod. Our scenes merge, and Ian begins to watch what I am watching. I pull my knees up and rest my chin on them to keep from shaking. I close my eyes.

"That one guy's looking at us," Ian says softly, and I open them again. "Do you know him?" Levent is staring right into the mulberry tree. He is looking at me and I am looking at him, and Ian is also looking at him. Levent doesn't wave, but out of the corner of my eye, I see Ian wave, and my two lives, so neatly divided, crash into each other like a shipwreck.

Levent gives a sad sort of smile and walks back to his car. He starts the engine, pulls out of the pergola, and we watch him drive away to İstanbul.

"No, I don't know him," I answer Ian. "But my mom does."

I get up to leave but then sit back down, because Ian doesn't know that we were watching Levent, so why would the show be over when he leaves? I stay where I am for a while longer, watching the family. Bits of their conversation float over to us.

"Good riddance. What an annoying man he was . . ."

"There's more to the story, Semra said that there's something with Mukadder . . ."

"There's always more to the story, you can't stick your nose into everything . . ."

"Pop in, pop out. Didn't he know that this wasn't the type of town for a man like him?"

When enough time has passed, we emerge from the bush and continue down the street instead of heading back toward the main road. In front of Levent's villa, I turn around. Even in this dim evening light, the view directly into the hollow of the bush is perfectly clear. I imagine Levent smoking cigarette after cigarette, spreading lemon jam over his toast, acting like he doesn't know. I am startled at how much has happened simply through the act of pretending, of me spinning up my own truths.

The entire fantasy now crumbles before me. All that's left is a girl so frightened by her inheritance of fate that she convinces herself to rewrite the past, but ends up repeating it instead.

And though I now know that doesn't work, that it never would have worked, I still don't know what does.

Ian and I make our way back to the shoreline and walk toward the abandoned beach and the *sites* beyond. The architecture shifts entirely—what a difference the invisible borders make. Previously brown shutters are now painted blue. The more expensive terraces jut outward for landings large enough for a small pool. There they know me; here they don't. Everything I need is in my own *site*. Never had I felt the need to cross a border. Ian, on the other hand, stretches out the leash.

"So tell me, Ada," Ian asks, breaking the silence we've walked through the last few minutes. "What's your favorite thing about this town? Let me live it through your eyes. I want to know what it's like from someone who lives here."

His gaze holds his full trust in it, a trust that he's placing in me to tell my story. It's the first time that someone has requested to hear the tale of this town from me, a fair-weather visitor. I start by telling him about the evenings in the children's park, when all the kids turned their backs to me as I came up to play beside them, and how I would spend the hours until sundown drawing with my toes in the dirt, swinging alone on the swing set. How Aslı had retrieved my emerald hair tie and bought me a Cornetto and told me that I belonged. I tell him about the sense of freedom I feel wandering the town's streets well past midnight, in my cutoff shorts and flip-flopped feet, safe with the sounds of familiar voices in conversation everywhere I turn. I love the way that time works here in the summer, I say, when we look at the moon or look at the sun or look at what is happening, and that's how we determine where we need to be, if anywhere. I tell him how everything here is an extension of our own villa—the market as an extended kitchen, the sea as an extended backyard. I tell him how even though nobody really sees each other out-side of summer, when we come back, we start again where we left off, as if no time had passed in between. "The film ends, but starts again from the end," I say, half remembering a Turkish adage. "But I don't know if it will start again after this. I think this might be my last full summer here."

"Oh," says Ian. "Why's that?" There is more curiosity than sadness in his tone, an unexpected ratio that plunges me back into my misery. Of course Ian would never understand. Our closeness the morning of the *Moonlight Sonata* had me fooled. Of course it's easy to lapse into loving someone again when they don't expect anything of you or see what you're striving toward, all the ways in which you're not yet whole. How can some-one only love the one small part of you that they know? It can't be true, and their lack of understanding will only lead to suffering.

"I'm pretty hungry," I say, changing the topic. "There's a famous *tost* stand a couple *sites* down. It's about a ten-minute walk, you up for that?"

"A famous place, here?" Ian isn't convinced.

"They make double stacks," I explain.

"And how about you?" I ask, careful to draw attention away from his unanswered question about my future summers. "You still haven't told me about your experiences in this country, how you spent your days in İstanbul."

My mother had helped him plan it all, he tells me. He had arrived via Frankfurt and booked a ticket on the same flight back to San Francisco as us. On the way here, he sat next to a man who was heading to Tirana for his father's funeral, who complained about airline food as he ate stale, buttered bread rolls and requested can after can of tomato juice.

If airports are at all representative of the cities whose entrances they guard, Frankfurt was nice enough, he felt. Despite the fact that in in-ternational airports, nobody is ever anywhere they want to be—in fact, they are quite far from it—he would say that the overall experience was pleasant. He sat down somewhere and ordered noodles that tasted like wet paper, garnished with carrots cut into slices so thin they were nearly translucent. The noodle dish was a valiant effort, and Ian does not nec-essarily need the best of the best, but he does hold a certain respect for valiant efforts. "I just knew I could live in that city if I had to," he tells me. "For like a year or two."

The longer he speaks, the more Ian's voice sheds its previous hesitation and curiosity that it suffered in this town during the conversations with my family, my friends. It grows into its own power, handling the cuts and curves in the story with finesse, moving forward to its intended direction with an unexpected boldness. The outline of his body sharpens against the reeds standing between us and the sea. When the tale turns to İstanbul, I imagine that it will be the tale of a traveler for whom the city is but a play in three acts, its set collapsing once the last tourist tucks himself in under his hostel sheets, then rebuilds itself in the night. The chronicles of, say, a spectator.

But Ian does not talk about İstanbul as if it were a piece of theater constructed for his enjoyment. He does not assess it as he did the Vietnamese eateries of a German airport. He tells me a different story entirely.

Ian reserved a hotel room in Old Pera and stayed in İstanbul for two full days before taking the bus south to Ayvalık. The first day, he wandered the streets alone, swerving toward attractions when he found himself drawn to them, but only if they happened to be en route, visible from the road he walked on. This was not something planned, or a self-guided tour. There was no destination to conquer as much as there was an atmosphere in which to indulge. He wandered the courtyards of Topkapı Palace, stroked the necks of stray cats napping atop restaurant tables, waited patiently outside the Blue Mosque for prayer time to end so that he could cover up his board shorts with a large cotton cloth and hobble inside. On the historic peninsula, he overpaid for tiny cups of pomegranate juice. On İstiklal Avenue, he stood in a line so long that he had no sense as to its endpoint, and when it was his turn, he ended up buying a sauce-drenched "wet" hamburger, which he ate for lunch. He rode the red-and-white tram up and down the length of the avenue.

But on the second day, Ian left Europe. A taxi took him across the first bridge to the Anatolian side, where he knew my grandmother lived, and he spent the day strolling up and down the Caddebostan promenade that skirted the Sea of Marmara. He crisscrossed from the promenade to the Avenue and back, seeking out restaurants that served İnegöl-style meatballs and *mantı* and eating them from to-go boxes with plastic cutlery while sitting on the raised stone wall along the sea. He remembered everything I had told him about where I had been. At sunset, teenage guitarists strummed and sang and tapped empty beer bottles for a tinny percussion on the grassy fields nearby, and when Ian returned via water, he marveled at the orchestral flight of seagulls dipping and soaring as they trailed the ferry (yes, those were the words he used, orchestral and dipping and soaring, a man who had never been to the split city before, a man who had crossed the Bosphorus for the first time).

"The first day was for İstanbul itself," he says. "And the second day— well, that was for you."

Ian reaches out for my hand, but I delay the rhythm of the pendulum that is my arm, and he grasps only the night air.

"And how was yours?" he asks. I stare at him. My what? "Your own trip to . . . Cheshire. That beach town?"

"My trip to Çeşme," I correct him, while keeping him in the wrong. The slowness of the evening weighs down on me; there is a heat and heaviness to the night, moonlight sludging in thick through the clouds. Sweat pools at the backs of my knees. I open my mouth to continue, but time passes, and no words arrive. The moment has condensed into a great big mass to be pushed, inch by inch, a deep slog through the minutes in order to arrive at the future, where everything will have been said and settled. I want instead the clarity of water, strokes slicing cleanly through. Ian keeps turning on me; my mind keeps changing; he refuses to stay in the spaces where I place him.

I can't start from the beginning, I realize. It's too hard. But maybe I can start from the middle, and somehow find my way out.

"Last week," I say, "I went to a spa in a hotel in İstanbul. Do you know who I ran into? Deniz, that girl I hate. A woman compared us once at the Republic Day Ball. Said that for us, this is nothing but a holiday country. Can you believe that anyone would say anything like that?"

"You mean you saw her in Çeşme," Ian corrects. He takes care to pronounce the name of the city correctly, exactly in the manner in which I had said it earlier. We cannot stop correcting each other in ways that do not allow us to go anywhere except in circles.

"I am repeating everything my mother does. Everything," I continue. "She resents me because when I was born, I became an anchor, and she became tied to a place she never should have been tied to. When the boat drops anchor, you swim, jump in the water, explore. That's what you're supposed to do.

"Do you know what my mother did, when she moved to California? She thought it was an adventure, she thought she was running away from a life. Not because she didn't want it, but because she didn't succeed in securing the life she thought was waiting for her. In her mind, if you did nothing and still didn't get what you wanted, then you were on the wrong path. But then I was born, and I ruined everything. The boat had anchored, but all she did was stay on the boat. Didn't make any American friends, rarely ventured beyond Palo Alto. I couldn't go to sleepovers because she didn't know any of the parents. I'd tell her, 'So meet them!' Never. Didn't even know what the PTA was, kept mixing up the numbers of the highways—85, 280, 101. They were all the same to her because all of them went elsewhere. Her location in time and space was so precarious that she was afraid to leave. She could never feel the heaviness and safety of that anchor. All she thought about was home, which kept changing the more she wasn't there. That's why I did it," I say finally, and I can feel tears running down my face, but I do not feel trapped or broken at all. I feel light and wild like a fire in the wind.

Ian stares at me with concern. "What did you do," he asks, but not as a question. Ian is precise. Ian is like needlework. He does not leave room for misinterpretation. Ian and I watch two different movies at the cinema. That's what people like him do; they think about all the facts and act rationally, according to the pros and the cons and what has actually happened and taken place. They pay no attention whatsoever to what has never happened, what could have maybe happened. It makes me angry, this lack of consideration for all the other possibilities.

Two more strokes and I can cut through the fog; I am almost at the end, even though I cannot see it. "I slept with him," I say. "I slept with the man my mother wasn't able to marry."

"You slept with—when did this happen?" His words are slow and measured, but he moves us forward in the stillness. A straight line through. The moon passes beyond the clouds, and its clear light dissipates the oppressive heat. My body begins to cool and harden in its outline, the significance of everything I've done taking shape in front of me.

"Eight days ago," I repeat, bringing us back around again. "In İstanbul. While you were walking along the Marmara, thinking of me."

26

THE WRONG BEACH

I am waiting outside with a glass of water when the phone rings. In front of me is a taxicab, and inside the taxicab is Ian. He made arrangements to leave very quickly, in the span of a day, rescheduling the flight that he was supposed to take with us the following week. The handful of days that remained seemed intolerable to him. Yesterday, he asked my mother to help him plan his bus trip back to İstanbul, and she booked him a seat on the blue-and-white coach up the coast for this morning. He did not tell her what happened, only that we had had a disagreement and he no longer felt comfortable staying here.

My mother is watching the scene from the porch with my grandmother. She lifts her hands from the railing and walks inside to answer the phone, kicking off her outside slippers. From where I stand, on the street in front of our garden, the ring sounds shrill, ghostly. The engine starts and I toss the water from the glass. *May your trip flow smoothly, leave and return like water.* A graceful arc descends on the back window of the cab, splashes off the trunk. Too early. But it's okay, I say to myself, trying out kindness for a change. It's a common mistake for first-timers. After all, I'm not used to people leaving. Only leaving people behind.

So this is what it feels like. Empty and senseless. And I can't complain, and I can't cry, because I've done it all to myself.

I had thought that we would walk back under the moon in contemplative silence that night, after I told Ian, but the first thing he wanted to do was make absolutely sure that it was my decision. *Did he force himself onto you, was it manipulation, was it your own doing, how could you ever want something like that?* Then, unable to control himself, he spit out: "Jesus Christ, Ada, this is disgusting." I collapsed on the road, pulled reeds by the fistful as I cried and said I was sorry, and yes, that it was my decision, it was completely my decision, and Ian would open and close his hands, like he wanted to tear something apart but could not bear to. His fingers spread and retracted, pulsing with an invisible violence that he kept tempered down.

Everyone was asleep when we got home, so there was no option to change rooms. We slept in the pushed-together beds, and it was easy not to touch each other, even though I tried. Ian shuffled away from me under the pretense of sleep. The night passed excruciatingly slowly and I spent it staring at the moonlit ceiling. I listened to the crickets and every single pop song that played from the Small Club until that empty space between night and sunrise silenced it all. I thought about all the power I had given Levent that he never had in the first place. *But who, then, or what*, I asked the half-light, *gives you the permission to belong? We have tried everything. What is left for us to do?* It is always *us* I think about, I realized as I drifted off to sleep. Never just her, never just me, but *us*. Everything I do is for us.

The taxi disappears from view. My mother walks back out to the porch, and she is crying.

Oh no. My hand goes limp and the glass falls, shattering at my feet.

That was Eliza, I say, wasn't it.

⚓

"What happened to you?" my grandmother says. "Go wash your face!" My mother steadies herself with the back of the chair she can't find the strength to fold her body into, her eyes wet and her face pulsing, her neck flushing like a poisonous rash is blossoming its way up to her head. She has dressed formally for Ian's departure, jeans and a pistachio-toned blouse with a gold necklace, a last-ditch effort for him to remember the family fondly.

My mother continues to cry, her hand trembling. My grandmother, unable to make sense of her deteriorating composure, turns to me. I am watching my mother, but I am cold and firm, my body in shock. I am in my swimsuit and sarong, my feet bare on the road, because I didn't want this day to be different from any other. Our triangle stands solidly for a while in that way, staring, crying, questioning. The Small Club starts up the first pop song of the morning, and that breaks us apart.

The rattle of the chair under my mother's hand slows to a silence. She draws her chin to her shoulder, looking at no one. Then she says, in a voice barely loud enough for anyone to hear, "Ada wasn't in Çeşme last week."

"Well then, in which hell was she frolicking?" asks my grandmother. She is starting to get haughty. She does not like someone else having the information or the control in the room.

"She went to the city with Levent."

"What city?" my grandmother asks, missing the point entirely. "You mean to town?"

My mother could say his name, but she could not say the name of the city. And only as I watch her mouth open and close with that dumb-founded look of dead fish on ice do I feel the full force of the consequences.

"İstanbul."

Two fish in the icebox. But only for a moment. My grandmother comes to life quickly—she is comfortable navigating the waters of shame and punishment. She nods at me, and I know that I must walk over the glass in my bare feet up the steps of the porch and stand in front of her. I do that. I look into her hard blue eyes. I can answer all the questions as long as they come from her, but not if they come from my mother. I can't even look at my mother. The heat of her sadness emanates from her body, and its warmth is different from the early sun's. It clutches at me and my body spasms in a series of futile efforts to shake it off.

"You went to İstanbul with Levent," my grandmother says. She nods after each word, assessing its weight as it falls from her mouth.

"Yes."

My grandmother closes her eyes and smiles, as though what I said could not possibly be true. She opens them again, but there's the same scene right in front of her. Nothing imagined.

"What did you do then, together in the city?"

"We, um, ate kebabs. It was raining. I walked to Mom's old high school."

My grandmother scoffs at what I've chosen to share, and then turns serious again. "And did. And did. And did." She tries one more time. "And did anything happen between you two?"

The truth will come out, eventually. It may as well come from me. "Once, and it was because I wanted to. I wanted it to happen."

My grandmother gasps. My mother stares at me, then gathers her strength. Her hand stops trembling. "Ada," she says. "This doesn't make sense—how could you do something so senseless? Don't you remember when we spoke, we were at the Big Club, and I told you that man was nothing but bad news?" She covers her face with her hands, so completely afraid to look at me. "Please, God, tell me what has happened in your life that has made it so you cannot even trust your own mother." Then she falls silent.

My grandmother points to me with a quivering finger. "You," she says, "are an absolute disgrace to this family." She is wearing her sapphire necklace, and the sunlight flashes on the stones, and so many blue eyes are staring at me with their knife-sharp glints. "Is that why your boyfriend left, he found out you were two-timing him with a man old enough to be your father? Is this how your mother raised you, to be the town slut?"

Her voice is shrill, and becoming too loud for this *site*. My grandmother is publicly airing our disgrace when she would otherwise go to great lengths to hide it. She does not even line-dry the intimate laundry outside, as all our neighbors do. A woman who makes no cultural allowances on revealing who we are underneath our clothes.

"Do you realize what you've done, Ada?" my grandmother continues. "All my efforts are now in shambles. The futures I had planned out, the lives that I thought you would live. I worked so hard to get Levent back here, to make your mother see what's right and what's wrong, and you go ahead and you raze all of it to the ground." She suddenly stops talking, having noticed a passerby heading to the Small Club, head tilted toward us, listening. I recognize the older woman, a transparent blue cover-up flowing over her brown swimsuit. She's walking with a slant, unable to control her posture.

"Emine!" my grandmother yells. She waves her hands in the air, as if her voice is not commanding enough. "Hey now, you're at the wrong beach! You don't live in this *site* anymore, remember? Why don't you go to your own beach? All you do here is drown, you old woman! Do you know that you've lost your marbles?" My grandmother frantically taps a finger against her temple. "You've lost all your marbles!"

Emine smiles at us, then turns in to the oleander path and wobbles down to the beach. My grandmother works out the societal calculations, her brows knitting as she arrives at the gravity of the insult. Emine may have lost all her marbles, she may have nearly died in the sea she has been swimming in her whole life, but at least she's not causing a scene.

"It's the most difficult task," my grandmother says. She can't look at either of us. "Having a daughter. May God grant patience and grace to all those who choose to raise donkeys like you."

"Who needs the patience?" snaps my mother. "Who needs the grace? You think it's easy, having you as a mother? People like you aren't fit to have children, especially not daughters. You look at them, and everything in their face is a reflection of you. A you that could be better, an opportunity for another chance. We fall for your version of the world—you *are* our version of the world—and look where it gets us. Every time I manage to make my own decision, it's like I have remembered how to breathe again. Severance is not a threat, Mother. It is an inevitability."

As she speaks, the cords emerge. I can see them, really see them, in the clarity of late-summer sunlight. They are thick and wormlike and wrapped around our necks like an unfortunate birth. Nothing had been cut, I realize. My mother is wrong. Severance in our family is an impossibility.

"I will never have a daughter," I say to my mother. I repeat it, louder. "I will. NEVER. HAVE. A. DAUGHTER."

My voice has called forth all those hesitating on the periphery. On the diagonal, the sailor's mother leans over from the balcony, elbows resting on the railing. Ozan peeks out from the entrance of the Small Club. Aslı comes up from behind to pull him back in, but they don't go all the way— her curls reach out like curious creatures from among the oleanders. The grocer's boy, on his way to a delivery, hits the back pedals on his bike and turns his gaze toward the sea, his ear toward us.

"Don't you see?" says my grandmother, noticing our audience. "There is no such thing as a secret."

"You shouldn't have a daughter," says my mother. "If you're going to be like Madame Mukadder here and play your children like chess pieces in the great game of your life, if you're going to pump them with guilt about how they should have lived and ensure that they never appreciate or believe in the lives they have, if you're going to beg your daughter to visit you for three months out of the year instead of investing in her own relationship and home and community, imprisoning her in a purgatory masquerading as quality time and making it so she cannot enjoy one place or the other, if you are going to constantly pierce her mind with deep regrets the moment she experiences happiness, happiness with the life that she has chosen and built on her own, if you're going to curse her in that way, then yes, my dear Ada, you should never have a daughter!"

"Why is it so hard for everyone to just stay where they belong?" wails my grandmother.

"It's not hard," says my mother. "It's easy. But listen to me, you can't choose what that is. You can't choose for other people. And besides, Mother, the places you choose don't even exist anymore. Do you understand what I'm telling you? I need you to stop it."

I am astounded by my mother's articulation. She has pulled words out from under the blanket of an untouched vocabulary. This, I realize, this is who she is. Not what she used to be like—that's not it. This is her, now, and I am seeing it. I need more time to make sense of it all but my grandmother cuts in to take back control of the conversation, and it slips my grasp.

"Another thing, Ada," my grandmother says. "The main thing, in fact. Soon all the neighbors will know what happened. You can't run away from something like this, you can't go back to America on your little flight and forget what happened. These summers aren't a throwaway. This country, it might seem like a playground to you, but this here, it's real life. Every day in your life is real, no matter where or when it happens. Can your thick head make sense of that?"

"I want to go home," says my mother. She looks up at the sky, where there are no planes. "Ada, let's go home."

Her expression is neither helpless nor hopeful; it is steady and determined, as if all matters are in her own hands. I can no longer recognize her. Every June, when I rattled through my winter-dusted Turkish, I was not trying to step into myself so much as I was trying to become who she had once been, and to live correctly this time. She doesn't need me anymore, but I have nowhere else to go. Moving toward her was the only way I knew to get closer to my country. There is still so far left to travel and all the lands are completely unknown.

I leave them there on that cursed terrace where they can argue with each other until the end of time. I walk quickly through the empty morning streets of the *site*, every single street, and end up at the children's park. I collapse near the slides, unable to bear the burden of my displacement. Its sudden, extraordinary weight is not unfamiliar to me. Many years ago, when I first came to this town, I arrived with that same heaviness. Nothing had changed.

27

THE LONG SWIM

The day of Ian's flight back to San Francisco, I wake up very early, though not as early as the last time I did what I am about to do. I gather up my sun-stiffened bikini from the porch, and walk out without glancing at yesterday's paper for today's weather. If there is any wind on my face, I do not notice it. Now is not the time for decisions; all the decisions were made long ago. As I walk past the entrance to the Small Club, my fingers brush against the oleander leaves, their fragile petals bending into a series of greetings: *Hello, good morning, goodbye.*

At the Small Club, it's the hour of the grandparents. All the bodies crawling around the beach are in various forms of decay. They navigate gingerly from sun beds to the wooden pier, pull themselves from wave to ladder, stumble from here to there. One of the men at the tables I pass salutes me, and I wince at the gesture of power attempted by such a trembling arm. I salute back. "Good morning, Miss Island," he says in English, but I still can't remember his name. I skip down the stairs out of the café, moving quickly as my indecision lurches to catch up with me. Not fast enough. I pass the changing rooms, pass the showers. I go all the way to the edge of the dock and step down the ladder. One, two, three, dive.

In the distance, the moon landing of Barren Island calls to me. I lift my head from the water and counter its gaze, kicking softly to orient myself in its direction. The sea is cold and shocking in the way that I expect it to be. There are two options when heading down a path of discomfort: to continually be alarmed and disappointed, or to accept the punishment of the path and seek solace in its consistency. I strike through the icy water to find my rhythm, and let my body enjoy the downhill sensation that my strokes and kicks pull me through. Down, down, down, into the darker patches of the seaweed fields.

At this very moment, Ian must be on his way to the Frankfurt airport, the place where nobody is where they want to be. Soon, he will be walking along the fluorescent hallways under glowing blue signs, wondering why he fell in love with someone who could not fit in. Someone who only belongs, if anywhere, among these people with slumped, fatigued figures and burdensome suitcases.

I butterfly-kick toward cooler depths, then let the water lift me back to the surface. Upon encountering a pile of floating seaweed, I sweep the leaves into eddies and gather them toward my chest as if welcoming children. A second later, I splash them away. I allow myself one glance behind. The pier has sunken into the land and the Small Club has collapsed into itself. The olive groves are nothing but a mist of pale green, leaves at the right angles shimmering in the sunlight. Yet the island is still so far. Four hours to the *Flughafen*, and still you are nowhere.

Waves—their spumes thicker, whiter—begin to emerge from the water, pouring in from all directions at once. They crash into the only thing they can find, which is me.

I thought my mother was directionless, that she could not tell her north from her south. But the truth is that my mother was imprisoned. I remember her fist curled up by the oak table in the dining room the night my car overheated. The knowledge sinking in that were my grandmother to die, maybe (here is the empty space, the silence, in which no one said, *God forbid*) it wouldn't be such a bad thing. My mother does not want to come back here; she is happy with the life she chose. When she fled to Paris to find herself and found my father instead, maybe "instead" was always the wrong word. Maybe she found what she was looking for and simply continued on. All my grandmother has done is confuse her every summer, in an attempt to keep her locked in.

The narratives I so carefully constructed about my mother are my own. Only one thought saves me from complete devastation: that even though I have not yet found my own footing, even though I have been unable to moor, I have at least made my grandmother stop meddling.

The good thing about crying in the sea is that you can't tell it's happening. Or you can pretend that it's been happening forever and now you are swimming in your own salt. I pretend that it's been happening forever. That seems to be the right amount of pain. I feel alone, and cold, and tired, and I miss Ian. Despite everything, never had he once thought that I might be better if I happened to be someone else. I think it will take a long time for him to forgive me. I cry harder, accidentally swallowing seawater in my desperate gulps for air.

There is a tingle underneath my chin. Like electric fish swimming inside me, nipping, the tiny shocks of their tiny teeth. Something is wrong. I pause to tread water, trying to pinpoint the pain. Then it sears. My chest is a backgammon board, and someone is rolling dice on fire, over and over. The pain expands from my neck to my rib cage, from one shoulder to another. I look down at my chest, leaning back into the water. My eyes take a minute to adjust to something that is not blue, or deep, or moving. Upon my skin are large red welts, glistening in the sunlight like slick newborns. In the middle of the sea, I let out a scream.

Nobody hears me. I slam my face back in the water and swim as fast as I can. I do not stop. I imagine I am swimming the 200 freestyle, my most difficult race, over and over again. Coach's voice in my ears: *They're going to have to pull your dead body out of the water. But don't worry, they've got another one waiting for you at the finish line.*

Hours, months, or years later, I am somewhere. I know this because my foot hits the sharp edge of a rock. Water leaks into my throat, and

I cough as the sides of my stomach turn against the boulders, pricked by the sea urchins. I crawl onto the rocks and make it up the short incline. The land levels out and I vomit all over my feet. What have I even eaten today? I don't have time to consider the issue because I immediately fall to the ground, and everything goes black.

I wake up sometime when the sun is high in the sky with dirt on my face. Dirt? Ian must be approaching the Atlantic by now. The welts on my chest have shrunk to scales. In my delirium, I think that perhaps I have become a sea creature, and inch back toward the water, crawling on my elbows as they scrape the dirt. Again, the dirt! There is no dirt; the island is barren. I sit up to try and collate the wavering components of my consciousness. My body hurts; there must have been multiple jellyfish. Hidden among the seaweed, perhaps, that I had welcomed into my chest. The pain will fade, I know. It's only a matter of time.

The sea may throw me its obstacles, but I am still a swimmer.

I force myself up and hobble around the island. There are plants and fruit trees and trash from previous visitors who have come here by boat. Gristled grills, busted bottles of Fruko and orange Fanta, the faded labels peeling. It takes about five minutes to circle the perimeter, and I do it three times, for good measure. This is not the island I thought it was from the distance. From the distance, I saw only rocks, no life at all. I saw two mounds like mighty volcanoes pointing up toward the sky, dormant but brimming with the threat of eruption, much like that island there, out at sea, back toward the east. That one closer to the mainland. Something rustles in the grass, then waddles over. It protrudes its neck from a giant shell and looks up at me with curious, beady eyes. A turtle. I am on Turtle Island.

I swam to the wrong island.

It takes a while for me to understand the extent of my achievement, that I swam to the farthest island off the coast. It takes even longer for the reward to present itself. When it does, it comes with a freedom that I have not felt in a long time. There is no need to trick myself this time, seeing only what I want to see, or remembering only what I want to remember. I am absolutely, exactly where I need to be.

I rest until the sun turns into a softer fire and begins its descent. Then I slip into the water again, hungry and lighter, to head back to the mainland. It's easy to swim toward the lights; it's always faster on the way back home. As I cross the street and unlatch the gate, my wet footsteps stay dark in the moonlight.

28

THE LAST GAME

The next day, we're all at the Small Club, almost as usual. There is a tangible sense of finality that hums over us. Ozan swats at it, looking for the invisible fly. Tomorrow the cousins are heading back to their family homes, the twins to Bursa, Ozan to Ankara. Most of the tables around us are empty, the lack of beach towels and elbows and backgammon boards revealing the tea and ketchup stains on the white plastic. The waitstaff has thinned out. The winds—and not the important kinds with names, like the *poyraz*, but the common winds, those that naturally appear when their time has come—have picked up enough velocity to thicken up the waves. Those of us who have spent summer after summer here, we can see the precision of the dateline between August and September. For some, the months may slink silently into each other, but our senses are sharper. The slightest shift in the wind has us lifting our heads like hounds on the scent. Our ears perk up. Fall is afoot.

Most of the young girls have already gone. Only a few are scattered about here and there, walking with their stomachs stuck out like pumpkins. The strings of their bikinis dangle like wayward threads down their skeletal backs, or wrap twice around their sheet-flat chests. I'm no longer working out my clock fortunes, not anymore. The last clock fortune I told for myself was in Levent's apartment. My mother is free, and I will be fine.

We set up for another round of Okey, and I signal for coffee, medium sugar. I keep the demitasse upside down and from time to time check whether it's cooled. Aslı begs to let her read the grounds for me. "I've gotten so good," she says. "I'll see birds and white spaces, I'll see so much good *kısmet* for you, you'll absolutely lose your mind." There's not much other chatter throughout the game. The boys are keeping quiet, afraid to say something out of line. Aslı probably made them swear that they wouldn't ask me any questions about why Ian isn't here anymore. I did tell them most of the truth: that Ian and I had an argument and he couldn't live here in the house any longer with me, so he rebooked for an earlier flight to San Francisco. I didn't cry as I told them. I held it in.

Aslı knows the truth, of course, and maybe when I'm gone for the winter and they are taking weekend trains to see each other in their cities, cousins gathering together for dinners and *bayrams*, when it's cold and there's snow on the ground, she'll fill them in over *salep* and hot chocolate. I'll be far away by then, and the summer will be long gone. It will seem like a safe story to tell.

"Which one was wild again?" I ask. I peer over at the sets of tiles, and look at the one that was overturned at the beginning of the game.

"Blue two," says Bulut.

Blue two . . . I've got them both. I quickly neutralize my expression to conceal my hand. Instead, I furrow my brow as I clack through my tiles, rearranging them into various sets.

"We'll see you next in Ankara, then, for Republic Day?" Aslı asks Ozan. Aslı's question turns meek at the end, as she realizes that it's a conversation that exists among only the three of them, and excludes me. I keep my head down on my tiles; I need to concentrate. Ozan nods. In late October, I'll be back on campus as a crisp fall settles in. Walking along the redwoods, at the open-air shopping center with my mother buying gowns for the annual ball. We'll laugh together at Deniz's inflated self-importance, amaze ourselves at the shift in dignity between the crowd's deference during the national anthem and their frenzy on the dance floor.

It's a different Turkey, the one we have in California. It's not an experience trying to be another experience. I know this because I have lived them both. I look at the faces of Aslı, Ozan, and Bulut, smile at how Ozan sneers at Aslı putting down an "absolute piece of shit" tile for him and pulls from the stack, how Aslı leans over to observe Bulut's board and sighs yet again that he doesn't understand the game at all and begs him to let her fix up his pieces, even though Aslı's sitting across from me and we are technically playing against the boys.

I will miss them.

"Idea!" I slap the table. "Next summer, let's plan it out so we're all together in Çeşme for a week." Three heavily tanned faces beam at me. "Even if we don't get the full three months here, and let's face it, we won't as we continue with school and work, I think we can probably plan a one-week getaway, no?" Everyone nods, and I can already see the fantasies taking shape in their minds. Adults on vacation, shots of sambuca.

"This place is getting too juvenile for us anyway," says Ozan, watching a girl in a younger group walk past us who sneers at him for staring. "I think we're ready to hit more of the big time when it comes to summer towns."

I look at my sets, and I am almost there. In fact, I *am* there. But I would like to go one step further. I wait for Ozan to set down his piece. Today I'm taking the pieces that Ozan sets down, because we have decided, for our last game and our last day, to reverse direction. The piece he provides me is useless, so I draw for myself. There we go. A green nine that I can add to my green eight and my green seven. Not that I needed to add it on, but it's always good to go above and beyond. To go out with a bang.

"First round of flaming shots on the beach will be on me," I promise. "But for now . . ." I flip around my completed board, "I believe each of you owes me a beer?" Then I gently set down a tile, covering it with my hand. I lift it to reveal the blue two.

Everyone gasps. They don't like it—they don't like it at all. Ending with the wild card is a power move. It knocks down the points for everybody else, even though we never keep track of the points because Ozan always wins. Almost always. They stand up and clap and call for beers, signaling to waiters, causing a ruckus. A few people at the tables around us look at me and smile. "Bravo, Ada!" someone yells. My friends march me down to the pier and click open the drinks, then pour them over my head as I stick my tongue out for the drops. Before I know it, Ozan's grabbed my arms and Bulut's got me by the legs, and my face is up toward the sun, which is late in the sky. Aslı counts to six. Her voice draws out the words with each swing of my body: "Threeee. . . . . . Fouurrr . . ." On six, they *altı okka* me into the Aegean. The temperature of the water is so shocking that it's painful to tread in place, so I swim to the raft. Every distance seems short after where I swam to the other day. From the pier to the raft, from Turkey to California. These distances are nothing. "It was nothing!" I yell out to sea, pulling myself onto the raft in a matter of seconds. Here and there is a false dichotomy.

The three of them laugh and wave to me from the pier. I wave back and curl my toes over the edge of the raft, shivering. The faraway islands are intricately contoured in the clear light. I haven't told anybody, not even my friends, about my swim. They would be impressed. Even Bulut's genuine happiness would be enough for him to bite back any jealousy. But the truth is that my story wouldn't do anything more than that. It wouldn't establish me here any more than I'm already established, or give my presence in and love for this town any greater validity. I'd gaze expectantly into three confused sets of eyes, who would tell me that they have nothing to give me that I cannot already give myself. They would pour another beer over my head for being such a fool.

To the north of the pier is the sharp pebbled stretch of what might generously be called a beach. Just small enough for a pink-and-green tent, for a young girl to play outside in the sand beside her mother, who keeps an eye on her daughter from the shadows of the nylon fabric. But my mother is not in the tent today, nor do I see her with her wide-brimmed sun hat, fighting the waves. Today, she has spread a towel over the rocks, and shoved away the seaweed that crawls up the shoreline. Leaning up against the seawall, she holds a bright orange hardcover in her hands—an end-of-summer gift from Ozan that matches her new swimsuit, a bikini she bought in town just this morning. For a moment, my mother lifts her head up toward the sun. Then she raises a hand to her lips, licks a finger, and turns the page.

29

THE END

My mother and I take our last walk together along the sea. We are not speaking to each other, not yet, but have reached a tacit agreement. It is this: When both of us are ready, we will see the betrayals for the declarations of love that they were.

We head down from the market between the soccer field and the basketball courts, past the children's park where the grass grows wild and free. At the end of the park, we make a left at the shoreline and continue on southward, turning our backs to the Big Club. We leave behind the abandoned beach of Sıfır and the *sites* beyond. We pass the oleander-lined entrance of the Small Club. Then we turn in to our own villa, where an open-mouthed suitcase awaits each of us in our respective rooms.

We help my grandmother pack the summer into its boxes. We throw old bedsheets on furniture as dust covers, roll mothballs deep into drawers. We carefully separate out the bills necessary to close our accounts.

We prepare for the off-season.

ACKNOWLEDGMENTS

Thank you first and foremost to my agent, Andrea Blatt, who is a dream come true. Thank you to my editors, Megan Lynch and Kukuwa Ashun, and the team at Flatiron for your enthusiasm. Special thanks to Katherine Turro, Maris Tasaka, Claire McLaughlin, Alexus Blanding, Emily Walters, Frances Sayers, Jen Edwards, Jason Reigal, Mary Beth Constant, and Ken Diamond.

Thank you to everyone who read my drafts over the last ten years, attended my open mic nights, and encouraged my writing. There are so many of you, and I am so lucky. Thank you especially to Erol Ahmed and Elena Czubiak, who were there from the very beginning with unwavering enthusiasm, and to Ayten Tartıcı and Duygu Ula, whose incredibly thoughtful notes helped take this book to the next level. To Scott Pack, Thalia Suzuma, Rachel Stout, and Jesse Coleman, for seeing potential in my writing. Thank you to my professors at Wellesley, especially Dan Chiasson, Marilyn Sides, and Colin Channer, for the guidance and practice. An enormous thank-you to Alyssa Bereznak and Martin Vera for dealing swiftly and deftly with every major (and minor) crisis in my life so that I could quickly get back to work. You are my favorite places to moor.

Thank you to my father for the precision and support, my mother for the stories and the questions, and my brother for the music. Thank you most of all to my grandmother, for the Aegean.

ABOUT THE AUTHOR

İnci Atrek holds a BA in English and creative writing from Wellesley College. *Holiday Country* is her first novel.